BOB COLE

BETTY"S BABY

ISBN 0-7414-2422-3

Published by:

INFINITY
PUBLISHING.COM

1094 New DeHaven Street, Suite 100
West Conshohocken, PA 19428-2713
Info@buybooksontheweb.com
www.buybooksontheweb.com
Toll-free (877) BUY BOOK
Local Phone (610) 941-9999
Fax (610) 941-9959

Printed in the United States of America

Printed on Recycled Paper

Published March 2005

BETTY'S BABY is a story of motherhood. The characters do not represent people in the real world. They exist only within this story. They are distinct individuals with their own personalities and characteristics. Their opinions are their own and not necessarily those of the author, publisher, or others involved in the production, distribution, and sale of this book.

I gratefully acknowledge the expert editing and other assistance provided by my sister, A. D. D., Master of Arts in English Literature, to Will Wright (www.wrightmediaonline.com) for the excellent design of the book cover, and to C. E. for her encouragement in the writing of this book.

Bob Cole

ONE

July, 1962

"ANGEL'S A BITCH!"

Dr. Charles Crawford summarized his troubled thoughts as he turned his sparkling red sports car into the parking garage below the Professional Office Tower. He waved to the attendant as he drove to his reserved space on the first tier.

At forty-two years of age, he was a physician board-certified in obstetrics and gynecology. He had a successful practice and was widely respected in his field. Late again, he was on his way to his office suite. His hospital rounds had taken longer than he had anticipated.

He parked his car and locked it as he got out. Briefcase in hand, he hurried to the elevator. He knew his waiting room would be full of anxious patients.

Leaving the elevator at the seventh floor, he strode down the hall to his private office and entered with a key. He paused momentarily at his desk to look over his messages. There was one from Ralph Stone, the attorney handling his pending divorce. Reading it, his thoughts returned to his estranged wife and their failed marriage.

"ANGEL'S A BITCH!"

He had long regretted the evening she had entered his life. Devil Woman! Oh, what a fool he'd been. He had only himself to blame.

Alone that evening twelve years ago, he was attending a high society reception at the country club in honor of John Clarke, the wealthy new chairman of the board of Memorial Hospital.

1

He had a few drinks at the bar as he looked out over the crowd. In the background, the orchestra played soft, romantic music.

With a drink in his hand, he strolled out on the front porch to get away from the endless chatter. He leaned against the rail near the steps and watched the fountains spraying water into the night air.

A limousine drove up the circle. The driver opened her door, and Angel got out. She shifted her fur coat from her shoulders to her arms and came up the walkway.

Astonished by her beauty, he waited for her to pass by.

"Good evening," she said as she paused at the top step. She smiled seductively as she looked him in the eye.

That moment they were alone. Still, he should have known. But the music was so romantic, and she so enticing in her stunning, low-cut gown.

She laughed wickedly, luring him on. His heart was gone. She was temptation. Like a fool, he fell for her then, hook, line, and sinker.

He had little prior dating experience then. An orphan, he had worked nights during his college years to pay for the courses he took during the day. Medical school had been a difficult struggle. He had spent every available moment studying to keep from falling behind in his classes. The long, grueling hours of internship and residency had left little room for a social life. His third year of residency was coming to an end, and he was preparing to take the board exams in obstetrics and gynecology. After board certification, his plans were to set up his own practice and to re-join the human race.

Once inside, he followed Angel at a distance as she went from room to room observing what the ladies of distinction were wearing. She was the new fashion writer for the city's largest newspaper.

Later that evening, he introduced himself and asked her for a date.

"I'm busy." She laughed softly as she turned and walked away. "Ask me again." She looked back over her shoulder and smiled. "I like chocolates. Ask me again."

Rejection was a bitter blow to the young physician, but he didn't heed the warning. He couldn't get her out of his mind.

It took him a month to gather enough courage to ask her out a second time. To his surprise, she accepted.

"I thought you had lost interest," she said with an encouraging smile, and she nibbled on one of his chocolates.

He took her to dinner at an expensive restaurant and afterwards to a play at the new performing arts center. He wanted to ask her for a goodnight kiss, but he couldn't say the words.

He took her out again. This time she let him kiss her on the cheek at her apartment door but wouldn't let him come inside.

His courtship was elaborate. She had expensive tastes. Only the best was good enough for her. "I like chocolates," she constantly reminded him.

After a year he proposed, and she accepted. She put him off another year before she would marry him. His medical practice had to build up so he could afford her elegance, and he had to buy a classic residence in a prestigious neighborhood.

Their country club wedding was a high society event. Cameramen and reporters were there from the local newspapers. It was a catered affair, and he willingly prepaid the expenses.

On his wedding night, he found out physical sex wasn't Angel's ballgame. He was disappointed. She was a wife he could show off but not one he could enjoy.

During the early years of their marriage she kept their romantic moments to a minimum, allowing him attention only to keep him from straying. When she became pregnant for the second time, she decided to cut him off from physical sex completely. Two babies were all she wanted. There was no need to risk another pregnancy. It might ruin her youthful figure.

He met a young, single nurse at the hospital who relished his attention. She senses his unhappiness in his relationship with his wife. He resisted her for a while. But, out of spite, after a domestic fight, he yielded to her bedroom charms. This was the first of his many affairs.

Charles took his dates to dine in private corners of crowded restaurants and clubs. They watched plays and performances from secluded seats, and they ended these evenings romancing in expensive hotel rooms.

But there was something missing in these relationships. Charles could not become attached to any of the women he dated. He was a married man, and he had his two young children to consider, Charles Jr., nicknamed Chuck, and Ellen.

While Angel didn't want intimacy in their marriage, she did encourage her husband to lust after her. She expected her flirtations to be enough to keep him on the string. She sensed his declining interest but was unable to understand why.

Then Angel learned he was having affairs with younger women. She tried to catch him, but he was too careful. She referred to his patients and

3

nurses as "those sluts you play with every day," but he refused to let her shame him or make him feel guilty.

Then Syndipore Chan came into his life. Syndi was his new chief nurse. She was the daughter of a Chinese-American military doctor and his Thailand-born wife. Syndi was an RN with specialized training in obstetrics and gynecology, She was unmarried, twenty-four years old, and intelligent. She had dark eyes, straight black hair, and beautiful tan-brown skin.

"Only dinner, nothing more," she said the first time he asked her out. "There's no future in my dating a married man."

He courted her for more than a year with roses to "someone special" from "guess who". He slowly won her over, but not to bed. He was still a married man.

When Angel learned of her husband's feelings for Syndi, she was furious.

"WHO DOES THAT SIAMESE CHINK WHORE THINK SHE IS? I'LL FIX HER!"

At thirty-six. Angel was more physically attractive than Syndi, but Charles wasn't concerned. Angel's disposition had so clouded his thoughts he could no longer see her as a beautiful woman.

Not to be outdone, Angel acquired a boyfriend, a freshman university football player barely half her age. Charles came home one day and found them in bed.

"I'm glad you caught me," she laughed. "Now you know I can be unfaithful, too."

"It's ridiculous to continue this farce," he said, and he stomped out of the house.

He spent that night alone in a motel room. The next morning he went to see his attorney, Ralph Stone.

"I want a divorce!"

The fight was a bitter one with Angel constantly on the attack. Her attorney scheduled endless court appearances designed to take him away from his medical practice. Angel claimed he was not a fit father and should have no visitation privileges. She insisted that he be examined by her psychiatrist, Dr. William Peabody. Her sessions with Dr. Peabody were amorous affairs, and she was certain Peabody would reach the conclusions she desired.

4

Judge Cargile ordered psychological examinations by a neutral doctor. The psychiatrist reported that there was no reason to deny Charles visitation.

"Professional courtesy!" Angel screamed at the judge. "Charles Crawford is an immoral man!"

Like a leach, she hung on for more than a year. Her attorney filed trivial motions over imagined incidents. She hired private detectives to follow him and report on his activities, and she tried to make life hell for Syndi.

Confused by the conflicting rhetoric, Judge Cargile pressured both sides to reach a negotiated settlement. "I hate divorce fights," he said. "Judge Chaney should have gotten this case. It was his turn, not mine."

"Why do we have to negotiate with that bitch?" Charles asked his attorney in private. "She makes agreements only for the purpose of binding me. She's broken every one she's made."

"We must try," Ralph Stone said. "If the judge thinks we're dragging our feet, he'll rule against us."

Charles had to bend more than he wanted, but Angel screamed he wasn't bending enough. Ralph Stone hammered away at the other side. Slowly the pieces of a settlement fell into place. Angel would get the house, a car, alimony, custody of the children, and child support. Charles would pay for the children's medical insurance and have visitation rights. It was expensive, but he would get his freedom.

Charles' freedom was hard for Angel to accept. She refused to agree on the terms of visitation and on the amount of alimony and child support.

Angel was in no hurry to settle the case. She lived in their classic home with the children while he had to rent an apartment. He had to pay the utility bills, the house payment, and an amount for her living expenses. No matter how much she got, she demanded more and more while her standard of living became more and more extravagant.

"This can't go on forever," he said out loud. "ANGEL'S A BITCH!"

The door leading into his medical suite opened. To his relief, it was Syndi. He wondered if she had heard what he had said.

TWO

X   X   X

"What's Angel up to this time?"

"I'm sorry, Syndi." Charles Crawford turned toward the doorway. "I didn't know you were there. Ralph Stone called this morning and left a message. I'll have to call him back to find out."

"She's always up to something."

"Who's the first patient today?" The doctor went into his medical suite and closed his office door behind him. He was trying to get his mind on his day's work.

"Mrs. Lewis."

"What's wrong with her this time?"

"The usual."

"Let's get started." He picked up Mrs. Lewis' chart out of the rack on the door of her treatment room, and they went inside."

A divorcee in her early thirties, Mrs. Lewis had taken off her dress and was wearing a scanty slip over her panties and padded bra. She was sitting on the examination table impatiently waiting.

"You're avoiding me," she said as the doctor entered.

"I'm not avoiding anyone."

"You spend so little time with me."

"I have an office full of patients, many with serious problems. You don't seem to be that sick."

"You never come in without HER!"

"I need Syndi to make entries on your chart. I must have a nurse with me when I examine a female patient, and she has to be a female nurse. It's required by the licensing board."

"Can we talk alone?"

"Not now. I have other patients to see. What's wrong today?"

Julie, the office receptionist, knocked on the door. The doctor opened it.

"It's John Clarke on the phone. It must be an emergency."

"Take a message," the doctor said. "Tell him I'm with a patient. I'll have to return his call."

"I told him that. He told me to remind you he's chairman of the hospital board. He insists on talking to you now."

The doctor shook his head and frowned.

"You look cute when you frown," Mrs. Lewis smiled trying to attract the doctor's attention.

"I'll take the call in my office." He ignored Mrs. Lewis' remark.

"Syndi," he said when they were in the hallway, "have Julie phone in the order for lunch for the staff. See what everyone wants. Get me the usual. They'll deliver. Julie can pay for it with an office check."

"How's the money situation?"

"Tight, but my staff has been loyal. I want to continue this as long as I can. It's a tax-deductible expense."

"Mrs. Lewis has the hots for you."

"She's got the hots for any man wearing pants. She's nothing but a pain. She needs a psychiatrist. I'd love to palm her off on Peabody."

"You're not that cruel, are you?"

"It's not cruelty. He deserves her. Angel could stand the competition."

"The X-ray you ordered at the hospital yesterday is here," Syndi said as they reached his office. "It shows the Riggioletti baby is anencephalic." She handed the X-ray picture to him. "It has no head. If the baby's born alive, it can't last long."

"I was afraid something major was wrong." the doctor looked at the picture. "Among other things, the heartbeat has never been regular. I feel sorry for Betty. She's been a good patient."

"I feel sorry for her, too. She wants that baby very badly."

7

"I'll have to tell her husband," said the doctor. "Maffi's not a pleasant person. Have Julie call him and set up an appointment. I need to see him here in the office tonight by seven if it can be arranged."

"I'll tell Julie."

"I let this go on too long. I don't like to use X-rays in a pregnancy. They're dangerous to an unborn baby. It was wishful thinking on my part. I was hoping for the best."

"I was, too."

"We'd better get this meeting over with as soon as we can. It won't take long. Maybe we can still go to dinner and see the play tonight like we planned. I still have the tickets."

"Will we find you in the river?" Syndi asked, halfway joking.

"You might. Maffi's that kind of man. Keep an eye on Mrs. Lewis. She gets impatient."

"I'll watch her."

Dr. Crawford entered his office and closed the door behind him. He sat down at his desk, took a deep breath, and picked up the telephone.

"Yes, John, what's up?"

"Deborah's pregnant."

"Is that your daughter?" The doctor asked.

"Yes, and I want an abortion."

"How old is she?"

"Seventeen."

"Who's the boy?" Dr. Crawford turned uncomfortably in his chair.

"Steven Cortez, a boy in her class in school."

"Why don't you have a wedding?"

"I don't want that boy for a son-in-law. He's Mexican. His father's a bricklayer. They're trash."

"Has she seen a doctor?"

"No."

"How far along is she?"

"Five months."

"How do you know?"

"She told me. She's showing."

"An abortion is risky at that stage, John."

"But you can do it!"

"Yes, but it's illegal. She's too far along."

"Charles, I'm depending on you!"

"It's too damn risky, John. It'll cost you plenty. Think it over. I don't advise it. Give the baby up for adoption.

"We're going to have this abortion, one way or another!" John Clarke was angry. "What will it cost for you to do it?"

"John, I don't want to do it!"

"YOU'LL DO IT! STATE YOUR PRICE!"

"Thirty big ones in cash up front and you blinding people's eyes and ears at the hospital. I don't want to do it."

"YOU'LL DO IT OR YOU'LL LOSE YOUR HOSPITAL PRIVILEGES! I'M A POWERFUL MAN. I'LL RUIN YOU! YOU'LL WISH YOU HAD NEVER HEARD OF ME!"

"But, John, it's illegal as hell. We can get into serious trouble. I could lose my license."

"YOU'LL LOSE YOUR LICENSE IF YOU DON'T DO IT! What time can you see her today, or do I take her somewhere else?"

"Don't take her to the butcher shop! They'll kill her. She's too far along for a coat hanger. I can see her late this afternoon."

"When?"

"Here at my office at five o'clock."

"What about before then?"

"No! Don't come sooner! The office closes at four. It will take us an hour to get everybody else out of here. Syndi and I can do the work-up for her. You will have to shut up the lab people and keep this out of accounting. Tell Deborah as little as possible until we know for sure what we're up against. This is risky business. I don't like it. I don't want to do it."

"YOU WILL DO IT!"

Julie knocked, then opened the door and came inside.

"I've got to go, John. We'll talk more later. I'll see you at five."

"Doctor," Julie said, "your lunch is here. Ralph Stone is on line two."

9

"I'll take it in here."

She set his tray on his desk and closed the door as she went back to the reception desk.

"Hi, Ralph, what's up?"

"Rough day?"

"Yeh, rough day. I went to the hospital at five this morning, and I've been going hard ever since. I'm up to my eyeballs in alligators. I haven't had time to relax a minute, much less have lunch. What's new?"

"I received a letter from Angel's lawyer," Ralph said.

"What did she say?"

"Angel will give you the divorce for fifty thousand more than what you offered her."

"Fifty thousand! Good God! What does she think I'm made of? Money? I don't have it, and she knows that. She's already getting everything as it is."

"Think about it and tell me what you want to do."

"I'm in debt to my limit now. I don't know how I could come up with fifty thousand. But even if I could, what's to keep her from trying to get more? There's got to be a stopping point. This is blackmail!"

"I have the offer in writing. She can't back down if we accept it. Think about it some more and get back to me."

"I'll think about it and get back to you, but I don't know where the money can come from."

Harried, the doctor came out of his office. Syndi took him back inside and closed the door.

"Honey." She sensed his anger. "What did Ralph say?"

"Angel's a greedy bitch. She'll give me the divorce for fifty thousand more than what I offered. It would be worth every penny to get rid of her, but I don't know where the money can come from."

"What did John Clarke want?"

"His daughter's five months pregnant. He wants an abortion."

"Who's the father?"

"Steven Cortez, her classmate in school. The boy's father is Hernando Cortez, a bricklayer. He's a widower. He did some work for me a few years back. He's ok. I don't know the boy."

"Why don't the kids get married and have the baby?"

"The boy's Mexican and not country club caliber. Clarke's threatening to take her to the butcher shop if I don't do it. They'd kill her."

"Five months is too far along for their coat hanger methods. They've killed and maimed too many girls already. I don't understand how they stay open."

"Not all abortions are legal, and sometimes the girls don't want their parents to know they've been fooling around. I insist the parents know about the abortion and approve of it or I won't do it. This greatly reduces the number. I'm not fond of doing them anyway."

"When are they bringing Deborah in?" Syndi asked.

"Clarke's bringing her here at five. She hasn't seen a doctor yet. We'll have to stay late. We'll do a quick work-up and send it to the lab. I'm going to try to talk him into placing the baby up for adoption."

"But I have a dinner date with a handsome doctor," she teased. "Then we're going to see a play."

"We may have to put it off. If Clarke weren't chairman of the hospital board, the answer would be 'HELL NO!' I would have washed my hands of this mess. I'd rather see a play. Please help me in this."

"I will if I can."

Julie knocked on the door, and Syndi opened it.

"Doctor, Maffi Riggioletti is on the phone," Julie said. "He can come at seven."

"Tell him to meet me here at the office. I want to get this over with. Damn, what a day. Who's next?"

"Mrs. Lewis," Sindi reminded him. "I've kept an eye on her. She doesn't like to wait."

"Of course. Why not?"

"Why not what?"

"She's one headache I'm going to get rid of."

The doctor and Syndi went into the treatment room to see Mrs. Lewis.

"Mrs. Lewis, I am referring you to Dr. Wilson Peabody. Julie will call his office and get you an appointment. He'll be able to handle your problem much better than I can."

Stunned, Mrs. Lewis did not answer.

At four forty-five that afternoon, Dr. Crawford sat down at his desk to eat his cold lunch. His last patient had just left. He picked up the telephone and placed a call.

"Hi, Ralph, this is Crawford."

"Finished for the day?"

"No, the day's not over. I've two more to see. Call Angel's lawyer and offer her ten. Tell her I don't have it. See what she says. Call me back when you get an answer."

He tried to relax while eating his lunch. The telephone rang a few moments later. It was his private line.

"Hi, Ralph, what's the word?"

"Angel's lawyer says no dice. It's the entire fifty or fight."

"Let me think on it some more. I don't know where I can come up with that much money."

"We've got to get rid of that damned woman," the doctor grumbled to himself as he hung up the phone. "Maffi was right. I'm sorry I didn't hire a hit man. It would have been simpler, cheaper, and over by now. Angel's a bitch."

THREE

X   X   X

"John Clarke and his wife are here with Deborah," Julie said over the intercom. "I'm leaving for the day."

"Thanks for staying late," Dr. Crawford said.

"I envy Julie," he said to Syndi. "When her day is over, she can leave the office behind. My day is never over."

The doctor went to the waiting room. "Come in," he said pleasantly to the Clarkes.

Deborah got up first. She was in tears. Carrying a briefcase, her father followed her into the medical area. Her mother remained in the waiting room crying.

Syndi took the girl to a treatment room to get blood and urine samples while the two men went into Dr. Crawford's office.

"We'll have to see what the situation is," the doctor said as he sat down at his desk. "I'll also need a blood work-up and the lab reports. I think you should reconsider. Not only is this illegal, it's dangerous to Deborah. She should have seen a doctor before now."

"YOU'LL DO IT OR ELSE!" Clarke put the briefcase on Dr. Crawford's desk. "The boy's Mexican. Victoria and I couldn't face our friends at the club if they knew about this."

Clarke opened the briefcase and turned it towards the doctor. "Thirty big ones up front, cold, hard cash. Count it! You'll get anything you want out of the lab and any other department of the hospital. If you don't get cooperation, you know how to reach me! Nothing will go to medical records or to Accounting unless you say so. I MEAN BUSINESS!"

13

Dr. Crawford paused momentarily looking at the open briefcase. He had never seen that much in cash before.

"I'll take your word for it." He closed the briefcase. "I'll hold the money in case you change your mind. I need to examine Deborah while she's here. We'll have to get the lab reports before we can schedule anything. I still don't like this business. Tell the girl as little as possible, and don't let her eat anything before I call tomorrow morning. Time is critical."

John Clarke went back to the waiting room to join his wife.

"How's it going?" Dr. Crawford asked Syndi. They had gone into the hallway where the girl could not hear them.

"She doesn't want an abortion," said Syndi. "She's cooperated so far because she feels you won't do it. She's too far along."

"Her father isn't backing down. He had thirty thousand in cash in his briefcase."

"Here is what I have so far," said Syndi. She handed her notes to the doctor.

"The baby's a good six months instead of five," said the doctor as he read the notes. "You know more obstetrics than most GPs. I'll tell John I'll call him when the lab results are in."

X   X   X

Michael Thomas Riggioletti arrived promptly at seven. Better known as Maffi, he was the vice lord of the city. His father, brothers, uncles, and cousins had all been killed in rival gang warfare, leaving him as the sole heir to his grandfather's underworld empire, and he ruled it with an iron hand.

Betty Riggioletti was very much a part of her husband's organization. Always in the background, she laundered their gangland profits and handled their finances.

Maffi was over fifty, and Betty was in her late forties. They had no children. It was only through a new medical technique that Betty had been able to conceive. This was her last chance to have a baby of her own.

"Good evening, Mr. Riggioletti." Dr. Crawford said as he came into the waiting room. They were alone.

Maffi put down the magazine he was reading. "What's it with Betty and the baby?"

"Bad news. Betty's had trouble with this pregnancy from the beginning. The baby's anencephalic. It doesn't have a head. She's carried it for six months. I'm surprised it's gone this far. She can lose it at any time. It probably won't go to term. If it survives delivery, it won't live two minutes. I'm recommending we end the pregnancy now. We've got medical grounds to do it."

"You don't understand. You're not going to abort that baby!" The gangster got to his feet.

"The baby's a lost cause."

"It'll kill her if she finds out. There must be something you can do. I'll pay any amount."

"It's not a matter of money."

"CRAWFORD, YOU DON'T UNDERSTAND! SHE MUST HAVE THAT BABY! IT'S GOT TO BE NORMAL! YOU'RE GOING TO MAKE IT THAT WAY!" He glared at the doctor.

"I've done all I can do."

"YOU'RE GOING TO DO MORE! YOU'VE GOT TO COME UP WITH SOMETHING!" Maffi Riggioletti doubled his fists. "I'LL NOT TAKE 'NO' FOR AN ANSWER!

"I'll call you in the morning, and we can talk about this further."

"NO! YOU THINK OF SOMETHING!" Maffi raised his doubled fists. "I DON'T CARE WHAT IT COSTS! SHE MUST HAVE THAT BABY! IT MUST BE NORMAL! YOU FIX THAT BABY! IF YOU DON'T, YOU'RE IN THE RIVER!"

The mobster turned and stalked out the door. Tears were in his eyes.

"I've never seen a fifty-year-old gangster cry," Syndi said as she came into the waiting room. "They really want that baby."

"He took it hard," said the doctor. "There isn't anything else I could say. He doesn't want to understand."

He paused for a moment and then looked down at the floor.

"This is a medical problem. He's trying to handle it in a gangster way."

They went down the hallway to his office.

"I have the Clarke results from the lab." She handed him a folder. "They did a rush job on the blood work. It's not complete. You're private line's ringing."

"I got it." Dr. Crawford picked up the phone. "Hello."

"This is Ralph. Is the day over yet?"

"No, the day isn't over. I've got mountains to climb and miracles to perform. That's what you get for being a board-certified physician. What's up?"

"Angel's lawyer is threatening to withdraw the offer."

"I can come up with half of the money now. See if that will satisfy her. I don't know where the other half can come from."

"It won't. She says it's all or none."

"I'll have to call you in the morning."

"Syndi," he said after hanging up the phone. "I wish I'd hired a hit man! Let me have those reports." She handed him the files. He paused momentarily before continuing. "Sorry about tonight. Here's some money. Please get our supper."

"What do you want?"

"It doesn't matter. Angel is trying to crush me. Maffi threatens to put me in the river. Clarke is going to ruin me. I'm really not hungry, but I should eat something."

"I'll go to Wilma's," Syndi said "It's just around the corner."

"I wish I hadn't given Clarke a figure," Charles said. "Thirty thousand is to him like thirty dollars to an ordinary person. I should have known he'd come up with the money."

"We can talk more after I get back," Syndi said as she went out the door.

The telephone rang. It was his private line, and Charles answered it.

"Charles Crawford! You come up with that money NOW!"

"Angel! How did you get this number?"

"You come up with that fifty thousand NOW! I won't take a penny less. I want it NOW!"

"I don't have it, and you know that."

"You get it NOW!"

"Go eat a chocolate-covered rat!"

Angel slammed down the receiver.

Crawford shook his head in dismay as he hung up the phone. "Maffi was right. I should have hired a hit man."

He picked up the Clarke and Riggioletti reports and tried to read them.

Angel's voice was still ringing in his ears.

"You come up with that fifty thousand NOW! I won't take a penny less I want it NOW! You get it NOW!"

He knew John Clarke would carry out his threat. "I'M A POWERFUL MAN. I'LL RUIN YOU! YOU'LL WISH YOU HAD NEVER HEARD OF ME!"

And Maffi Riggioletti would be true to his word.

"YOU FIX THAT BABY! IF YOU DON'T, YOU'RE IN THE RIVER!"

"What a mess I'm in."

Charles Crawford shook his head as he tried to read the reports a second and then a third time. He leaned back in his chair as if he were meditating.

"I'm back," said Syndi as she came in his office with their supper. "I got you an extra order of that fried chicken you like. It's part of a dinner special. I'll reheat it for you in the oven. I also got you a piece of apple pie."

"I've been looking at these blood types and test results." He hadn't heard a word Syndi had said. "They're compatible!"

"What do you mean?" Syndi asked.

"If Betty Riggioletti were carrying the Clarke baby, it could go to term and be born normal and healthy."

"What are we going to do?" Syndi asked.

"I don't know," said the doctor. "It's a bad deal any way we go."

"What are our options?" Syndi asked.

"If we don't do the abortion, Clarke will be mad. He'll take Deborah to the butcher shop. They'll botch it up and probably kill her. Clarke will blame us."

"And Betty will still lose her baby," said Syndi.

"If we do it," the doctor continued, "a perfectly good baby will be dead."

"It's too bad we couldn't give Deborah's baby to Betty," Syndi said.

Charles paused momentarily.

"Your idea isn't a bad one. They discussed this at the obstetrics and gynecology meeting last month at New York."

"Yes."

"A doctor from Denmark gave a presentation. I took notes on it." Charles got up and went to a filing cabinet. He opened the top drawer and found a file.

"Here it is."

He took a few moments to review his notes.

"What happened?" Syndi asked.

"The doctor was in Africa serving as a missionary. A pregnant mother came out of the bush. She was in poor health. He didn't expect her to survive delivery."

"Could he abort the baby?"

"She was too far along, and the religious denomination he represented opposed abortions."

"Not even to save the life of the mother?" Asked Syndi.

"Not even to save the life of the mother."

"What did he do?"

"He had another mother in good health at about the same stage of pregnancy carrying a dead fetus. He investigated the possibility of transferring the baby to her."

"Did it work?"

"His tests indicated that the baby would not be compatible with the new mother, so he didn't try it. There was the question as to whether the first mother could survive the operation."

"What happened?"

"The first mother and her baby died in childbirth. The second mother lost her baby in a natural abortion."

"How sad." Syndi said.

"In our case, the baby and new mother would be compatible. Both mothers are in good health." Charles took the notes to his desk and sat down.

"What about the ethics question?"

"We wouldn't have to tell anybody," said Charles. "If we could do it, it would make John Clarke and Maffi both happy, and we would be saving the life of the baby."

"But Deborah wouldn't have her baby," Syndi said.

"At least she and the baby would be alive. Betty would be a good mother. I wish Deborah could have her baby and keep it, but John Clarke isn't going to let that happen."

"Can we do it?" Syndi asked.

"We can try. The plan is outlined here in my notes. We don't have much to lose. I'll need to make some quick arrangements."

"I'll do my best to help," Syndi said. "It's the best of a bad deal."

The doctor picked up the telephone and called John Clarke at his home.

"John, this is Dr. Crawford. Bring Deborah to the hospital tonight. Don't let her eat or drink anything. I hope she hasn't had any supper. Meet me there at ten-fifteen. Tell her it's for more tests. Don't tell her anything else. If we do the abortion, it has to be done tonight. Be there at ten-fifteen sharp. Don't be early, and don't be late. It's now or never."

He hung up the telephone and looked up a number in Betty Riggioletti's medical file. He dialed it and leaned back in his swivel chair.

"Maffi, this is Dr. Crawford. I've been looking through your wife's file and test results. There is something we can do. It's a long shot. I don't promise it will work, but I'll do my best. It involves surgery on the baby. You have nothing to lose."

"When will you do it?" Maffi Riggioletti asked.

"If we do it, we need to do it tonight. Betty could lose her baby at any moment."

"We'll do it. What will it cost?"

"Thirty thousand in cash. Can you have it tomorrow sometime?"

"That's pocket change. I'll be there tonight. You fix that baby!"

The doctor hung up the phone and turned to Syndi. "We'll need three OB nurses and an anesthesiologist who will keep their mouths shut. I know who we will call. We're going to give Deborah's baby to Betty."

FOUR

X   X   X

Dr. Crawford entered Betty Riggioletti's room promptly at ten o'clock that evening.

"Betty, your husband will be in to see you but only for a few minutes. We're going to operate on the baby tonight. If we don't, we'll lose it. I make no promises. We may lose it anyway. It'll be touch and go. Just do your best."

"I will." Betty took Dr. Crawford's hand. "I knew there was trouble. So did Maffi. You'll do your best, too, doctor, I'm sure."

"We will," he said. "We'll have to put you to sleep."

"Do what you have to do."

Maffi Riggioletti came into his wife's room. He set down his briefcase and his unopened newspaper and went to his wife's side.

"I'll leave you two together." Dr. Crawford said. "The anesthesiologist will be here soon. When he comes in, Maffi, you go to the waiting room."

The anesthesiologist came a few minutes later with two nurses and gave Betty an anesthetic through her IV. When she was unconscious, the nurses took her to the first of two adjacent OB-GYN operating rooms. Maffi picked up his briefcase and his newspaper and went to the waiting room where John Clarke and his wife sat with Deborah."

"Do we have to be in the same room with that hoodlum?" Victoria Clarke whispered to her husband as Maffi entered.

20

"Leave him alone. He can be dangerous. We have more important concerns tonight."

"Paying no attention to the Clarkes, Maffi Riggioletti sat down. He took the latest edition of 'THE GANGSTER CHRONICLE' out of its plain, paper wrapper and began to read it.

He noticed an article on the tommy gun, a type of submachine gun popular in gangster circles, on one of the inside pages. He marked it for Betty. She would want to read it after she came home from the hospital. She always read the 'CHRONICLE' cover-to-cover.

X   X   X

"Deborah, we're ready," Syndi said as she opened the waiting room door.

Deborah followed Syndi into the operating room next to Betty Riggioletti's. There was a closed door that connected these two rooms.

"Change into this gown," Syndi said. "Let me help you."

"Do I have to?"

"Yes, you have to."

Deborah hesitated for a moment, and then with Syndi's assistance, she took off her clothes and put on the gown.

"Lie down on the examination table and follow instructions," Syndi said. "This won't take long."

The anesthesiologist came in. He held a soaked cloth near Deborah's nose. When the girl was unconscious, a nurse inserted an IV into her arm, and gave her more anesthetic through the IV.

Dr. Crawford came into the next room to see Betty, and then he opened the door connecting her room to Deborah's.

"Betty's ready," he said.

"Deborah's under," said Syndi.

"Now we'll induce labor," he said.

The doctor gave Deborah a shot in her abdomen. "Contractions will begin in a few minutes. She'll deliver at about eleven. The baby will be partly anesthetized. We don't want it to start using its lungs. We need to watch closely for problems. We'll start Betty's surgery now. Our timing must be perfect."

X   X   X

"Scalpel." The doctor reached out for the instrument. He was standing over Betty Riggioletti in the operating room. Tipped to her right side, her legs were strapped to the table. One arm was outstretched with an IV. The other was tightly wrapped to her side. She was receiving oxygen.

"Scalpel." The nurse gave him his surgical knife.

Crawford's hand was steady as he made the abdominal incision. He cut through the body wall quickly. Then he opened the uterus, exposing the baby inside its amniotic sac.

"Draw out most of the fluid with that large syringe," Dr. Crawford said to one of the nurses. "Save it in those sterile bottles on the counter. We'll need it later."

"That's enough. I'm going to cut the amniotic membrane," he said to the second nurse. "Hold the edges apart. We don't want them to stick to each other."

"I'm ready," said the nurse.

"What time is it?" The doctor asked.

"Five 'till eleven."

Dr. Crawford slit the membrane, and he clamped the umbilical cord.

"Watch out for the blood vessels," he said.

The nurse held the edges apart.

Leaving the clamped umbilical stub inside the amniotic sac, he cut the baby free and lifted it out.

"A headless baby boy," he said as he put it into a jar of preservative. "There's no way it could survive."

"Deborah's baby is coming out," Syndi said as she stood in the doorway connecting the two rooms.

The doctor hurried to Deborah's side.

"It's out!" Syndi caught the baby.

The doctor clamped the umbilical cord twice, about six inches apart. Then he cut the cord about halfway between the clamps.

"Get those plastic tubes," he said to a nurse, pointing to the sterile package on the cart. "We're in the most critical part."

The doctor hurried with the baby to Betty Riggioletti's side. He inserted two tubes, one halfway into the baby's umbilical artery and the other halfway into the vein.

"The fluid inside should keep the membranes from sticking to the baby," he said to the nurse as he put the baby inside Betty Riggioletti's amniotic sac.

The doctor connected each tube in the baby's cord to its corresponding blood vessel in the umbilical stub. He stitched the ends of each vessel together tightly around its tube. Then he removed the clamps and paused momentarily to observe.

"Blood flow has been re-established. The baby didn't start using his lungs. His heart seems to be beating normally. Let's hope he wasn't deprived of oxygen long enough to do damage to the brain."

He attached the cord ends together with stitches. "Now add more amniotic fluid."

The second nurse injected more fluid.

"That's enough, Let's overlap the cut edges of the amniotic membrane, They'll stick together."

He stitched the edges together as the first nurse held them in place, and he pressed the overlapping portions to seal them tight.

"That should hold. Add more fluid."

Using a syringe, the second nurse finished filling the amniotic sac with fluid.

The doctor wiped his brow. "The membranes aren't leaking."

He closed up the uterus and then the body wall. Then he stepped back for a moment.

"The surgery's done. How's Deborah?"

"Deborah's doing fine," said Syndi. "Her placenta is out. It's Betty and her new baby I'm worried about."

"So am I," said the doctor. "We're in uncharted territory. The next goal is to get them through the night."

"At least the baby has a chance," said Syndi.

X   X   X

At one o'clock that morning, Dr. Crawford met with the Clarkes outside the OB-GYN operating rooms.

"It's over. The baby's gone."

"I diagnosed it as anencephalic," the doctor continued. "It didn't have a head.

"How's Deborah?" John Clarke asked.

"The nurses have taken her to a private room," the doctor said. "She'll recover nicely, but we have to keep her for a couple of days."

"The girls at the club will never know." Victoria said.

"The paperwork will be finished this morning," the Doctor said. "Syndi got Deborah's signature on the necessary papers yesterday afternoon, but she's underage. I need for you and your wife to sign, too. For the record, Deborah had a miscarriage, not an abortion. The result is the same."

"I knew you could do it," said John Clarke. "Can we see her?"

"She's asleep. We have her sedated. Her memory of tonight will be blurred by the anesthesia. Go home and get some rest. You'll need to come back at about one o'clock this afternoon. I expect her to be upset when she wakes up and finds out she's no longer pregnant."

"Where do we sign?" Asked John Clarke.

"Here on the dotted line."

"This is a relief," said Victoria Clark as she and her husband signed the form. "I can't stand that wop in the waiting room. I hope he doesn't know anything about this."

"This is all confidential," said Dr. Crawford. "His wife's a patient here. He's waiting to see her. He knows nothing about Deborah's situation."

"He's trash. Can we go home now?"

"You can leave by the staff entrance. It opens directly into the hall near the elevators."

X   X   X

At one-thirty, the doctor met with Maffi Riggioletti in the waiting room. They were alone.

"The surgery's finished. Everything's gone well so far. Your wife has a good chance of carrying the baby to term. Chances are good it will be a normal C-section delivery and a normal boy."

"I'm relieved. When can I see Betty?"

"You can't see her until this afternoon. She's still sedated. It's not over yet. I'll spend the rest of the night in the doctor's lounge. Syndi will be sitting in the big chair in Betty's room. I'll check on Betty every two hours. We'll be here in case she needs us. She could still lose the baby."

"I brought your briefcase, doctor," said Maffi. "The money's all there. I'm sorry I threatened you. You've always done your best."

"I'll take your word on the money. We're all tired. Everything tonight is off the books. Your apology is accepted. No hard feelings."

"I want Betty to have a normal baby. It'll mean a lot to her. Good night."

"What are you going to do with the money?" Syndi asked after Maffi had gone. She had come into the waiting room, and they were alone. "You got thirty thousand from the Clarkes and thirty thousand from Maffi Riggioletti. That's sixty thousand."

"Fifty thousand is what we need to get rid of Angel. Ten thousand will pay the people we needed tonight."

"Will anyone talk?"

"No way. That was understood before they came. Anyway, they're getting cash. There'll be no taxes."

"What about the baby?" Syndi asked. "Will it look enough like Maffi Riggioletti to pass as his?"

"The father's Mexican. He's short, stocky, and dark like Maffi. Both mothers are White European ancestry. It's a fair match, but not perfect."

"You're tired. You'd better get to bed."

"I'll be paged every two hours to come in and check on Betty. Call me anytime she has problems. You can sleep. The monitors will alert you to trouble.

"What about Deborah?" Syndi asked.

"The floor nurses will check on her. She'll be all right."

"Somehow, I feel like a traitor," Syndi said. "She trusted me."

FIVE

X   X   X

Tired, Dr. Crawford paused momentarily in front of Betty Riggioletti's room and looked down at his notes. It was almost ten o'clock. He had entered the room at four, six, and eight o'clock that morning according to schedule. Syndi and Betty had been asleep. Each time he had checked the monitors and listened to the unborn baby's heartbeat with his stethoscope.

"No sign of rejection so far," he said to himself. "Let's hope the baby's vital signs are still normal."

He knocked softly on the door, opened it, and then entered the room.

"Syndi," he whispered, "its ten o'clock."

Syndi was awake and sitting in the chair.

"Betty's still asleep. She's rested peacefully so far."

The doctor checked the monitors and the baby's heartbeat as before.

"The baby's vital signs still appear to be normal. Everything seems to be ok."

"What about Deborah?" Syndi asked.

"She's still asleep. I'll check on her again later. She'll recover fine. It's Betty and the baby I'm worried about."

"What happens when Deborah wakes up and finds out her baby's gone?"

"That's the next problem," the doctor said. "Her parents are coming to help. She can't prove anything. Her memory about last night will be blurred."

26

"You go back to bed," Syndi said. "You look tired. I'll take over. I'll get you up if there's trouble, and I'll look in on Deborah."

X   X   X

"Nurse, what am I doing here? Deborah awoke in an angry mood. "It's daylight. What time is it?"

"Its two o'clock in the afternoon," said the nurse.

"What did they do to me last night?"

"You have a tray soft food here if you want to eat something."

"I don't feel like eating." Deborah sat up.

"Your doctor will be in soon. He'll talk with you then."

"I want to go home. I hurt like hell. What did they do to me last night? WHAT HAPPENED TO MY BABY?"

"Calm down," said the nurse. "They can hear you all over the hospital. I'm sure everything's all right. Your doctor will be in to see you soon."

"I don't care who hears me. I want to see the doctor NOW!" Deborah lowered the rail and got out of her bed. "WHAT HAPPENED TO MY BABY?"

"Get back into bed," the nurse said. "You have no business being up and about."

"NO!"

"Good afternoon, Deborah," Dr. Crawford said as he entered the room. "You'd better get back into bed. You still have an IV."

"DID YOU GIVE ME AN ABORTION!"

"Nobody gave you an abortion. You had a miscarriage."

"A WHAT?"

"A miscarriage. Your baby was anencephalic. It had no head. It died about two seconds after it was born. I have the X-ray of your baby here." The doctor took the picture of the unborn Riggioletti baby out of an unlabeled folder and handed it to her.

Deborah looked at the X-ray in disbelief.

"We still have the baby if you want to see it. It isn't a pleasant sight. Now go back to bed. You need to rest."

"What did you do to my baby?" Deborah burst into tears.

"Nobody did anything to your baby," the doctor said. "You need to stay another day or two in the hospital. You'll be fine if you take it easy for a day or two."

"YOU MURDERED MY BABY!"

"Your baby wasn't murdered." Dr. Crawford pointed to the picture. "Had you gone to a doctor earlier, you would have known there was trouble. Your baby had no head. There's no way it could have survived even if it had gone to term. You had a miscarriage, not an abortion. Things happened for the best."

"I don't believe you." Deborah took the X-ray and threw it at the doctor's face. "You did something to my baby! I HATE YOU! YOU"RE A BUTCHER!"

"Don't say that," her mother said.

Deborah had not seen her parents come into the room.

"You had him murder my baby!" She said to her parents. She burst into tears. "YOU"RE ALL MURDERS!"

"Don't talk that way," her mother said. "It's over now."

"NO, IT ISN'T!"

"Nurse," the doctor said quietly, "see that she gets more sedative."

He turned to her parents. "She needs to remain quiet for a day or two. She'll be fine."

The doctor picked up the X-ray and put it back inside the folder. "Let's get her back to bed. She needs to lie down."

"NO!"

"Be a good girl," her mother said.

The nurse and Mrs. Clarke assisted Deborah back to her bed. She continued to cry as the nurse gave her more sedative through her IV. They talked softly to her as she drifted off to sleep.

X   X   X

"How did I do, doctor?" Betty Riggioletti was awake when he entered her room.

"You did fine." Dr. Crawford placed his stethoscope on Betty's abdomen and listened to the baby's heartbeat. "Things went well last night. The baby's heartbeat and vital signs are normal. You have a good chance of having a normal baby boy, but we're not out of the woods yet. You'll probably have to stay here until the delivery. We need to keep a close eye on you and the baby."

"I'll do my best, Doctor. You're tired, I can tell. You need to rest."

"You're a good patient, Betty. You don't complain. I appreciate that. Maffi's in the waiting room. I'll send him in, but he can't stay long. You need to rest, too.

"I'll be fine."

"I'll leave now. Maffi will be in soon."

X   X   X

"Betty, are you asleep?" Maffi said softly as he came into her room. He had a dozen roses in his hand.

"Maffi, is that you?" Betty had her eyes closed.

"You must be tired from the operation."

"Yes, I am, but it's worth it. Dr. Crawford said the baby is all right." She didn't open her eyes.

He lowered the side rail and sat down on the edge of the bed beside her.

"I brought you more roses." He kissed her forehead."

"I appreciate them." She took his hand.

"Dr. Crawford said the baby is a boy," he said.

"We'll name him Michael Thomas after you."

"I'll try to be a good father to him. I want him to have the best. The Doctor told me not to stay long. I'll leave now. I love you."

"I love you, Maffi."

He kissed her forehead again and then got up from the bed. He raised the rail and put the roses on the table. Then he quietly left the room.

X   X   X

"Ralph," Dr. Crawford was calling from his office, "I got the fifty big ones. I'll bring the money by your office this afternoon, but you'll have to launder it."

"Launder it?"

29

"It's all cash, off the books, but don't let Angel or her lawyer find that out."

"I won't Where did you get it?"

"Midnight medicine, Ralph," Charles turned nervously in his chair. "You wouldn't believe me if I told you. The money's not stolen. You don't have to worry. Just launder it and pay the bitch off."

"Bring over the money. I'll call Angel's attorney and accept her offer. Did you hear the news?"

"What news?"

"Dr. Peabody proposed to Angel. She's wearing a big engagement ring. That may be why she wants to settle."

"Poor fool, I hope he marries her. Serves him right."

X   X   X

"John," Victoria Clarke said. "I'm worried about Deborah." The Clarkes had eaten dinner at the Golden Garden Restaurant and were returning home.

"She'll get over it." John Clarke turned their Rolls Royce into their driveway.

"She keeps saying we killed her baby. It was for her own good. I don't want to lose her. She's our only child."

"She'll settle down."

"I certainly hope so. If she married Steven, I couldn't face the girls at the club."

"He's trash. We don't want him for a son-in-law."

"Can you imagine having Mexican grandchildren? The girls would never forgive us."

John Clarke stopped the car in front of the garage and turned off the engine.

"We're both tired. Let's go inside and get some rest. I've got a rough day at the office tomorrow. I'll be glad when this is all over."

X   X   X

"It's been a rough two days," Dr. Crawford said to Syndi over dinner. They were at the Golden Garden that evening.

"I'm glad we came to see the play tonight. It's the last performance. You needed a night off."

"I gave Ralph the fifty thousand this afternoon. He contacted Angel's lawyer and accepted her offer. He said Peabody gave Angel an engagement ring."

"That's interesting." Syndi looked at her own ring and smiled.

"That's Peabody's problem. If things go well with Betty and Deborah, maybe we can go away and have this weekend to ourselves."

"Let's wait until we're married, dear."

Charles dozed during most of the performance. Syndi said nothing until the final curtain.

"The play's over, Charles."

"Huh, huh, I must have fallen asleep. He yawned.

"Let me drive," she said when they reached the car. "Give me the keys. I want to see how it drives."

She didn't want to risk him dozing at the wheel.

"All right."

Syndi drove them to his apartment.

"Shall I take you home?"

"May I come in? You're too tired to drive. I can stay here tonight."

"I thought we were going to wait until we were married."

"We are."

Once inside, Syndi helped him find his pajamas. After he had changed into them, she helped him to bed. Tired, he fell asleep almost as soon as he lay down. She took a blanket and pillow to the couch.

"We'll wait until after we're married," she laughed. "He's too tired anyway."

SIX

X   X   X

"How's Deborah doing?" John Clarke asked Dr. Crawford. They were standing outside the doctors' lounge at the hospital. Victoria Clarke was standing beside her husband.

"She's calmed down since yesterday," the doctor said.

"What does she say about the baby?" John Clarke asked.

"She realizes its gone, and there is nothing she can do to bring it back. Keep reminding her the baby didn't have a head, and nobody murdered it. In time, she may accept it. Be patient with her but firm."

"When can she come home?"

"She's ready. I'll finish the paperwork now." Dr. Crawford turned to go to the nurses' station.

X   X   X

"Steve," Deborah whispered over the phone in her hospital room.

"Where are you?"

"I'm in the hospital. My parents tricked me. They murdered our baby!"

"What!"

"They murdered our baby. They're coming down the hall. I've got to hang up." Deborah hung up the phone as her parents reached her room.

"Deb," Victoria Clarke said, "we're sorry about the baby. It's for the best. The doctor says you can come home. Are you ready?"

"I don't want to stay here. I hate this place."

"Your mother brought you some clothes," her father said. "I have business to tend to for a few minutes. Your mother can help you get dressed."

"Close the door behind you. I can change myself."

"Your mother will stay with you."

X   X   X

"The doctor has released you," John Clarke said to Deborah when he returned. "He says you'll recover in time to start school. Are you ready to leave?"

"I'm ready."

The Clarkes went to the elevator and rode down to the parking garage. Without a word, they got into their Rolls Royce, and John drove them out to the street.

"Deb," he said, breaking the silence, "stay away from Steven! I know he'll be at school. If you don't stay away from him, I'll have him arrested. You're both underage. Do you understand?"

"I understand," she said resentfully.

"We should have sent you to a private girl's school," her mother said.

"You've got your last year of high school ahead of you," John Clarke said. "Keep your grades up, and leave the boys alone. No nonsense! We want you to go to college."

"I understand."

"We have some colleges picked out," her mother said, "Ivy League schools. You'll meet boys there. They'll be from the best families. They won't be foreigners. Once school is underway, we'll start applying."

"I understand."

"You need to stay home all next week," her father said. "Dr. Crawford says you need to rest."

"I understand."

"You'll go back to the doctor for a checkup at the end of the week and, if things are all right, another one just before school."

"I understand."

"Can't you say anything else?" Her mother asked.

"No."

X   X   X

"Did Angel sign the papers?" Charles Crawford asked his attorney. He and Syndi were in Ralph Stone's office.

"She signed, but things did not go well."

"What happened? Did she count the money?"

"I gave her lawyer a check from my escrow account. Angel won't get it until the divorce is final."

"What did she say?"

"She wanted to know where you got the money."

"What did you tell her?"

"I said it was none of her business."

"Then what?"

"She said she wasn't going to sign until she found out where it came from. She said you must be hiding assets, and she wanted the rest of what you had."

"What did I tell you she'd do, the greedy bitch."

"I told her you weren't hiding anything. Her lawyer said it didn't matter one way or the other. She had made the offer in writing, and we had accepted it in writing. She couldn't change her mind. She had to sign. The judge would rule against her if she didn't."

"When will the divorce become final?

"About a month after the judge signs the order. We hope he'll set the date Tuesday when he rules on it. There'll be a court hearing then.

"Will Angel be there?"

"I don't know, but if she is, I don't want you available. I don't want you there."

"When can I see the children?"

"Let's wait until the divorce is final. It has provisions for visitation."

"But I'm supposed to be able to see them now."

"Don't rock the boat. Let's take things one step at a time. Let's get this hearing over first."

X   X   X

"I wonder how Mrs. Lewis and Peabody are getting along," Syndi said to Charles as they were driving out of the parking lot.

"I haven't heard."

"I'm surprised," Syndi said. "We should hear something soon. Mrs. Lewis doesn't waste time when another woman is in the picture."

"Deborah left the hospital this morning," Charles said.

"Is she still mad?"

"Mad as a hornet."

"Can she cause trouble?"

"She can't prove anything. The baby that went to pathology was anencephalic. All of the documentation is in place. What about this weekend?"

"Let's wait until we're married."

"You'll never give in on that?"

"No."

"Thirty days is a long time to wait."

"We've waited this long. A few more days won't matter."

X   X   X

"Hello." Hernando Cortez answered the phone in his kitchen. He was Steven's father, and he had just arrived home from a hard day of work.

"This is John Clarke, Deborah's father. Deborah miscarried the baby yesterday. Tell Steven to leave her alone."

"What!"

"See that Steven leaves Deborah alone. If he doesn't, I'll have him arrested, and I'll see that no contractor in town will use you."

"I will tell him what you said." Angered by John Clarke's threat, Hernando Cortez slammed down the receiver.

"Dad, I listened on the phone in the bedroom." Steven came into the kitchen. "Deb called from the hospital this morning and had to hang up. I thought that might be her. She said they murdered our baby. I'm sorry I caused all this trouble."

35

"Clarke doesn't know it yet. I'll be out of his reach in a couple of weeks. Lay low until then. I'll be on a new job where he can't touch me. It'll last a couple of months until things cool off. After that, the other contractors will use me in spite of John Clarke. They can't find good brick masons."

"I will, Dad."

"Another Hernando Cortez was our distant ancestor. He captured Mexico for Spain in 1519. Our ancestors were proud people. We're proud people. The Clarkes are no better than we are."

"I agree, Dad."

"I don't care how much money they have. Don't ever apologize because your mother and I were not born in this country. Don't ever be ashamed of being Mexican."

"I won't, Dad."

"I don't like being threatened. John Clarke can go to hell!"

X   X   X

"More roses from your husband," a nurse said as she brought them into Betty Riggioletti's hospital room. "You've been out of the recovery room a week, and he's brought you roses every day. He's dedicated to you. I wish my husband was like that."

"If Maffi likes you," Betty joked, "he gives you roses. If he doesn't like you, he puts you in the river. Take some of these home. I have plenty. It's the thought that counts."

"I'd like to, but it would make my husband furious. He'd think I had a boyfriend."

"Mine wouldn't care," another nurse said as she picked out a few to take home. "All my husband is interested in is my paycheck. Wait until I tell him who these roses came from."

X   X   X

"Hi Ralph, what's up? Dr. Crawford answered the phone in his office.

"I got a call from Angel's attorney. Angel has thrown a fit. She wants to eliminate your visits with the children."

"No way! Tell her I'll fight. She isn't going to use this to extort more money out of me. She agreed to the settlement last week. We paid the money. She needs to abide by her agreement."

36

"That's what I wanted to hear. I'll be back in touch."

The doctor hung up the phone. He began reading a lab report on one of his patients, but his thoughts were elsewhere.

"Hello." He picked up the phone on the first ring. It was his private line.

"DAMN YOU, CHARLES CRAWFORD!"

"Angel!" He wasn't expecting to hear from her.

"You know what you did!"

"What is it this time?"

"That damned Lewis woman! She's after Peabody, AND YOU SENT HER!"

"Can't you stand a little competition? I've been told she puts out. She's supposed to be terrific in bed."

"I'LL GET YOU FOR THIS! IT WILL BE A COLD DAY IN HELL BEFORE YOU SEE THE CHILDREN!" Angel slammed down the telephone receiver.

Oh, dear me," Charles Crawford laughed as he hung up the phone. "I have done it this time. I couldn't help myself. Syndi was right. Mrs. Lewis doesn't waste time."

He picked up the lab report and read it with greater interest.

SEVEN

X   X   X

"I talked to Ralph this morning," Charles Crawford said to Syndi. They were in his office. He had just returned from making hospital rounds. "The divorce will be final on the Thursday after Labor Day. Then I can begin seeing the kids."

"Has Angel cooled off about Mrs. Lewis?" Syndi asked.

"No, but she can't stop the divorce. She signed the papers and accepted the money."

"Has she broken off with Peabody?"

"I don't know," answered Charles. "That's their problem. We can get married that Friday, but we won't have time for much of a honeymoon."

"Let's go somewhere private."

"The waiting room's full. We'd better get started."

September, 1962

Tuesday, the day after Labor Day, was the first day of the school term. Steven Cortez started down the hallway on the way to his first class.

"Psst, Steve!"

"Deb! Meet me in the auditorium. It's empty now. We can talk in private."

"I'll be there in a few minutes."

38

X   X   X

"Over here," Steve whispered as Deborah entered the auditorium. "It's safe here."

They hurried to each other and embraced.

"I missed you," she said, almost in tears.

"I love you, Deb." He kissed her forehead, then her lips, and he held her close to him.

"I love you, Steve."

"What happened?"

"My parents tricked me. They took me to see Dr. Crawford for an examination. He put me to sleep and caused me to have a miscarriage. They said our baby didn't have a head. I don't believe it. They murdered our baby."

"I'm glad you're all right."

"They said I miscarried naturally. We can't prove anything. My father said he'll have you arrested if I see you any more."

"He told my father that, too," answered Steve. "I didn't try to contact you because he'd cause trouble. What did he do with the baby?"

"The doctor kept it. I don't even know whether it was a boy or a girl. My parents wouldn't let us bury it. People at the Country Club might find out,"

"That's stupid," said Steve.

"They're watching me every minute. They're afraid I'll see you. They want me to marry someone rich. Mother says she sorry they didn't send me to some snobby girl's school. I want to run away."

"You're under eighteen. If they caught us, they'd put me in jail and punish you."

"What can we do?"

"We're both seniors. If we wait until we graduate, we'll be eighteen, and we'll have high school behind us. We can run away then. They can't stop us."

"Where will we go?" Deborah asked.

"We can go to college somewhere out west. We'll have to work our way through school, but we can do it."

"Oh, Steve, I love you."

"We'll have to plan this carefully," Steve continued. "We'll see each other in secret. They mustn't know."

"I'll be at the football game Thursday night."

"We've got to go now, before we're late to class. I'll see you at the game."

X   X   X

"You have been here to see me every day," Betty said to Maffi. They were in her hospital room. "I appreciate it very much."

"I love you, Betty. I want you and our son to be all right. You're the only family I have left."

"My family's gone, too. At least we have each other."

"The doctor sees you a lot, doesn't he?"

"At least twice a day. Syndi sees me that much, too. I haven't felt like reading since the operation on the baby. Please take these financial magazines home. I'll read them later."

"You know the stock market better than most professionals."

"I have lost touch with the market. I have a lot to catch up on, but I haven't felt like doing it. I haven't tried to work any of my crossword puzzles either. Please take them home, too. I don't feel like concentrating."

"You can catch up later. Our son is more important."

X   X   X

"Deborah, I have been waiting for you." Victoria Clarke was standing beside the Clarke Rolls Royce in front of the high school. "Classes were over fifteen minutes ago. What took you so long?"

"Fifteen minutes? It took me that long to get here. Where do you think I have been?"

"Was Steven at school today?"

"I don't know. Steven and I aren't going together any more."

"I wish you could choose boys from better families."

"Why can't I ride the school bus like everyone else?"

"You don't meet boys from the best families on the school bus."

40

Without answering, Deborah opened the door and got into the back seat. Her mother got into the car and drove home.

X   X   X

"The divorce is final," Ralph said to Charles. Syndi was by his side. Ralph had returned to his office from the court hearing. "Let's wait a week before we try to arrange a visit with the kids. Are you current with your child support payments?"

"Yes, I am. What's Angel trying to pull this time?"

"Peabody eloped with Mrs. Lewis. Angel's boiling mad. She blames you. She now says the kids can't be yours, they're Peabody's."

"Peabody wasn't in the picture back then," said Charles.

"Chuck looks too much like Charles to be Peabody's," Syndi said.

"Let's let her cool off a bit," said Ralph. "If you aren't the father, you won't have to pay child support. When she realizes that, she'll change her tune. Do you mind taking a blood test?"

"No, I don't," answered Charles, "but the people giving the test must be independent. Angel will try to fake things if she can to have the results come out the way she wants them. I want honest, accurate results."

"You keep paying the court clerk's office the child support and don't be late," said Ralph. "Don't give her any excuses. I don't think we'll have to resort to blood tests, but we might."

"Whatever you say. Did Angel return Peabody's ring?"

"She hocked it and gave him the pawn ticket."

"Serves them both right."

"One last word," said Ralph. "Don't say bad things to the kids about Angel. They're old enough to make up their own minds. If you try, it will backfire. She's their mother regardless of her bad qualities."

"Ok."

"I know you think she's a bitch, but go out of your way to be nice to her, no matter how rude and ugly she is. Let me handle the problems."

"Is tomorrow still on?" Charles asked Syndi as they left the lawyer's office. "Can we finally have a weekend to ourselves?"

"If it's a honeymoon. How's Betty Riggioletti?"

"Doing fine so far."

41

"How's Deborah?"

"Last I heard, she's calmed down a bit. She'll get over it. Let's go to the courthouse and get the license now. We can get married tomorrow morning and be on our way."

"Let's go."

X   X   X

"Deborah, what are you doing?" Victoria Clarke demanded. Deborah was upstairs in her room combing her hair. Her mother was standing in the doorway.

"Billy Stamperson asked me to go to the football game with him tonight. I'm getting ready."

"I'm going with you."

"Mother, you can't! What will Billy think?"

"I don't care what he thinks. I'm going with you."

"Why?"

"Steven will be at the game."

"I'm not seeing Steven anymore. I'm dating other boys. I don't know whether Steven will be at the game or not. If he is, he might be with another girl."

"I'm going with you anyway. We want to know who you're dating."

"You'll embarrass me! I'll call Billy and tell him I can't go." Deborah went to the telephone in the upstairs hall and dialed Steven's number. "Is Billy Stamperson there?"

"Deb." Steven recognized her voice. "What's up?"

"Billy, I'm sorry I can't go to the game tonight. My mother has other plans for me. I'm sorry to call so late."

"Thanks, Deb. I'll call Billy and tell him not to stop for you. Is everything all right?"

"Maybe some other time. Thanks for asking me."

"I'll see you at school. Be careful, Deb. I love you."

"Bye, see you around." Deborah hung up the phone.

"I wish you would choose a better class of boys," her mother said. "Why don't you date the Hampleton boy? I can arrange for him to ask you out."

"He's rude. He's nothing but a snob. He won't keep his hands off of you. None of the other girls like him."

"Don't say that. He's descended from English royalty. His mother and I are friends."

"His parents are members of your country club. That's all that matters to you."

"We're descended from English royalty, too," said John Clarke. He had heard the discussion and had come up the stairs.

"Through an illegitimate line," Deborah said under her breath.

"If a boy isn't from a good family," her father continued, "throw him back. Let the other girls have him."

"I can run my life!"

"Deborah," her mother said, "we're not trying to choose for you, but we want you to marry right."

"His family had better be Republican, rich, and WASP," her father said.

"The English royal family is German," Deborah answered as she returned to her room, "not Anglo-Saxon."

X   X   X

"Our wedding plans will have to be changed," Charles Crawford said to Syndi. They were at the hospital. He was doing morning rounds.

"You look like you didn't get any sleep last night," Syndi said. "What happened!"

"Betty Riggioletti had a bad night. Her membranes haven't broken, but they might at any time. We almost had to take the baby. I stayed up with her all night."

"How's Betty now?" Syndi asked.

"She's stable now, but she's in intensive care. Dr. Hennessy is with her now. I hope the baby can go to term."

"How's Maffi taking this?"

"He's concerned, but he's not a problem."

"What about us?" Syndi asked.

"We already have the license," said Charles. "There's a military chaplain visiting on the next floor. He's a personal friend of mine. He could marry us in the hospital chapel, but we'd have to wait until Betty's crisis is over before we can have a honeymoon. I have already mentioned it to him."

"How soon can he do it?"

"We would have to give him at least an hour's notice, but he could do it anytime. They may call me away from the wedding if Betty's condition were to deteriorate."

"Let's get married in two hours. That will give me time to call mother and get my things together. We've waited long enough. Once we're married, you can go to the physicians' lounge and get some sleep. I'll sit with Betty. We can have the honeymoon later. If they call you out of the wedding, I'll understand. We must stay here until Betty's out of danger."

"I'll call the chaplain."

X   X   X

The chapel was dark when Syndi opened the door.

"We're early," she said as she turned on the lights.

Syndi's widowed mother, her two sisters, Jan and Joie, and her older brother Dan were with her. They were carrying flowers to decorate the chapel.

"I'll go change while you arrange the chancel for the service," Syndi said to her mother. "Jan can come with me. We won't be long."

Syndi left for the ladies' room with Jan. She carried a bag with her wedding apparel.

Wearing a black tuxedo, Charles arrived with the chaplain and Dr. Hennessey, a new ob-gyn physician at the hospital. Dr. Hennessey was to be the Best Man.

When Syndi returned, she was wearing a simple white bridal gown with no train. She had a white veil. Jan was her maid of honor.

After brief introductions, they took their positions. Syndi's mother turned on a tape player. The wedding march began, and Syndi started down the aisle with her older brother Dan.

"Dearly beloved, we are gathered here...."

Charles tried to block out thoughts of Angel and his first wedding. It was a gala affair. This wedding wouldn't be a circus. It wasn't being put on for public display.

44

Syndi is different, he thought. She wasn't so concerned with social status and material things. He had dated her for about two years. She accepted the fact he had been married before, and she liked his children. This marriage would work. He would do his best to see it did.

Syndi concentrated on the chaplain's words. Yes, she was marrying a divorced man. She had never been married before. She loved him. She would try hard to make this marriage a success.

"Do you take this woman to be your lawfully-wedded wife?"

Tired, he would be glad when it was over. Their honeymoon would be later. He had a critical patient. He was glad Syndi understood. He would go to the physicians' lounge after it was over to sleep, but could he sleep? He wasn't sure.

"I do."

His commitment was made.

"Do you take this man to be your lawfully-wedded husband?"

The world was full of uncertainties, but for Syndi, this was not one of them.

"I do."

Her commitment was made. In a moment, they would be married. Syndi wondered if Betty Riggioletti would understand if she told her she and Charles Crawford had just gotten married. No, she thought, Betty would feel bad about their delaying the honeymoon because of her. She'll tell Betty they were married after her crisis was over.

"I now pronounce you man and wife. You may kiss your bride."

Charles and Syndi put their arms around each other and kissed.

EIGHT

November, 1962

It was in the afternoon, and Charles Crawford was seeing patients in his office suite.

"The hospital called," Syndi said. "Betty Riggioletti's going into labor."

"I'm on my way there." He reached for his medical bag. "Tell everyone in the waiting room it's an emergency. Call Dr. Hennessey and ask him to cover for me here. Join me as soon as you can."

"I hope things go well," Syndi said.

"So do I."

X   X   X

"Betty," Dr. Crawford said, "it's time."

They were in her hospital room.

"The anesthesiologist will be here in a few minutes. We've called Maffi. You've been a good patient."

"Thank you, Doctor."

The anesthesiologist entered the room with an assistant.

"I'll see you in the delivery room." Dr. Crawford turned to leave.

X   X   X

46

"How is she?" Maffi Riggioletti asked as Dr. Crawford came out of the delivery room.

"Congratulations," the doctor said. "You have a son. Betty is fine. The baby has breathing difficulties and jaundice. We've moved him to neonatal intensive care."

Maffi looked disappointed.

"He'll make it," Dr. Crawford said. "He was born with clenched fists. He's a fighter for sure. I'll arrange for you to see him now."

"Thank you, Doctor. You've done your best. I'm grateful to you, regardless of the outcome."

"Weren't you a bit optimistic?" Syndi asked after Maffi had left.

"What else do you tell him?"

"I don't know," Syndi said. "This is a major scientific achievement. The baby went to term and was born alive. Is there a way you can publish this in a medical journal? Your experience might save another baby's life."

"The situation would have to be different," the doctor said.

"Maybe some day you can get credit for it."

"It's not over yet," Charles said. "He's in intensive care. He'll probably make it, but other problems can develop, even after he's grown."

"What do you mean?" Syndi asked.

"We still don't know if there was any brain damage."

X   X   X

Dr. Crawford was at Betty Riggioletti's bedside when she awoke in the recovery room.

"Congratulations, Betty," Dr. Crawford said. "You are the mother of a baby boy."

"Is he all right? I'm still groggy."

"He has jaundice and breathing difficulties," said the doctor. "We'll have to watch him closely for a while, but he should be fine."

"We're going to name him Michael Thomas after his father. We'll call him Michael T."

"Michael Thomas Riggioletti, that's a nice name. Maffi is in the waiting room. He's already seen little Mike. He's a proud father. He's got dozens of roses for you. I'll send him, in."

"Charles." Syndi was in the hallway laughing and holding a dozen of Maffi's roses. "You are going to be a father, too. Are you going to give me roses when our baby is born?"

"Are you serious?"

"I'm expecting. You can see the test results for yourself. Dr. Hennessey just handed them to me. Here they are."

"You'll get roses." He looked at the report.

"Charles, are you upset?"

"No, just surprised. I haven't thought about being a father again this soon. I've been too involved in Betty's situation." He paused for a moment. "I've also been concerned about Deborah. The last time I talked with John Clarke, she was still giving them trouble."

"I'm sorry for Deborah," Syndi said, "but I'm glad for Betty. I hope little Mike is all right. Betty will be a good mother. Do we get the kids this afternoon?"

"As far as I know, but let's not tell them your pregnant. Angel will have a fit when she finds out."

X   X   X

"I love you Steve."

Alone in the gym at school, Steve and Deborah embraced.

"I love you, Deb."

"I'm sorry we have to meet like this. Mother follows me everywhere."

"Deborah! Deborah!"

They heard Victoria Clarke calling as she came down the hallway towards the gym.

"Quick! Hide!" Deborah said.

Steve hid under the bleachers.

"Deborah, what are you doing here?" Victoria Clarke came into the gym.

Deborah moved away from Steve's hiding place. "Waiting for you."

"Why didn't you answer me when I called?"

"I'm not a puppy."

"Where's Steven?"

"Steven?" Deborah answered. "I don't know where he is."

"Who were you with?"

"Nobody."

"Then why didn't you answer me when I called?"

"I'm a grown girl now," Deborah answered. "Why can't I ride the school bus?

"I'll talk to your father about this when we get home."

X   X   X

"Hi, kids," Charles Crawford said to Chuck and Ellen as he and Syndi arrived to pick them up. The kids were out on the porch with their bags. Charles and Syndi were in her four-door sedan, and Syndi was driving.

"Hi, Dad." They picked up their bags and came to the car. Charles got out and opened the back door for them.

"Where's your mother?"

"Inside." Chuck pointed toward the house.

"Should we tell her we're here?"

"I don't think it matters," said Ellen. She did not want to see a confrontation between her parents.

As a courtesy, Charles rang the doorbell, but no one came to the door.

"Oh, well," he said to Syndi as he got back into the car. "Ralph will be proud of me. I tried to be nice to Angel."

It was late Friday afternoon, and Charles had the children for the weekend. This was the first time they had visited him since he and their mother had separated more than a year earlier.

Syndi drove them to a rented three-bedroom house in a middle-class neighborhood.

"This is where we live," said Charles. "It isn't a classy place. We don't have a pool or a patio, and the yard is small."

"That doesn't matter," said Ellen.

"You each have a bedroom," said Charles. "Chuck, you take the back room. Ellen, you can have the front room. While you are unpacking, I'll call the hospital and check on a patient."

49

"I called while you were talking with the kids," said Syndi. "Betty and the baby are fine. I talked with her a minute. If they need us, they will call. Why don't you and Chuck throw a football while Ellen and I fix supper."

X   X   X

"You need to fill out these application forms," Victoria Clarke said to Deborah. They were in the den of the Clarke home. "They are all to ivy-league universities."

"Do I have to do it now? I have homework to do."

"I'll help you. These forms need to be submitted early. You can do your homework later."

"Yes, Mother."

Deborah began filling out the forms according to her mother's dictations.

"It must cost a lot to go to these places, more than many families make a year."

"It screens out the riffraff," said Victoria Clarke. "Your first choice is Schnobbe University. It's close, and I'm certain you will meet boys from the best families there."

"Yes, Mother."

"John," Victoria said after Deborah had gone upstairs to do her homework. "I'm concerned about Deborah. She still doesn't understand."

"Does she mention the baby?"

"No, it's Steven. I think she's seeing him, but she denies it. Will you talk to her?"

"How do you know she's seeing Steven?"

"I suspect it. It's her smug attitude."

"Have you seen them together?"

"Not yet."

"Have you seen Steven anywhere?"

"Not since before the baby."

"What am I to say to her?"

"I don't know," said Victoria. "I hope we haven't lost her."

"Once she's in college, she'll come around. I don't think she's seeing Steven. If she is, it won't last long. If they were going to run away, they would have done it before now."

X   X   X

It was Sunday afternoon, and Charles and Syndi had taken the children home. Syndi stayed in the car while Charles got out. He opened the trunk and handed Chuck and Ellen their bags.

"Well, I see you brought them back." Angel was sitting in the swing on her front porch. "I'm surprised."

"Things went well." Charles was trying to avoid a fight.

The children went inside with their bags.

"You weren't supposed to have HER involved. Couldn't you find an American whore to shack up with this weekend?"

"We're married," answered Charles. "She's a native-born American. She's not a whore."

"Married? Where do you live?"

"On Poplar Street near the railroad."

"You're not paying me enough money if you can afford HER. Where did you get the fifty thousand?"

"That's none of your business."

"Next time don't bring HER. You can see the children here. I'll be present while you do. I don't want my children exposed to HER. You're a bad influence on them by yourself. She's worse."

"We'll see about that."

"Where did you get that fifty thousand?"

"Go eat a chocolate-covered rat!"

"I'm going to ruin you, Charles Crawford, if it's the last thing I do. I'M GOING TO BE YOUR WORST NIGHTMARE!"

Charles walked away without answering. Angel glared at him as he got back into the car, and Syndi drove off.

"More trouble with Angel?" Syndi asked nicely.

"Probably another attempt at blackmail. I'll call Ralph in the morning."

"How long will this crap continue?"

"Until Chuck's eighteenth birthday."

"Will it stop then?"

"Not really."

NINE

X   X   X

"Little Mike's feet and hands were bluish until yesterday," Betty Riggioletti said to Dr. Crawford. They were in her hospital room. "I'm worried. I feed him whenever he's hungry. Yesterday, I nursed him twelve times. Is he getting enough to eat?"

"The Jaundice is almost gone," Dr. Crawford said. "He's breathing normally. I called Maffi and told him you and the baby would be ready to go home this afternoon. He's on his way here now. You may want to consider switching to a bottle once you get home."

"His eyes are blue. I wasn't expecting that."

"All babies have blue eyes when they're born. They'll probably change to brown in a few days. You and Maffi both have brown eyes. It doesn't matter if they stay blue. You need more self-confidence."

"But I'm an older mother. This is my first baby. I have had no experience with babies."

"Being an older mother has its advantages. You have more experience in life and more forethought. You are more financially stable. Concentrate on the positive and think things through. You'll do fine."

"Thank you," Betty said. "I'm glad you have confidence in me. I didn't expect to leave so soon. I have been here so long. It's almost like home here."

"It was a normal C-section delivery. You did very well considering the circumstances. Mike is five days old now. He's been out of intensive care for two days."

The doctor paused and turned towards the doorway.

53

"There's something happening in the hallway," he said. "Let's see what it is."

Dr. Crawford went to the doorway and then burst into laughter.

"It's Maffi. He's got a florist passing out a dozen roses to each of the nurses."

"My husband will be jealous when I bring these home," one said.

"I don't care what my husband thinks," said another. "I'm glad to get roses."

"Take these roses home." Maffi laughed. "Tell your husbands you want roses from them when these are gone. Tell them they'll be in the river if they don't."

Seeing Dr. Crawford in the doorway, Maffi came to his wife's room.

"Thank you." He extended his hand to the doctor. "You don't know how much we appreciate this. I hired a live-in nurse to help Betty like you suggested."

He paused for a moment as he entered the room.

"Give your wife roses," he said to the doctor. "You don't belong in the river."

X   X   X

Maffi and Betty Riggioletti took their baby home from the hospital that afternoon. Betty was surprised to find her husband had hired Molly, a registered nurse.

"Dr. Crawford recommended it," he told her. "You need to rest. Molly will do the work. She's a live-in. She has her own room, the one next to the housekeeper's room. The nursery is all set up like you planned it."

"Is he getting enough to eat?" Betty asked Molly. "I have considered switching to a bottle. Maffi said it's up to me. At the hospital, I fed him whenever he was hungry, sometimes as much as ten or twelve times a day."

"He's doing fine," Molly answered.

"But he's reddish around the neck."

"It's prickly heat. Baby powder will help."

"He cries when he's wet or hungry. He sleeps the rest of the time."

"That's not unusual."

"I don't know much about caring for a baby. Little Mike is my first."

"Don't worry. I'll teach you."

"How many do you have?"

"Three and three grandchildren."

"But you are younger than I am."

"That doesn't matter."

X   X   X

"Ralph," Dr. Crawford said over the telephone. He was calling from his office. "I'd better set up an appointment. The visit with the kids went too well to suit Angel. She says that from now on I can only visit them for a few hours at her house with her present. Syndi can't come. Angel called Syndi a whore."

"The judge won't like this. You're supposed to get the kids every other weekend. Are you current with your child support?"

"I have never been late with a payment."

"If I can't work it out with her lawyer, we'll go back to court. Plan on a regular visit in two weeks. I don't know if I can stop the name-calling but don't reciprocate."

"There's something else you need to know. Syndi is expecting. The kids don't know it, and neither does Angel. All hell will break loose when she finds out."

"I can understand your concern. You and Syndi are married, and that's none of Angel's business. This won't affect visitation or the divorce settlement. The judge won't care. He may even offer you his congratulations."

"Angel will try to make trouble over it."

"That shouldn't be your problem. You be careful. You let her be the one to pull crazy stunts."

"What are my chances of getting custody of the kids?"

"Perhaps sometime in the distant future, but not now. Don't even hint that you are thinking about trying to get custody. That will only make matters worse."

X   X   X

"Deb, I missed you."

Steven and Deborah were alone in the band room at school.

"I missed you, too. We just have a moment. Mother will be here soon."

"I have the information on Pacific City and Pacific Coast University."

"I'll have to look at it later. I hear Mother coming. I'd better meet her before she finds us together."

"See you later," Steven said as Deborah went out into the hall. He hid inside one of the instrument lockers in the band room.

"Here I am, MOTHER." Deborah's lack of enthusiasm was obvious.

"There you are. Who were you with?"

"Nobody."

"I don't believe you." Mrs. Clarke opened the door to the band room and looked inside. Seeing no one, she closed it and glared at Deborah.

"Why can't I ride the school bus like the other kids?"

"Let's go home!"

Deborah started down the hall towards the front entrance, and her mother followed."

X   X   X

"Hi, kids."

It was Charles Crawford's second visit with his children. It was a sunny day. Wearing coats, they were sitting on the porch with their bags. He came up to the steps and started to the door.

"Don't ring the bell," said Ellen. "It will only make Mother mad."

"Anything I do makes her mad. Let's get off of disagreeable subjects and have a good time this weekend."

The children got into the back seat of Syndi's car. Charles got in the front beside Syndi, and they drove away.

"Syndi's going to have a baby," Charles said. "You'll have a baby brother or baby sister in another seven months."

"Neat," said Ellen.

"Champion football is on TV tonight," said Chuck. He wasn't interested in babies. "Can we watch it?"

"Probably."

When they arrived home, they got out of the car and went inside.

"This room hasn't changed since our last visit," Ellen said as she unpacked her clothes.

"It's your room," said Syndi.

"Even when we're only here every other weekend?"

"We may use it occasionally, but it's still your room."

"Can I leave things here?"

"Sure."

"Neat!"

December, 1962

"Maffi," said Betty Riggioletti, "I'm surprised." She was standing in their den. "A Christmas tree and presents."

"Some of the presents are for Molly and the staff."

"This is the first year we've celebrated Christmas like this."

"We have a good reason to celebrate. This is little Mike's first Christmas."

"Little Mike has made you a softer, kinder man."

"He's our only child. I want to be a good father."

"Maybe I shouldn't ask, but does little Mike have to grow up as part of the mob?"

"No, he doesn't. I have been thinking about that. Our way of life will eventually end. We'll talk more about that later. Let's get ready for midnight mass."

X   X   X

"I'm glad we can have Christmas together," said Charles. He, Syndi, Chuck, and Ellen were in the living room of their rented home. "It's a small tree, and the presents aren't expensive."

"That's ok, Dad," said Chuck. "I like the baseball glove."

"It's neat, Syndi's having a baby," said Ellen. "Have you picked out any names yet?"

57

"Would you like to help me?" Asked Syndi. "Your father gave me a book of names."

X   X   X

"Deborah," Steven whispered, "over here."

They were in the stockroom of a large department store. As planned, Deborah had slipped away from her mother who was shopping.

"I have a Christmas present for you," Steven said.

"You shouldn't have done it." Deborah took an engagement ring from his hand and tried it on. "It's so expensive."

"But we're engaged."

Tears came to her eyes.

"I can't wear it because of my parents." She handed the ring back to him. "Keep it for me until we run away. I'll wear it then."

She put her head on his shoulder.

"I'll keep it for you," he said. "I understand."

He put his arms around her and kissed her forehead.

"I'm sorry we have to meet this way," she said.

"I'm sorry, too."

"I love you, Steve."

"I love you, Deb."

X   X   X

"It's Christmas, Deborah," Victoria Clarke said. They were in the dining room of their home. "Do you have to be so solemn? We have nice presents for you."

"I don't feel well. I'm going to my room."

"Why don't you open your presents?" Victoria asked. "Are you sick?"

"Yes, I'll open them later."

"Do you need to go to the doctor?"

"No, I'm not pregnant."

58

X   X   X

"Mother," said Ellen, "I appreciate the nice clothes you bought me, but they're so expensive."

Ellen and Chuck were beside the Christmas tree in Angel's living room.

"It beats what your father gave you yesterday," said Angel.

"It's not a contest, Mother."

"Your father and his CHINK WHORE are scum. I wish you didn't have to see them. No telling who is the father of the baby. Maybe it's Dr. Hennessey."

"Don't talk like that, Mother. It's Christmas."

"You shouldn't take his side. He's not your real father. He can't have children."

"I'm not taking sides, Mother. I just don't like being in the middle."

TEN

March, 1963

About seven o'clock that evening, Maffi Riggioletti's limousine stopped in front of a brick building in the older part of the city. Seemingly abandoned, its windows were boarded up, and there was a padlock on the front door. A barricade blocked the driveway leading behind the building.

"Who put that there?" Maffi's driver asked, referring to the barricade.

"I don't know," Maffi answered. "Let's take it down."

Maffi, his two bodyguards, and his driver got out to remove it.

A black sedan was parked a block away. Its driver and passenger had been waiting for this opportunity since the middle of the afternoon. The driver started his engine, and the black sedan pulled out into the street without attracting attention. As it passed Maffi's limousine, the passenger pointed a tommy gun out the back window and opened fire.

Maffi and his men reached for their revolvers, but it was too late. They fell to the sidewalk dead, and the car disappeared down the street at a high rate of speed. A crowd gathered, and someone called the police.

X   X   X

"Nobody will talk," a police detective told a news reporter in a TV interview. "No license plate number, no description, no nothing. They are too frightened to say anything."

"The vice lord is dead," said the reporter. "Who is going to take his place?"

60

"Who knows," answered the detective.

There was an explosion inside the old building about an hour before dawn the next morning. It caught fire and burned to the ground. Its brick walls collapsed on top of the rubble.

"Arson," said the fire authorities. "The fire was too intense for it to be anything else. It was probably related to the murder."

"Maffi had an office hidden in the basement," an informant told police. "Everything of value had been removed before the fire."

A power struggle began over control of Maffi's criminal empire. Maffi's lieutenants were the contenders.

Three minor gangsters were gunned down the next day, and the police expected more bloodshed.

"Mrs. Riggioletti was upset," a police spokesperson told the press. "She has cooperated with us so far. We're convinced she has no connections with the mob."

Word on the street was that certain members of the mob were concerned about what Betty Riggioletti might know, and they were afraid her infant son might some day try to claim his father's empire.

X   X   X

Betty went into Maffi's study the afternoon after Maffi's murder. She ignored the telephone on his desk because she knew the police would be listening. Instead, she pressed a concealed lever inside a bookcase built into the wall. A panel opened, revealing a hidden wall phone. It was a private, unlisted line to a fictitious address. She dialed a number from memory.

"Hello."

"Tonio, who made the hit on Maffi?"

"Mari said he had it done." He recognized Betty's voice.

"That's what I heard," Betty continued. "What about Al, Frank, and Bugs?"

"So far, they're supporting Mari. They had to be involved."

"I'll handle this after the funeral," Betty said. "Stay out of it! I don't want you stung. Have an ironclad alibi and be ready to take over. Nobody messes with Maffi."

61

"I'm sorry about Maffi," said Tonio. "He taught me everything I know. When is the funeral?"

"It's the day after tomorrow at nine in the morning," Betty said. "It's at the high school football field. Tomorrow is visitation at the funeral home."

Betty hung up the phone, closed the panel, and left the room.

X   X   X

The next day, over ten thousand people passed through the undertaker's chapel to pay their respects. Maffi was dressed in an expensively tailored suit and lay in a made-to-order bronze and silver casket. The room was packed with roses sent by crime figures from across the country. In accordance with mob custom, they included envelopes filled with hundred dollar bills.

It was the grandest funeral in underworld history. Bankers, lawyers, judges, businessmen, clergymen, and politicians were in the crowd. Many of the mob stayed away because they knew the FBI and local police would film everyone in attendance, and they were wanted criminals. The pallbearers were all nationally known mob leaders, and some had defied the threat of arrest to come. The funeral procession was over a mile long, and over five thousand people followed the hearse to the cemetery.

Police guards were everywhere. Anonymous threats had been made against Betty Riggioletti and her son. Authorities feared assassins might try to kill them at the funeral. Protection continued after the service.

X   X   X

"Mrs. Riggioletti, I'm Detective O'Hara." He was at her front door the morning after the funeral. "Four of Maffi's lieutenants and some twenty of their henchmen were found in the river this morning. The shooting apparently took place at Riverbend Park last night or very early this morning. Do you know anything about it?"

"Why, no! I haven't had contact with any of the mob people since Maffi was murdered. Who got hit?"

"Mari, Al, Frank, and Bugs were the major ones. They were all shot with a tommy gun like the one Maffi used. Did Tonio do it?"

"I don't know who did it?

62

"An informant told us Tonio has taken over Maffi's place with your blessing."

"I don't have any authority in the mob. My blessing would be meaningless."

"Tonio denies the murders. He has an ironclad alibi. It looks like Maffi's handiwork. Are you sure he's dead?"

"Didn't you see him in the casket? You were there when we buried him."

"When Maffi had someone wasted, he always had an ironclad alibi. The river, the tommy gun, and the alibi were his trademarks."

"Maffi always got blamed for other people's deeds. This happened after his death. He couldn't have done it."

"I didn't mean it that way. Where were you last night?"

"I was here. Your people have been watching me twenty-four hours a day."

"We've been watching this house twenty-four hours a day."

"If I had gone anywhere, you would have seen me leave."

"No one saw you leave the house."

After the officer had left, Betty called Tonio on the secret telephone line.

"The police were here. They told me about the bloodbath."

"What did you tell them?"

"Nothing," Betty said.

"Is Maffi really dead?" Tonio asked.

"He's dead. Why do you ask?"

"Maffi once said you were good with a tommy gun. How did you get them all together?"

"I never tell my secrets." Betty smiled. "The police don't know anything. They think you did it. Be careful. Maffi's death is avenged. He was careless. I won't be. It's your ship now. Put out the word. Nobody messes with Maffi's widow. I want to be left alone."

"You'll be left alone. Let me know if anyone bothers you. He'll be in the river, and you won't have to do it."

"Thanks," Betty said as she hung up the phone.

X   X   X

63

"You have been accepted at Schnobbe University," Victoria Clarke said to Deborah as she handed her the opened letter. They were in the hallway at their home.

"Mother! You opened my mail again!

"It was from Schnobbe. I wanted to see what it said."

"I have been accepted at six universities. Does this mean I have to choose one of them and turn down the other five?"

"Schnobbe University is the one you were waiting for. I'll tell your father tonight. It will make him happy. You will meet boys from nice families there."

"Republican, rich, and WASP," Deborah said under her breath as she turned to go upstairs.

"What did you say?"

"Oh, nothing. I'll go to Schnobbe."

Deborah went upstairs to her room.

X   X   X

"Little Mike is four months old now, and I'm worried," Betty Riggioletti said to Dr. McCormick, his pediatrician. It was Mike's regular check-up.

"He's content to stay in his crib all day. He's beginning to turn his head and look around. He doesn't roll over yet."

"Every Baby's development is different," said the doctor. "He's just a bit slower, that's all. It's nothing to worry about."

"Would he be old enough to miss his father?"

"He was too young when his father was killed. He won't remember him."

"Little Mike made Maffi a softer, kinder man. Looking back, I can see it. Maffi let down his guard, and his enemies murdered him."

"What about you and the baby?"

"We're getting police protection. They guard the house twenty-four hours a day. There are two officers in your waiting room. We're careful about going out in public."

"Are two officers enough?"

"Enough for them to know I don't participate in mob activities." Betty Riggioletti opened her purse, and the doctor saw a pistol inside. "They follow me everywhere I go. Those two couldn't fight their way out of a paper bag. We're protected."

"Mike's doing fine." The doctor laughed. "See you in two months."

"Nobody messes with Maffi's widow."

On her way home, Betty stopped by the post office and got the mail from her post office box. One of the items was the latest edition of 'THE GANGSTER CHRONICLE' in a plain paper wrapper. She was anxious to get home to read it. This issue would report her late husband's death and tell about his funeral. She planned to save this copy for little Mike's family album.

May, 1963

"Are you going somewhere tonight?" Victoria asked Deborah, They were upstairs at home.

"MOTHER! It's the senior prom." It was late afternoon, and she was in her room getting ready for the prom.

"I'm going with you."

"Can't I go anywhere without you?" Deborah sighed.

"I'm your mother. I can't let you go out alone."

"But I have a date with Billy Stamperson. I don't need protection. You can't go."

"Yes, I can. I'm going. Billy Stamperson is Steven's friend."

"I won't go then. I'll cancel my date. You have ruined my senior prom. I hope you're happy."

"At Schnobbe, you will meet boys from better families," her mother said. "Some day you'll understand."

X   X   X

"Hi, kids."

Charles and Syndi had arrived to pick up Chuck and Ellen for the weekend. The children were on the porch waiting as usual. Angel was there with an escort.

"Charles, this is Reverend Marvin H. Whittingham, III," Angel said, ignoring Syndi. "We are going to the opera tonight after having dinner at the Golden Garden."

"Glad to meet you," Charles said, trying to keep from laughing. He stuck out his hand to shake hands but pulled it back when Whittingham did not reciprocate. "I hope you have an enjoyable evening."

Whittingham did not answer. He couldn't take his eyes off of the top of Angel's low-cut gown.

"He gives me chocolates." Angel smiled at Whittingham.

Charles put the kids' bags in the trunk. He opened the car door for them and then got inside with Syndi.

"He's strange," he said to Syndi as they drove away. "I'm calling Ralph tonight. We need to find out who he is."

X   X   X

"Ralph, Angel has a new boyfriend." Charles was in the bedroom where the kids could not hear him. "He's a preacher named Marvin H. Whittingham, III. He's probably in his early fifties. We met him when Syndi and I went to pick up the kids. He and Angel were going somewhere together. She was showing him off."

"How did things go otherwise?" Ralph knew it was serious or Charles would have waited until Monday to call.

"There wasn't any problem from my standpoint," said Charles. "I'm not concerned about him seeing Angel. It's the kids I'm interested in."

"What's the problem?"

"Whittingham wasn't very friendly. Angel was wearing a low-cut gown. He couldn't keep his eyes off of her boobs. It was funny. He'd love to get his hands on them. That was obvious."

"She may have a serious boyfriend."

"I hope he's got a lot of money. He's going to find out they're expensive boobs, but that's his problem. My concern is whether he'll harm the kids."

"Find out what the kids think about him. He sounds like a dirty old man."

"He's got to have money. Otherwise Angel wouldn't have any interest in him."

"Is he staying with Angel?"

"I don't know."

"Ask the kids. Call the office Monday, and I'll see what I can find out."

66

X   X   X

"Hi, kids," Charles said as he came into the living room. They were watching TV with Syndi. "What do you think of Whittingham?"

"He's OK, I guess," said Ellen. "He ignores us."

"He doesn't know much about sports," said Chuck. "He's more interested in Mom. I think they're going together. He brings her chocolates. Sometimes she shares them with us when he's not around."

"Does he stay overnight?"

"Sometimes," said Ellen.

"You and I had better have a private talk," Syndi said to Ellen.

"What did I do?" Asked Ellen.

"Nothing," answered Syndi. "I'm not punishing you. It's for your own protection."

X   X   X

"Charles," Ralph said over the phone Monday morning. Charles Crawford was in the doctors' lounge at the hospital in between seeing patients. "I checked on Whittingham. He's apparently harmless, at least as far as the kids are concerned. He's more interested in big boobs and bank accounts than in kids."

"What about his background? Is he dangerous?"

"He was a minister several years ago until he got involved with the young wife of an elderly deacon. He's been in and out of trouble ever since, mostly with younger wives of wealthy husbands. He's even been shot at a time or two. So far, he has shown no interest in harming children. He doesn't claim his own."

"What should we do?"

"Keep an eye on the situation, but don't become involved unless he harms the kids. Report any changes to me immediately."

"I will. Syndi and I are going house hunting tomorrow. We haven't told Angel or the kids yet. We'll need more room after the baby comes."

X   X   X

"We've looked at six places so far," Charles said to Syndi. "What do you think?"

It was late Tuesday afternoon, and they were out looking at houses for sale.

"I don't like any of them that much," Syndi said.

"It's getting late. Shall we look at number seven or shall we wait until another time?"

"Let's see it now."

Charles reached for the newspaper. "According to the address, this one is on the way home."

"What's the latest on little Mike?" Syndi asked as they drove away.

"I talked with Dr. McCormick last week. He said the boy was slow in developing, but it was too early to tell if this means trouble."

"I'm worried about him."

"So am I."

A few blocks later, they stopped in front of a colonial two-story house sitting back from the street. There was a for-sale sign in the yard, and the grass needed mowing.

"This is it," said Charles.

He paused momentarily while they looked at the property. Then Charles turned the car into the driveway.

"According to the description," he said, "it has five bedrooms and four baths. There's a pool and a patio, too. They must be in back behind the fence."

Charles and Syndi went up the front steps to the front porch and looked through the windows.

"It's vacant," said Syndi. "Let's go around back."

"It has a four-car garage," said Charles. "It's an older home, but it could be fixed up nice. What do you think?"

"It has privacy," said Syndi. "So far, I like it. I want to see the inside."

"It's beginning to get dark," Charles said as they returned to their car. "I'll call the agent when we get home. Maybe we can come back tomorrow."

X   X   X

"Ralph, we have made an offer on a house," Charles said late the next afternoon. He had called from his office. "Syndi wants it. She wasn't sure until she got inside. If we buy it, we won't tell Angel or the kids until it closes. She'll try to claim I bought it with hidden assets."

"That's none of her business. I'll be ready if Angel wants to cause trouble."

ELEVEN

June, 1963

"I'm ready, Steve." Deborah met him at the back door of the Clarke home. I packed everything I'm taking in these two bags."

"I have the tickets in my pocket," said Steve. "Are you sure you want to go through with this? It's not too late to back out. I can still get my money back."

"I'm sure. We can never be together as long as I stay here. They killed our baby."

"It will take at least a week to get across the country," said Steve. "Do they suspect anything?"

"Not yet. This is the maid's day off. Mother won't be back for at least two hours."

"Let me get your bags. Billy's car is out front.

Steve went to the driveway with the bags and motioned Billy to come. He put Deborah's bags in the trunk with his. He and Deborah got into the back seat, and Billy drove out the circular drive.

"So far, so good," Steve said as they turned into the street.

Billy drove Steve and Deborah to the bus station. They got their luggage out of the trunk and started to the door.

"Thanks, pal," Steve said to Billy. "You will hear from us."

"Good luck," Billy said as he drove away.

Steve and Deborah entered the terminal carrying their bags.

"We're due to leave in twenty minutes," he said.

The bus arrived on time, and they boarded it.

"How about here?" Steve asked. They were on the driver's side near the back.

"Fine, I want the seat next to the window."

The bus left the station, and they were on their way.

"Here's your ring." Steve handed Deborah the box.

"Thanks for keeping it. I love you." She kissed him.

"I bought a wedding band to match it. It's inside the box, too. Why don't you wear both of them? That way they won't get misplaced. We'll get married as soon as we can."

"Sure." Deborah put both rings on and looked at them on her finger. "They're pretty."

"Have you thought about the church?" Steve asked.

"I want to join," she answered. "I want us to go to church together."

"Are you sure?"

"I'm sure."

As the bus came to the highway, Deborah suddenly turned away from the window and ducked her head.

"What's wrong?"

"It's mother, she's coming home early. I hope she didn't see me."

"I don't think so," Steve said as he looked out the window.

The Clarke Rolls Royce continued down the street in the opposite direction.

"It's too late to stop us now."

X   X   X

"John," Victoria said over the phone. Her hands were shaking, and she was in tears. "Deborah's gone! She's run away!"

"What!"

"She left a note. It said 'You killed my baby!' The doctor did it for her own good. She hasn't mentioned it since it happened. I thought she had gotten over it."

"What did she take?" Her father asked.

70

"A few clothes. She said for us to give the rest to charity. She's not coming back!"

"I'll come home now," John Clarke said.

"High school graduation was yesterday," Victoria Clarke said. "We had her enrolled in Schnobbe University this fall. She would have met a better class of boys there."

"We'll find her," said John Clarke.

"I knew she was seeing Steven."

"Did she mention him in the note?"

"No, but I'm sure she's with him."

"I'll check on him, too."

X   X   X

"Hernando Cortez!" John Clarke said over the telephone. Calling from his office, he reached Hernando Cortez at his home. "This is John Clarke. Where's Deborah?"

"I don't know. She's not here." Hernando was in his kitchen.

"Where's Steven?"

"I don't know. He's not here either."

"Are they together?"

"I don't know."

"What kind of car does Steven drive?"

"Steven doesn't have a car. He drives my pick-up, but it's here."

"Deborah's run away. We think she's with Steven."

"I don't know anything about it. I expect Steven to be home tonight."

"Her mother's worried sick."

"I don't know any more than you do, Clarke."

"I'll get you for this, Cortez!"

"It won't do you any good to threaten me, Clarke. I'm minding my own business. I know nothing about Deborah's running away. I'm not bothering you. LEAVE ME ALONE!" Hernando Cortez slammed down the telephone receiver.

71

X   X   X

"John, I'm glad you're home." Victoria met her husband at the back door. "Any word?"

"I talked with our lawyer. Deborah's eighteen now. She's legal age. We can't stop her from leaving."

"What about that no-good Steven?"

"They're probably together. I have a detective agency trying to find them."

"John, I can't face the girls at the club like this. What will I do? It's all Steven's fault. He's trash. If only he'd left Deborah alone. They might be married by now."

"They'll have to get a license to do that. So far, they haven't. Detectives are watching the courthouses in the nearby counties. We'll find out if they try. Meanwhile, I need to call Jerry at my office."

John Clarke picked up the telephone and dialed the number.

"Jerry, this is John Clarke. Put out the word to the other contractors. Nobody's to use Hernando Cortez for anything, not even cleanup. He's got a matter to settle with me first."

"Does he owe you money? He's a good bricklayer. He can't pay you if he doesn't work."

"It's worse than that. Nobody uses him, you understand. If he wants work, he can go back to Mexico. These damn Mexicans think they run the country."

"I'll tell them what you said."

"I intend to make it stick! Nobody uses him for anything!"

X   X   X

"Charles, it's time," Syndi said, shaking him awake. They were at home in bed.

"But it's two o'clock in the morning. I didn't get to sleep until after eleven."

"I'm sorry, but the baby won't wait."

"I could deliver it here."

"We have time to get to the hospital. Are my bags still by the door?"

72

"They've been there for two weeks."

"I'll call Dr. Hennessey while you get the car. You're the father this time, not the doctor."

X   X   X

"Congratulations, Crawford, it's a boy," Dr. Hennessey said. They were in the maternity ward waiting room. "It was a normal delivery. You'd better get some rest. You're in worse shape than Syndi is."

"I did an emergency C-section last night. There were complications, and I didn't get to bed until eleven. I have roses coming for Syndi. I'd better wait until they get here. I'll get some sleep in the doctors' lounge after that."

"What are you going to name the baby?"

"Syndi likes the name Jason. I'd better call Syndi's mother before I forget.

"You get some rest."

X   X   X

"We made it, Deb," said Steve. "Pacific City at last. We'll be at the bus station in about twenty or thirty minutes."

"It's been a rough week," said Deborah. "I'm tired of riding."

"We've been through several states and seen a lot of the country."

"It's too bad we couldn't stop and explore some of the places we saw," said Deborah.

"Maybe we can go back later."

The bus made it's way down the streets of Pacific City to the station. It was almost dark. Steve and Deborah left the bus, collected their luggage, and caught a taxi.

"Do you know an inexpensive motel near the university?" Steve asked the driver.

"Why not the West Side Inn? It's a nice place, but it isn't a chain. It's on a side street, out of the way."

"Take us there," answered Steve.

Steve paid the driver at the West Side Inn, and they went inside with their bags.

73

"We would like a room for two," said Steve.

"Since you don't have a car, you'll have to pay in advance." The clerk handed him a form to complete.

Steve listed his father's address as their home address and signed it "Mr. and Mrs. Steven Cortez".

"Here's the money for one night."

X   X   X

The next morning, Steve and Deborah found an unfurnished apartment for rent within walking distance of the university.

"Are you both university students?" The landlord asked.

"We are," answered Steve. "Let's see the apartment."

"Is the apartment okay with you?" Steve asked Deborah after they had walked through it.

"It's fine."

"I have a lease. You have to pay in advance, and I require a deposit."

"Here's your money," said Steve as he and Deborah signed the lease.

"The apartment's nice," Deborah said after the landlord was gone. "Too bad we don't have our own furniture yet."

"I don't like sleeping on the floor either," said Steve. "The next thing is for us to find work."

"What about the fast-food place down the street?" Deborah asked. "There was a help-wanted sign in the window."

"Let's go," said Steve. "If we don't get jobs there, we can get a newspaper. We might find something in the want ads."

They went to Fast Fred's Hot Foods down the street. Steve looked at the help-wanted sign in the window as they went inside.

"We're looking for work," Steve said at the counter. "Is the manager in?"

"He's over there," said the counter clerk.

"I'm Mr. Lee, the manager." He took them into his office. "I'll get two application forms. You can fill them out. Then we can see what we can do."

Steve took the forms. They filled them out and gave them back to the manager.

Mr. Lee looked over the applications and the high school transcripts. He picked up the telephone and called the home office.

"I got a married couple here from the east coast," Mr. Lee said to the company president, Fred Gonzales. "They're kids. They want to work at night and take day classes at the university."

"What do you think?" Fred Gonzales asked.

"Their high school grades are good. The girl doesn't have any work experience. The boy's worked in construction. I'm short-handed on the night shift."

"Why don't you give them a try? It's up to you."

"Can you start this afternoon at five?" Mr. Lee said to Steve and Deborah as he hung up the phone. "There's some paperwork to be filled out, and we'll have to train you,"

"Sure," said Steve. "We'll be back at five."

X   X   X

Steve and Deborah applied for a marriage license at the courthouse the next day.

"There's a required waiting period," said the clerk. "You can pick up the license in three days."

"We'll be back," said Steve.

Three days later, they picked up their marriage license and took it to a priest at the university's Catholic Student Center.

"We want to get married," Steve told him. "I have been baptized in the Church. Deborah has studied the instruction material and is ready for baptism."

The priest looked over Steve's baptismal certificate, and then he questioned Deborah in his office about church doctrine and her beliefs. When he was satisfied, he called for Steve.

"We can have the baptism before mass this afternoon," he told them, "and we can perform the wedding before mass tomorrow morning. Is that all right with you?"

"We'll be back this afternoon before mass," Steve said.

X   X   X

Steve and Deborah didn't become students at Pacific Coast University. Instead, they registered as students at State University back home. Using Steve's father's house as a legal address, they began taking correspondence courses by mail.

"We won't have to pay out-of-state tuition," Steve said to Deborah. "We can study when we have time and can get required courses out of the way first."

X   X   X

"Hi, kids. You have a new baby brother." Charles opened the back door of Syndi's car for Chuck and Ellen. He was picking them up at their mother's house. He was driving as Syndi was at home with the new baby.

"Mamma knows about the new baby," whispered Ellen. "She's furious."

Angel came to the front door.

"Charles! Where did you get that fifty thousand?"

"That's none of your business."

"You are hiding something!"

"Hiding what?"

"I'll find out!"

"Is that a threat?"

"I'M GOING TO RUIN YOU IF IT'S THE LAST THING I DO! YOUR NAME IS MUD! MUD CRAWFORD!"

"The divorce is over, Angel. I'm sorry you still want to carry on the fight."

"YOU'RE GOING TO BE EVEN SORRIER!" Angel turned and went inside.

"What's the baby's name?" Ellen asked once they had driven away. She could see her father was angry.

"Jason."

"That's a nice name. What's wrong, daddy?"

"Nothing."

"It's Mamma, isn't it."

"I'm sorry the fight has to continue."

"So are we."

TWELVE

July, 1963

"Hi, kids." Charles and Syndi had arrived at Angel's house to pick up the kids for the weekend. They were waiting on the front porch. Charles put their bags in the trunk of Syndi's car. They got inside, and Syndi drove away.

"Can we see the baseball game on TV tonight, Dad?" Asked Chuck.

"We'll see."

"Leave me out," said Ellen. "I'd rather do something else."

"Syndi and I have bought a house," said Charles. "We'll close on it next week. We'll show it to you tomorrow."

"Neat," said Ellen. "Tell us about it."

"It has a pool and a patio in the back yard," said Charles.

"Does it have a place to play baseball?" Asked Chuck.

"You will have to see for yourself tomorrow."

"There's the Clarke house," Syndi said as they drove by. "Have you heard how Deborah is doing?"

"She graduated from high school in June," Charles answered. "I don't know where she's going to college. I'll ask John Clarke the next time I see him."

X   X   X

"Still no word," Mrs. Smythe from the detective agency said over the phone. "We're checking everything we can, but we still haven't found out where they went."

"Steven doesn't have a car," John Clarke said. He was at his desk in his den. "How did they leave?"

"We suspect Billy Stamperson knows, but he won't tell us. We know they didn't leave on a commercial airline. We think they borrowed a car. We don't think they have gone far."

"What about their other high school friends?" John Clarke asked.

"If they know, they're not talking," Mrs. Smythe said. "Do you have any idea where they might be?"

"No, but keep watching Hernando Cortez," he answered, "He knows something. They will contact him sooner or later."

"I put out the word," John Clarke said to Victoria after hanging up the phone. "As a favor to me, the major contractors are not using Hernando Cortez for anything, not even cleanup."

"I hope he starves," said Victoria.

September, 1963

"It's a package for you," said Julie. She handed Dr. Crawford a long, narrow box that had been delivered to the office. "There's no return address."

"What is it?" Syndi asked.

"We'll see." He took off the wrapping paper and opened it. "A dozen dead roses."

"Here's a note," said Julie. "It says 'MUD CRAWFORD! WHERE DID YOU GET THAT FIFTY THOUSAND?'"

"It's Angel's foolishness," Charles Crawford said. "We'll let Ralph have it. Answering it would only fan the flames."

"Mud Crawford?" Syndi laughed as she turned to Julie. "Have you been to the new office?"

"Yes," Julie answered, "but the people haven't moved out yet."

"The renovation will start next month," Charles said.

78

"I'm glad Dr. Hennessey is willing to join us," said Syndi. "He'll keep his own patients, but it will be easier for one doctor to cover for the other."

"What you mean is I'll be able to take a few days off," Charles said.

February, 1964

"Little Mike is fifteen months old now," Betty Riggioletti said to Dr. McCormick. It was a regular check-up. "I'm worried. He sits up now, but not well. He can stand, but he's not steady. He has trouble sitting back down."

"Has he taken any steps?" The doctor asked.

"Not yet."

"Keep him barefoot except when he's outside. Has he said any words yet?"

"No, he hasn't, but he makes sounds."

"He's doing fine," Dr. McCormick said after his examination. "See you next time unless he has problems."

May, 1964

"Your honor," said Andrew Walker. He was Betty Riggioletti's attorney, and they were appearing in court. "This petition is a simple matter. Mrs. Riggioletti is a widow with an eighteen-month-old son. Her husband died over a year ago leaving everything to her. The estate has been probated and closed. Mrs. Riggioletti wishes to have her last name and the last name of her infant son shortened from Riggioletti to Riggs. She doesn't want this to take effect until she moves to the west coast."

"Wasn't her husband a gangster?" Asked the judge. "Wasn't he murdered?"

"That's another reason, your honor," said her attorney. "Mrs. Riggioletti didn't participate in her husband's gangster activities. She wants to live a quiet life and to raise her son to be a law-abiding citizen. She doesn't want him to be labeled with the Riggioletti name. She doesn't want him to be part of the underworld."

"Are there any other children?"

"No, your honor. She and her husband do not have prior marriages. They were married over twenty-five years, and this son is their only child."

He handed a copy of little Mike's birth certificate to the judge.

"Does she have any gangster connections?" The judge asked as he looked at the birth certificate.

"No, your honor. She has broken all contacts with the mob."

"When does she plan to move?"

"As soon as her house sells."

"What does she do for money?"

"She has enough income from blue-chip stocks to provide for her and her son. She has no debts other than month-to-month living expenses, such as utility bills. She's not trying to escape creditors."

"I see no objections," said the judge. "The court approves the change. Prepare the order as soon as you know the effective date, and I will sign it."

X   X   X

"Look, the Riggioletti house is for sale," Victoria Clarke said as she and her husband drove by on their way to the country club. "Wonder why she's selling? The mob business ought to be making her a lot of money."

"I heard she got out of the mob business after her husband was murdered," John Clarke answered.

"Maybe she has to sell," Victoria Clarke said.

"I don't know what she does for money," answered her husband.

"Let's buy it, John. I hear it's a fabulous house, better than anybody at the club has. It would be great for parties. Deborah would like it. I know she would."

"It's a big house, all right."

"I like the tall stone wall and the iron gate," Victoria said. "The guard house at the driveway entrance is unique. Nobody at the club has one."

"I'll call the realtor and arrange for us to see it. I'm curious. I have never been inside the gate."

X   X   X

"The house is bigger than I thought," said John Clarke.

They had returned to the real estate office with the realtor.

"I'll offer her this," he wrote a figure on a piece of paper and gave it to the agent. "The deal is subject to our selling our present house at a satisfactory price."

"Your offer is less than what she's asking," the real estate agent said as he took the piece of paper, "but she might negotiate. I'll call her. She may be back home now."

The Clarkes waited patiently as the agent went into a private office to call.

"She'll split the difference," the agent said when he returned, "but she won't take anything less."

"We'll accept her counter offer," said John Clarke, "subject to our house selling. We would like to list it now."

"I know the house," the real estate agent said. "It won't be hard to sell."

"The Riggioletti house is fabulous," Victoria Clarke said once they were in their car. "The flower beds and yard have been well kept. We can have fantastic parties there. If only Deborah were here to enjoy it. Have you heard anything from the detective agency?"

"Not recently. I'll call when we get home."

X   X   X

"Hi, kids," Charles said as he let them in the back seat of Syndi's car. She was driving. Jason, the new baby brother, was in a car seat in front in between his parents.

"The Riggioletti place is pending," Syndi said as they drove by and saw the changed real estate sign. "Wonder who is buying it?"

"Mamma said she wanted to buy it," said Ellen, "but Dad didn't give her enough money. She blames Dad for everything."

"Mon hates the fact that I was named after you, Dad," said Chuck. "She wants to change my name, but her lawyer won't let her. She says you are not our father."

"She knows better than that," said Charles.

"Do you know where Mrs. Riggioletti is moving?" Syndi asked, trying to change the subject.

"No, I don't," said Charles. "Last week I asked Dr. McCormick how little Mike was doing. He said the boy was still slow in developing. He doesn't think there is any brain damage, but he is not sure."

"Did you tell him what happened?" Asked Syndi.

"No, I didn't. I haven't told anyone. I'm not sure they would believe it."

X   X   X

"How was your trip to the west coast?" Asked Andrew Walker, He was Betty Riggioletti's attorney, and they were in his office.

"I bought a private place at Ocean Spray," Betty said. "It's a suburb of Pacific City. I paid cash for it. I used the name 'Betty Riggs'. It has three bedrooms, one for little Mike, one for me, and one I plan to turn into an office. The property is on the beach. I can see the ocean from my back patio. It has a fenced yard."

"You will probably be safe there. We've kept your name change quiet. Apparently nobody has discovered it in the courthouse. It won't take effect until you move."

"I'm giving the staff and Mike's nurse a year's pay as a gift. It will help them in their transition to new jobs and living quarters. They're staying until I leave next week. They've been very good to me and little Mike."

"You are most generous."

"I am selling the furniture at a sale after I leave. A church charity is conducting it for me. I couldn't bear to do it myself. They get half of the proceeds. I may give them more if things go well. My new house is smaller, and I won't need much furniture. I'll buy new things out there."

"It's cheaper to sell old furniture and buy new rather than ship things to the west coast," said the attorney. "It's also less trouble."

"I'm starting a new life out there," Betty said. "While cleaning out a closet, I found a hidden compartment, one I didn't know about." Betty handed her attorney an old briefcase. "This was inside. It has over a hundred thousand dollars in it."

The attorney took the briefcase and opened it.

"I was hurt at first," Betty continued. "It wasn't like Maffi to hide money without telling me. But then I looked at the bills. They're all at least fifty years old. The money probably belonged to Maffi's father, or maybe his grandfather. I'm sure Maffi would have told me about it if he knew it was there."

"The briefcase isn't a new one. It could easily be fifty years old. I don't think we need to contact the police."

"I want to stay out of trouble with the tax authorities."

"I'll contact them and see what we can work out. I'm sure we will have to pay some of it in taxes. I'll keep it to a minimum with us being legal."

"That's what I want. My new house doesn't have any hidden compartments. I don't want to go through my new life having to hide things."

"But you want your past hidden, don't you?"

"Yes, I want a clean break with the past." Betty got up to leave. "I have turned down all requests for interviews. Angel Crawford has been persistent. She's a fashion reporter. I don't like her as a person. My answer to her is 'NO!'"

"Keep me informed of your whereabouts in case I have to contact you. I'm not telling anyone where you are."

"I'll keep in touch. If anyone asks, I went to Sicily to live with Maffi's people."

On the way home, Betty picked up her mail from her post office box. The latest edition of 'THE GANGSTER CHRONICLE' was there in a plain paper wrapper.

"I'll cancel this subscription," she said to herself as she drove home. "I'll subscribe in my new name after I move to Ocean Spray."

She always read this newspaper cover-to-cover. Though leaving the gangster world, she still wanted to keep up with what was going on.

X   X   X

"Our house sold," John Clarke said that evening. He had just come home from the office. "Once the buyer's loan goes through, we'll close on the Riggioletti place. The rest of our money is in escrow. It will be a cash deal."

"When can we move in?" Victoria asked.

"The realtor said we can begin to move things there before closing if we did it quietly, but we can't live there until after the sale takes place. He gave me keys to the gate and to the front door. We'll have all the locks changed after closing."

"But what about Mrs. Riggioletti?"

"She moved out after selling her furniture. Her lawyer has the power of attorney to sign the papers at closing. The grass needs cutting. I'll have to arrange for that tomorrow. Is dinner ready? I'm hungry."

"I'll see."

X   X   X

"I understand you bought the Riggioletti house," an expensively dressed lady said to Mrs. Clarke at a country club function. She had a pen and a notebook in her hand.

"Who are you?"

"Angel Crawford. I'm a member here. I'm a fashion writer. I wanted to interview Mrs. Riggioletti, but she's gone. This house has underworld charm. It must have a lot of secrets."

"The first thing we did after buying the place was to look for hidden compartments," Victoria Clarke continued. "Mrs. Riggioletti spoiled all the fun. She left them open for us to find. There was nothing inside them, not even spider webs. She even had a secret entrance and a secret telephone line. We're having a party next month. Please come. I'll show them to you. You will have a great time."

"I'll be there," Angel said. "Do you have her new address?"

"No, but I'm sure her attorney does."

"Is Deborah at home?"

"She's away at school."

"When does she come home for the summer?" Angel asked. "I would like to interview her. Perhaps she would want to model."

"She's staying in Europe this summer."

"Perhaps at Christmas?"

"She wouldn't want to be a model," Victoria Clarke said as she walked away. "She's dating a prince. We hope she will marry into European royalty."

THIRTEEN

May, 1964

Steve and Deborah were at the admissions office at Pacific Coast University.

"We're instate residents," Steve told the counselor. He had rent receipts showing they had lived in Pacific City almost a year, a copy of a state tax return they had filed, and their pay stubs since the previous summer from Fast Fred's Hot Foods.

"You qualify as instate students," the admission counselor said as she approved their applications. "Your high school transcripts came in last week."

"Thanks," said Steve. "When do we register for summer classes?"

"Here's a schedule. You need an appointment with a faculty advisor."

"We're transferring our correspondence courses from State University out here," Steve wrote his father. "It's the maximum credits Pacific Coast University will accept. We'll attend classes during the day and work at Fast Fred's at night and on weekends. Nobody else wants to work nights. It's different from home. Mexicans aren't discriminated against here like they are on the east coast. Why don't you move to Pacific City?"

August, 1964

"Charles," Syndi said, "number two is on the way." They were going home after evening rounds at the hospital. "Are you going to give me roses again?"

85

"You'll get roses. You've been very romantic the last few months. I shouldn't be surprised."

"Jason is more than a year old. If we have other babies, they need to come soon."

"Is that your way of telling me I'm getting old?"

"You're not getting old, Charles, you're getting better."

"You'll get roses." He laughed as he pulled into her mother's driveway. "I'll get Jason."

September, 1964

"It's a package for you," Julie said to Charles at the office. "There's no return address."

"What is it?" Syndi asked.

"We got a box like this last year." Charles took off the wrapping paper and opened it. "A dozen dead roses. This is more of Angel's foolishness. Ralph said for us to throw stuff like this in the trash. If she asks, don't tell her we received it. Who is our next patient?"

"Mrs Stonecipher. She's in room one."

October, 1964

"Someone broke into the office last night," said Syndi. "Julie discovered it when she got here this morning."

"What did they take?" Charles Crawford had just arrived at the office after completing his morning rounds.

"Nothing we know of," said Syndi. "They searched the old patient files in the back room.

"Whose files?"

"Apparently Betty Riggioletti's and Deborah Clarke's. Those were the only files they pulled out."

"Have you called the police?"

"Julie did that first thing."

"What did they do?"

"They came, asked questions, tried to find fingerprints, and left."

"What did they say?"

"They said it looked like a professional job."

X   X   X

"Dr. Crawford," Julie said the next morning. "There are two policemen here to see you."

"I can see them now if it won't take long. Send them back to my office."

The doctor went into his private office with Syndi.

"Good afternoon, gentlemen," Dr. Crawford asked the policemen. "How can I help you?"

"The medical records unit of the hospital was broken into last night," one of the officers said. "We're investigating."

"Nothing appears to have been taken," the other officer said. "The burglar or burglars searched closed patient files. They seemed to be interested in two of your patients."

"Who?" Asked Dr. Crawford.

"Betty Riggioletti and Deborah Clarke. Do you have any idea why?"

"No, I don't."

"If you think of anything," the first officer said, "please let us know."

"We will."

"What are you thinking?" Syndi asked after the police officers had left.

"The hospital break-in and the one here at the office are probably connected."

"What do you mean?" Asked Syndi.

"The culprits were interested in the same patients, Betty Riggioletti and Deborah Clarke. I suspect Angel is involved in this, but she must have had the help of a professional burglar."

"What could she be after?" Syndi asked.

"She knows I have been elected president of the state medical society. She would like to dig up enough dirt on me to block my taking office. She's still trying to find out where the fifty thousand came from."

"What does she suspect?"

I don't know," said Dr. Crawford. "There is nothing incriminating in those files. I made sure of that back then."

87

"Do you know where Deborah Clarke is? Asked Syndi.

"The Clarkes say she's in Europe."

"What about Betty Riggioletti?"

"Dr. McCormick said she moved away to break her ties with the mob. He sent a copy of little Mike's to his new pediatrician, a Dr. Westover in Pacific City."

"How is little Mike?"

"Still slow in developing. I haven't been able to keep up with his progress since Betty moved."

"We'd better get back to our patients. Syndi opened the office door. "I wish Angel would leave us alone."

"So do I."

X   X   X

"It's a call from John Clarke," Julie said.

"I'll take it in my office." Dr. Crawford was in between patients.

"What's up, John?"

"Did you hear about the hospital break-in?"

"The police were here."

"What was in Deborah's file?" John Clarke asked.

"The bare minimum. She had a miscarriage. The baby was anencephalic. It had no head. It died within minutes. There was an x-ray of the baby in the file."

"What about the baby's father?"

"There was nothing mentioned about the baby's paternity."

"What were they after?" Asked John Clarke.

"I don't know."

"I don't want any of this to be made public. Let me know if you hear anything."

"I will. You do the same."

"I'm worried," Betty Riggs said. She was in for Mike's two-year-old check-up.

"We have his records from Dr. McCormick back east," said Dr. Westover. "Does Mike talk any?"

"He says a few words."

"Sometimes unusually bright children are late in talking." The doctor made notes in his chart.

"He's quiet and is slow in responding to people or things around him."

"Can he walk now?

"He's just beginning to take steps."

"Let's see how he progresses," the doctor said as he examined Mike. "Keep shoes on him. That will help."

December, 1964

"I miss Deborah not being here for the holiday," Victoria Clarke said to her husband. They were in their den watching a movie on TV.

"I miss her, too," John Clarke said, "but we still have a lot to be thankful for."

"Will you be going away next week?" Victoria asked.

"I'll be going to New York for two days. I'll be back Wednesday morning."

"I want Deborah back. I wish she had married right. I was looking forward to being a grandmother."

"I miss her, too."

March, 1965

"Charles, it's time again." Syndi woke him up at seven that morning. They were at home.

"This time you let me get some sleep." He laughed. "What about Jason?"

"I have made arrangements with mother for Jason. We can take him to her apartment on the way to the hospital. We've got time. I'll call her and tell her I'm coming."

Syndi went to the phone to call her mother, and Charles took her bags to the car.

X   X   X

"Congratulations, Crawford," Dr. Hennessey said as he came out of the delivery room. It was early evening. "It's another boy. Everything's fine. What are you going to name the boy?

"Jeremy. Syndi chose the name. I have learned never to argue with her on these matters. I need to call her mother. Roses are on the way."

"She's awake," Dr. Hennessey said. "You can see her now."

"Hi," Charles said as he entered Syndi's room. "How do you feel?"

"Do you believe in dreams?" Syndi asked.

"What do you mean?"

"I dreamed Deborah Clarke was married and was going to have a baby."

"Could be," Charles said, "but I don't put much faith in dreams. I called your mother, and roses are on the way."

May, 1965

"Steve," Deborah said. It was midnight, and they had just come home from work. "I went to the doctor this morning. I'm three months' pregnant."

"Huh?" Steve looked astonished.

"I know we didn't plan it this way," Deborah said. "It's a bad time for a baby, but I want us to keep it."

"I want us to keep it, too," Steve said.

"I don't see how we can afford it," Deborah said, "not on the money we make. We're barely making ends meet, now. Your dad's having a hard time, too."

"I don't want to ask him for help," said Steve. "He's done enough already."

"If we go to my parents for help," Deborah said, "they'll try to split us up and kill the baby. I don't even want them to know I'm pregnant. What will we do?"

"Last night," Steve said, "the boss offered me the manager's position at the Fast Fred's across town. It's a full-time position. I told him I couldn't take it. I needed to stay in school. He told me to think about it. I'll tell him I have changed my mind. I'll take it if I can take this semester's final exams first. Then we'll have two years of college completed. The promotion will mean more money."

"But you will have to drop out of school," Deborah said.

"No, I won't," Steve answered. "I'll cut back to one or two courses each semester, whatever I can take. I'll go to school at night. You can take classes this summer. I want you to graduate, too. It will take longer, but we'll make it."

"I'll go to the prenatal clinic," said Deborah. "They use mostly interns. You have to take whoever is there. It costs less. We'll make it."

"I love you, Deb." He put his arms around her.

"I love you, Steve."

November, 1965

"Steve, it's time. I have had contractions for a couple of hours." Deborah was sitting down in the living room. Steve had just gotten home from work.

She grabbed the arm of the chair as another contraction began.

"I didn't call because I thought we had more time, but we don't." Deborah was almost in tears.

"Are your bags by the door?"

"They're ready."

They made a fast trip to University Hospital. Steve rushed into the emergency room. There was a long line ahead of him.

"Sorry, I need this." He grabbed an empty wheelchair and headed back to the car.

"Come back with that!" Two nurse aides followed him out the door. "That's hospital property!"

Steve didn't stop until he reached the car.

"This is the best I could do." Steve helped Deborah into the wheelchair. The nurse aides pushed her to the emergency room entrance as Steve led the way.

"You shouldn't have done that, young man," one of the Aides scolded Steve. "You should wait your turn."

"There isn't time! Her contractions are coming too fast!"

X   X   X

"Mr. Cortez," the doctor said as he came into the waiting room. "I am Dr. Sanchez. Congratulations, it's a girl. Both mother and daughter are fine."

"Thank you," Steve said as he turned toward the doctor.

"What's the baby's name going to be?" The doctor asked.

"Bianca Marie Cortez, after my mother. When can I see them?"

"In about thirty minutes."

"Where's a pay phone?" Steve asked.

"Down the hall, on the left."

Steve went to call his father.

"Dad, this is Steve. You're a grandfather. It's a girl."

"I hope things went well."

"Deborah and the baby are fine. Her name is Bianca Marie Cortez. When are you going to move out here and join us?"

"I don't know, son. It probably won't be long. There's little work for me here now. When was the baby born?"

"About fifteen minutes ago. She weighs six pounds and seven ounces."

"I'm glad to hear everything's all right."

"We'll talk more later, dad."

X   X   X

"Mr. Clarke, we have some word of Deborah."

"Just a minute." The Clarkes were at home in the den watching television.

"It's Mrs. Smythe from the detective agency about Deborah," he said to Victoria. "She has some information. Get on the other phone."

"It's about time." Victoria picked up the phone in the hall.

"My wife's on the line, too."

"We have been monitoring Hernando Cortez's telephone calls since Deborah ran away. We have had no results before now. Steven called to tell his father that Deborah had a baby girl this morning. Her name is Bianca Marie Cortez."

"Where did the call come from?"

"We don't know. We weren't able to trace it. All we have is the tape recording. There was some talk of Hernando joining them. We'll keep watching him."

"Thank you for the word. Keep trying."

"John!" Victoria Clarke burst into tears as she hung up the phone. "We have a Mexican grandchild! What will the girls at the club say?" Sobbing, she stumbled up the stairs to her room.

"At least Deborah's alive." John Clarke followed her up the stairs. "Maybe some day she will come home. She can bring her baby girl with her."

"What about Steven? Victoria continued to cry. "I HATE HIM! He stole our daughter. We have a Mexican grandchild. It's all his fault."

"He can come, too. I'll give him a good job. I would sent them some money If I knew where they were. I don't think Hernando Cortez will tell us."

"It's all Steven's fault!" Victoria was in her room crying. "WHY DOES HE HATE US SO?"

X   X   X

"HI, Mike," said Dr. Westover. It was Mike's three-year-old check-up.

"I'm worried," Betty Riggs said. "Mike was operated on before he was born. I would have lost him if they hadn't done it. I'm an older mother. Could that have affected him?"

"It's possible. What did they do?"

"They never told me."

"Dr. McCormick doesn't mention it in his notes. I can set up an appointment for Mike with a pediatric neurologist. We can also have him screened for motor development, hearing, speech, vision, and the works."

"Please set up the appointments," Betty said.

"I'll call Dr. Gomez and get a time. His office can arrange for the screening."

"Dr. Gomez wasn't able to detect any major neurological damage or brain disorders," Dr. Westover said to Betty Riggs. "The screening people say he's slow in developing, but they didn't find anything wrong with him."

"I would like to find a good nursery school. He needs to be with children his own age."

"I suggest you consider a Montessori school. My wife and I sent our children to one, and we're happy with the results."

"Can you recommend a school?" Betty asked.

"Try ours. It's certified by the American Montessori Association. It's church-supported, and preference is given to children like Mike. I'll call and get you an appointment. I know the director. Her name is Mrs. Santiago. Perhaps you can start Mike there after Christmas."

X   X   X

"Glad to meet you, Mike," Mrs. Santiago said as she shook the little boy's hand. Betty and Mike were in her office at the Montessori school. "I have read Dr. Westover's letter recommending Mike. His children have attended our school."

"He recommends you highly," said Betty.

"Would you like to see the school? We're proud of our program."

"Yes, I would."

"We have no competition, rewards, or punishment here," the director said as she took Betty and Mike from room to room. "Our goal is for each child to advance by small steps to the beginning stages of reading, writing, and arithmetic. Each child progresses at his own pace. Some are faster than others. No child is pushed or rushed in his work. It won't matter if Mike is slow."

"When could Mike start?"

"We have a vacancy in January."

"Do I need to pay something now to hold the place?"

"A deposit is required."

"I'll write a check for the whole term." Betty took her checkbook out of her purse. "May I observe?"

"Parents can observe any time they wish as long as they don't disrupt the program."

"Mike hasn't had much contact with other children his age. He is shy. May I stay the first few times until he becomes adjusted to being away from me? I can bring my crossword puzzles."

"Sure," said the director. "Mike, would you like to play with the toys?"

Betty put him down on the floor and pointed to the toys. He clung to her leg and would not leave her.

FOURTEEN

January, 1966

"Good morning, Mike," Mrs. Santiago said. This was Mike's first day at the Montessori school. He was holding his mother's hand.

"I have been telling him it's time to start school," said Betty. "He's been expecting it, but he's not sure. I can stay, but I need to leave by the middle of the morning. I can come back this afternoon if it would help."

"It might. Let's get him playing first and see what happens." The director took Mike's hand and led him to a play area.

Three other children Mile's age were there, and he joined them with some hesitation, and Mike became engrossed with the new toys.

"I'll wait in the office for a while," Betty said as they left the room.

"That's fine," said Mrs. Santiago.

While sitting in the office, Betty got out the mail she had picked up at the post office that morning. The latest issue of 'THE GANGSTER CHRONICLE' was there in its plain paper wrapper.

"I'd better not read this here," Betty said to herself. "It might scare Mrs. Santiago if she saw it."

Betty put it beside her purse unopened and read a financial magazine instead.

X   X   X

"Angel has an article in the paper about John and Victoria Clarke," Syndi said to Charles at dinner. "It's in the society section. His company has gone public. Deborah isn't mentioned."

"I asked John about her at his Christmas party last month. He said she was doing fine. He said she's in Europe somewhere. I asked where she was, but he changed the subject. I still feel they are hiding her. Have you heard anything?"

"No, I haven't," Syndi answered. "Maybe the Clarkes don't know where she is. What was her Mexican boyfriend's name? She might have run off with him."

"He's Hernando Cortez's son. I don't recall the boy's first name."

"Did you ever find out what happened to the boy?"

"I saw Hernando last week. He was working on the driveway entrance to the Corrigan house. He said his son was out west. He didn't say anything about the boy being married."

"Angel was at the party," said Syndi. "I heard her ask Mrs. Clarke about Deborah."

"What did Mrs. Clarke say?"

"She said Deborah's in Europe, but I'm not sure about that."

"Why?" Asked Charles.

"Deborah would come home occasionally if she were, and if she's dating royalty, Mrs. Clarke would splash it all over the society pages."

"You're right," said Charles.

"What happens if Angel finds Deborah?"

"We'll have to cross that bridge when we get to it," Charles said.

"She still calls you Mud Crawford." Syndi laughed. "I wish Angel would mind her own business."

"So do I."

X   X   X

Betty Riggs stopped at her stockbroker's office after dropping Mike off at the Montessori school.

"Please give these transaction orders to Mr. Tachonaka." Betty handed a piece of paper to Mrs. Wang, his new secretary.

"What is the account name?"

97

"You must be new. I'm Betty Riggs. I am trading for my own investment company account. The name, account number, and other information are at the top of the page. He'll know me."

"I'll give this to Mr. Tachonaka," Mrs. Wang said. "Do you want to wait for the confirmations?"

"No, he can mail them to me. Thank you."

After Betty had gone, Mrs. Wang took the transaction orders to Mr. Tachonaka who was at his desk, and he processed them.

"Who's she?" Mrs. Wang asked. "Most of our active traders are men."

"She usually phones in her orders. She's one of the smartest stock pickers I have known."

"She doesn't wear expensive clothes."

"No, and she drives an ordinary automobile. She doesn't need to impress people like some I know. She makes big money buying and selling stocks."

"How does she do it?" Asked Mrs. Wang.

"She studies the companies and the economy. She has the knack of knowing what to buy and sell and when to do it. She beats most of the pros."

"Is she good enough to manage one of our funds?" Mrs. Wang asked.

"We tried to hire her last year," Mr. Tachonaka said, "but she declined. She doesn't want to be responsible for other people's money."

"She's bought a thousand shares of Clarke Industries," Mrs. Wang said. "I haven't heard of that company before."

"It's a construction and engineering company on the east coast. She already owns the stock and keeps buying more on dips."

"Why?"

"It's one man, John Clarke," Mr. Tachonaka said. "He owns seventy-five percent of the company."

"Isn't that dangerous?" Mrs. Wang asked. "Isn't she at his mercy?"

"When the company went public, he promised to pay out at least twenty-five percent of the company's earnings each year in dividends. So far, he's kept his word. The company's gross revenues and earnings have more than doubled in the last two years."

"What else does she do besides stocks?" Asked Mrs. Wang.

"She works crossword puzzles and takes care of her small son."

"She looks old enough to be a grandmother."

The telephone rang, and Mrs. Wang returned to her desk to answer it.

X   X   X

"This is Hernando Cortez." He was calling contractors from his kitchen phone. "I'm looking for bricklaying or masonry jobs. Do you have anything available or coming up soon?"

"We don't have anything now, but we'll keep you in mind."

"It's that son of a bitch John Clarke," Hernando Cortez swore to himself as he hung up the phone. "I call the contractors in this area over and over again. They know I want work. The only jobs I find are little ones that don't go through them. No major contractor will touch me. It's been this way since Steven and Deborah went to the west coast."

"Steve's been asking me to move out there. I'm tired of building brick mailboxes and driveway entrances. I want to build houses and buildings like I used to. Maybe I should go west. I'll see what happens this year. John Clarke can go to hell!"

X   X   X

The last patient had gone, and Julie had left for the day. Charles Crawford sat down at his desk to finish his paperwork.

"Hello." He picked up the phone on the first ring. It was his private line.

"DAMN YOU, MUD CRAWFORD!

"Angel!" He was not expecting a call from her.

"That fifty thousand, you got it from that gangster Maffi Riggioletti, didn't you!"

"The divorce is over," Charles said.

"His wife was your patient, wasn't she?"   .

"That's none of your business."

"You bought that baby for them," Angel said. "Where did it come from?"

"You are crazy!"

"Who does the boy look like?" Angel asked. "Where did she move to?"

"Who?"

99

"Betty Riggioletti!"

"You leave my patients out of this!"

"That boy is your downfall, Mud Crawford! I'll find him yet!"

"Go eat a chocolate-covered rat!"

Angel slammed down the receiver.

"Was that Angel?" Syndi asked as she came into the office.

"She's still trying to find out where the fifty thousand came from."

She's persistent."

"She probably found out I have been appointed to the National Health Board."

"Your first board meeting is next Monday in Washington," Syndi reminded him. "Julie told me about it this morning. Do you know anything more about where Betty Riggioletti is?"

"No, I don't. Dr. McCormick said a Dr. Westover is Mike's new doctor. He's in Pacific City. There's no phone listing for the Riggioletti name in Pacific City."

"What about the doctor?"

"I called his office. His records clerk said he's never had a patient with that last name."

"What about Deborah?"

"I don't know."

June, 1966

"Steve, I'm sick again." Deborah was getting up to prepare breakfast.

"You were sick yesterday. What did the doctor say?"

"He said I'm two months' pregnant. I'm sorry I didn't tell you last night. You had to work late, and I didn't feel like talking when you came home."

"Can he do something about your being sick?"

"He gave me some prescriptions, but I didn't get them filled."

"Why not?"

"We don't have the money now."

"I know we didn't plan this, and we're tight on money, but we do have health insurance this time. You don't have to go to the clinic, and you can get the medicine you need."

"I'll still go to the clinic. If there's trouble, the medical school doctors take over. I want you to finish school."

"I want us both to finish school. We will have three years out of the way by the time the baby comes."

"We don't see much of each other now," said Deborah. "You come home from your job just before I go to work."

"One of us has to stay with Bianca," said Steve. "With both of us taking classes, we can't afford a baby sitter."

"I could baby sit other children this summer for a little extra money," said Deborah.

"You are not enrolled in classes this summer," said Steve, "but since you are pregnant,, maybe you should rest instead. You will have enough to do taking care of Bianca. We'll make it one way or another."

"We always have."

"I got a letter from Dad," said Steve. "He is thinking about selling his house and moving out here. He can't get jobs with the contractors. He's been black-listed by your father."

"I'm sorry," said Deborah. "That's the kind of people my parents are. I don't want them to know about Bianca and our new baby. They might try to kill them."

"Some day we may have to face your parents," Steve said.

"I don't want to see them," Deborah answered.

Let's get some breakfast. Do you feel like eating?"

"Not really."

September, 1966

"It's a package for you," said Julie. "It's like last year."

She handed Dr. Crawford the long, narrow box that had just been delivered. He was in between patients at the office.

He took off the wrapping paper and opened it. "A dozen dead roses. This is more of Angel's foolishness. Throw it away."

He handed the box back to Julie.

"She's done this every year since the divorce," said Syndi. "When will she stop?"

"Ralph says we should ignore it. She'll get tired of it eventually. Who is the next patient?"

"Mrs. Schwartz in room three."

December, 1966

"How is little Mike doing?" Betty Riggs asked Mrs. Santiago one afternoon at the Montessori school. "He enjoys coming here now."

"He plays mostly by himself," said the director. "He's slowly getting acquainted with other children. He's beginning to play with them some."

"Is he mentally retarded?" Betty asked.

"He's slower than the others his age, but he gets there. He tries harder than any other child I have ever known."

"I want the best for him."

"Don't give up on him," Mrs. Santiago said. "He might surprise you some day. He's in one of the back play areas. I'll get him for you."

X   X   X

John Clarke was reading a financial report at his desk at home that evening when his wife came into his office.

"Christmas is lonely without Deborah," she said. "I don't understand why they can't find her. I'm sure Hernando Cortez knows where she is."

"That reminds me," John Clarke said, "I put out the word to the other contractors that it's all right for them to use Hernando Cortez."

"Why did you do that?" Victoria was alarmed.

"I shouldn't have told them to stop using him."

"Why, John?"

"Punishing Hernando Cortez is not the answer. I'm sorry I did it. How are the plans for the Christmas party coming?"

"Everything is done." Uncertain, she paused for a moment. "We're using the same caterers as last year. Is Dr. Crawford bringing his CHINK wife? They are not members of the club."

"I have to invite him. He's the senior doctor in obstetrics and gynecology at the hospital. He was president of the state medical society last year. He's on the National Health Board. I don't mind him bringing her."

"BUT SHE'S A CHINK!"

"She's only half Chinese. Her mother is from Thailand."

"Half chink and half mud. Mrs. Cowan said she's the color of light mud. The girls at the club don't understand why he divorced his ex-wife to marry HER!"

"I wasn't involved in the divorce. I'm not going to engage in name-calling. His wife is a nice lady, as far as I'm concerned. I don't care about her Asian ancestry."

"I don't understand why anyone would marry a foreigner. What could Deborah see in Steven? I wish she were here. It's all Steven's fault. I don't understand why he hates us so."

"Blaming Steven isn't going to solve anything."

"Why don't we shoot Hernando Cortez? We could hire a hit man to do it. They'd come back for his funeral. We could shoot Steven, too. Then Deborah would come home."

"We're not going to shoot anyone." John Clarke got up from his desk. "Let's turn on the TV. It's time for the news. There was a plane crash in France. People were killed. Clarke Industries has a branch there now."

X   X   X

"I've barely made ends meet since Steven left," Hernando Cortez said to himself as he drove down the street in his old pick-up truck. He was tired from a hard day's work. "I finished my last job this afternoon. I don't have any more work lined up. How am I going to get through the winter? I wish I could go west this Christmas and see my son and granddaughter, but this pick-up wouldn't make the trip. The tires are worn out, and the motor's leaking oil."

He passed the Clarke mansion.

"Maffi Riggioletti lived there when he was alive. I wonder where his wife and son are?"

He pulled up to a stop sign and looked both ways. Seeing no oncoming traffic, he crossed the intersection and continued on his way home.

"John Clarke and his hateful wife live there now. They look so unhappy. They have all that money, but I've got the granddaughter. I wouldn't trade places with that son-of-a-bitch for anything."

He turned into his driveway and stopped. Getting out, he went inside his house and turned on the lights. There were no Christmas decorations were up, not even a tree.

"Steven and Deb are better off out there. I wouldn't want them to come back here for anything."

He turned on the television in his living room and then went to the kitchen to fix supper.

"I don't have any more work. It's the slow season. Why fight it any longer? I'll clean out this place and sell everything I can. Then I'm going to put this house up for sale. I'll sell the old truck, pay all my bills, and join Steve and Deborah out west. John Clarke can go to hell."

FIFTEEN

January, 1967

"Steve, I called a cab," Deborah said over the phone. She was at home, and Steve was at work. "The baby's on its way. Bianca's asleep. I'm taking her with me. I'm sorry I didn't reach you earlier. I couldn't find you. The cab's here. We've got to go. We're on our way to the hospital."

"I'm on my way. I'll meet you there."

Deborah hung up the phone. She picked up Bianca, and carried her out to the cab.

"Take me to University Hospital!"

X   X   X

"I'm sorry I couldn't get here any sooner," Steve said to Dr. Tsumura, the intern at the clinic. Bianca was asleep in his arms. He had found her at the nurses' station. "How did things go?"

"Congratulations," the doctor said. "It's a boy. Deborah and the baby are fine. She told us you would be late. She had a hard time, but she made it. You can see her now. What are you going to name the baby?"

"Juan Hernando Cortez. He's named after his grandfather and great grandfather."

Steve put Bianca down on the bed beside her mother. Bianca was asleep.

"Where did you find her?" Deborah asked.

"She was asleep at the nurses' station."

"She's not supposed to be in the room," Deborah said.

"The nurses told me they would look the other way."

"I'm glad everything's all right."

"I'll take Bianca home now. I'll find someone to stay with her tomorrow, and I'll come back. Carlos is covering for me at the office."

"I love you, Steve."

"I love you, Deb." Steve kissed her forehead. "Get some rest."

X   X   X

Steve brought Deborah and the baby home three days later. It was after dark. They went inside, and Deborah put Juan in his bed.

"This pregnancy was difficult for you. We have Bianca and Juan, a girl and a boy. They don't make any other kind. I think we should stop at two."

"I had a hard time," said Deborah. "It didn't seem like it was ever going to end. I don't like being constantly sick. Two children are enough. We don't have to have any more, but if I get pregnant again, I want to have the baby. I don't want to lose it, no matter what. They never told me whether the first one was a boy or a girl. I never even got to see it." Tears came to her eyes. "I try to not think about it, but sometimes I can't help it."

"I don't want to lose it, either."

"Mrs. Lopez from our church counseling center came to see one of the new mothers at the hospital. I'd like to talk to her. She may be able to help me. Do we have the money? Their fees aren't much."

"I don't think our insurance will cover it. Find out what it costs. We'll work it into our budget."

"Thanks, Steve."

"I'll go next door and get Bianca. It's her bed-time."

X   X   X

Hernando Cortez watched intently from his window seat as the bus drove through the streets of Pacific City. The driver announced their arrival as the bus pulled into the terminal. Hernando waited as the other passengers got up to leave. Tired from his long trip, he got his suitcases from the rack above his seat, and he took his place at the end of the line.

106

Leaving the bus, he entered the terminal and paused for a moment to look around.

"Over here, Dad." Holding Bianca, Steve was standing on the opposite side of the room.

Hernando turned and saw his son and granddaughter.

"This must be Bianca," he said as he approached.

Uncertain about the person who was coming, she clung to her father.

"She's a little timid in a strange place. She'll get to know you."

"I haven't had a bath or shaved since I left the east coast. Has the baby come yet?"

"Deb came home with him yesterday. His name is Juan Hernando."

"Thank you, but you didn't have to name him that."

"You're probably tired from the ride. Let's get your baggage and go home. Deb will have supper for us."

"I have only these two bags. I shipped the rest of my stuff the day I left. It should be here in a day or two. Let's go. I'd like a home-cooked meal."

"It's your home, too, Dad." Carrying Bianca, Steve left the terminal with his father. "Deb won't have it any other way. We want you to stay with us, at least until you get established and can get your own place. She's sorry for what her father did to you."

"She's not responsible for that. I don't hold it against her."

"She wants you to feel welcome."

"I appreciate that. I have enough money to pay cash for a new pick-up truck and new tools. I'll start looking for them tomorrow. Once I can, I'll get a place of my own."

"Don't be in a hurry to move, Dad. It's your place, too. You've helped us out. We don't mind helping you."

"As soon as I get to your place, I want to take a bath, shave, and put on clean clothes."

They got into Steve's car and went home.

February, 1967

Victoria Clarke was in the kitchen when the phone rang.

"Clarke residence, Victoria speaking."

107

"Mrs. Clarke, this is Mrs. Smythe at the detective agency. We have news of Deborah."

"It's about time! I'll get John on the extension."

"I'm listening." He had picked up the phone in the den.

"Deborah's in Pacific City. She married Steven Cortez about two weeks after she left home. We have a copy of the license. A Catholic priest married them. She may have joined the Catholic Church. They attend Catholic services regularly."

"Hernando Cortez is Catholic," said John.

"Steven and Deborah are part-time students at Pacific Coast University. They're both seniors. They work for a fast-food chain, Fast Fred's Hot Foods. He's a manager of one of their outlets. They have two small children, a girl and a boy. The girl's name is Bianca Marie. She's about fifteen months old. The boy's name is Juan Hernando, He's about a week old."

"How did you find them?" John asked.

"Hernando Cortez went out there. Apparently, he plans to stay. He sold his house here just before he left. He sold his old pick-up and his furniture. He shipped two or three boxes of things the day he left. We got the shipping address and contacted a detective agency there."

"I'll call Deborah," said Mrs. Clarke. She was in tears. "What is her telephone number?"

"It's unlisted. We haven't been able to get it yet."

"Can you get it for us?" Asked Mrs. Clarke.

"Eventually. Why don't you write instead? We have her address."

"It's been over three and a half years since she ran away," John said. "Her anger may have cooled down some."

"I will," said Mrs. Clarke. "I'll include a check. John, maybe you can get him a job here."

"I don't know if they would come back east now," said John. "I wish Hernando Cortez hadn't gone out there."

"We'll send you copies of the marriage license, birth certificates, and other papers."

"Is there any sign she was kidnapped?" Mrs. Clarke asked.

"We don't think she was. She's had opportunity to get away if she wanted to."

"Keep an eye on them, but leave them alone," said John Clarke. "If they get into financial trouble, let me know. If he loses his job, let me know. I'll send them money. I'll help them out."

"John!" Victoria Clarke came into the den after she had hung up the phone. "Don't help Steven. He's the problem. He took Deborah away from us. I don't know why he hates us so." She burst into tears.

"I'm going to call some business friends in the Pacific City area. I'll see that Hernando gets plenty of work. I'll also help Steven if I can."

"John! You wouldn't!"

"Yes, Victoria, I would!"

"No! John, no! Don't do this to me!" Crying, she ran upstairs to her room.

March, 1967

"Bad news, Steve," Deborah said. He had come home after work.

"What is it?"

"My parents found us. Here's a letter from mother. I haven't opened it, but I held it up to the light. There's a check inside, too. I can't tell how much it is for."

"Do you want to open it?" Steve asked.

"I know we need money, but they killed our first baby. If we cash their check, they'll try to own us. They may even try to split us up. I don't want anything to do with them. I don't want their money, and I don't want to move back there. I wish they would leave us alone!"

"They're your parents. I'll respect your decision, but don't tell Dad this letter came. What he'd say about your father wouldn't be very nice."

Deborah printed "NOT AT THIS ADDRESS, RETURN TO SENDER" on the envelope.

""I'll drop this in the mail tonight on the way to class. Maybe they'll get the message."

"What happens if they don't?"

"I don't know, but I'm not going back. They killed our first baby. I don't want them to kill Bianca and Juan. I don't want them to split us up."

"I'm sorry they found us."

"I'm sorry, too." She put her arms around him.

"Have you seen Mrs. Lopez yet?" Steve asked.

"No, I haven't."

"Call her and see if you can get an appointment."

"Thanks, Steve."

X   X   X

"I'm worried." Betty Riggs was at the Montessori school that afternoon to pick up Mike. "How's he doing?"

"Mike makes friends more easily now," said Mrs. Santiago. "He's a slow learner, but he's making progress."

"He enjoys coming each day," said Betty. "He watches the children's TV programs he's old enough for. Can I do anything more to help him here?"

"It's best to let him progress at his own pace. Don't give up on him. He may surprise you some day."

X   X   X

"John," Victoria said over the phone. She was at home, and he was at his office. "My letter to Deborah was returned unopened. It's marked 'NOT AT THIS ADDRESS, RETURN TO SENDER'. It looks like Deborah's printing. She wouldn't do this to her mother. Are the detectives sure they got the right address?"

"I was afraid this might happen. We can check the address, but it's probably correct. Get the papers the detective agency sent us."

"Just a moment. I'll find them."

Mrs. Clarke put down the phone and went into her husband's study. She saw the folder from the detective agency on his desk and took it back to the phone.

"John, I found the file. The two birth certificates, the marriage license, and the Pacific Coast University records all have the same address as the one on the letter. Could they have moved?"

"If they moved and left a forwarding address, the letter would have been forwarded. They probably refused it."

"John, please come home. I feel so hurt. I'm her mother. Why would she treat me this way? Steven must have made her do it. It's all Steven's fault. Why does he hate us so? We have two Mexican grandchildren. What do I tell the girls at the club? I don't know what to do!"

"I'm coming home now. I don't know what to do either."

110

SIXTEEN

January, 1968

"I bought my own place today, son," Hernando Cortez said. It was evening, and he had just come home. "It's a two-bedroom house in an older neighborhood. I'll get some furniture and move in as soon as the deal closes."

"You don't have to hurry," said Steve. "You're not in our way."

"I know, son, but with two small children, you need the room. I need a place of my own. I appreciate your help. You're a good son."

"Work's better here than back east."

"I do more stucco here. There isn't as much brickwork. As soon as I finish one job, I have another one. I have to turn down jobs even in the wintertime. I wouldn't go back east for anything. John Clarke can go to hell."

"We wouldn't go back there either. We're staying on the west coast."

"Don't worry, son. I'll keep in touch."

"Dinner's ready," Deborah announced as she came into the room.

X   X   X

"I missed Deborah not being home for Christmas," Victoria said as she came into the den. John was watching the news. "I want to see our grandchildren."

"I'd like to see them, too." John Clarke's attention was on the news. "Brazil has a new president. Clarke Industries is considering buying a construction company there. I'll be going there next week."

"It's all Steven's fault, John. If only he'd left Deborah alone. He should have known his place. Steven is making her behave like this. Without him, she would read my letters. She would write to me. She would come home if he would let her. I know she would. I'm her mother." Victoria burst into tears. "JOHN! WE HAVE MEXICAN GRANDCHILDREN!"

"I don't know what to do, but blaming Steven isn't the answer." He looked at her momentarily and then back to the TV.

"What happened to the boy Deborah dated in junior high school? Why couldn't she have married him? There would have been a country club wedding. They wouldn't be Catholic."

"I don't remember his name," John Clarke said.

"Things would be different if she had married him."

"Maybe so," said John, "but she didn't. There's no need to think about it now."

"It's all Steven's fault, John. "Why does he hate us so?"

"Blaming Steven isn't going to solve anything. The news is over. Let's see what else is on TV. Maybe there's a good movie on tonight."

"JOHN!" Victoria burst into tears, and she fled to her room.

February, 1968

"Steve," Deborah said. "I'm at a pay phone at the hospital. Bianca had a fall on her tricycle. She broke her arm. The doctor said it's a simple break. She'll be all right."

"How is she taking it?"

"She cried the whole time, but she cooperated with the doctor. He's putting a cast on her arm now."

"I'll be home soon."

"I got another letter from mother. I didn't open it. I'm sending it back like the others."

"Some day we may have to face them."

"I've been talking with Mrs. Lopez about it."

"What does she say?"

"She tells me I must learn forgiveness, but it's hard to forgive someone who isn't sorry. I have to go now. They're bringing Bianca out."

X   X   X

Mrs. Clarke picked up the phone. She was in the living room.

"Clarke residence, Victoria speaking."

"This is Mrs. Smythe from the detective agency."

"I'll get John."

"I'm on the line." John Clarke had picked up the phone in the den.

"Bianca broke her arm in a tricycle accident," Mrs. Smythe said, "but she's going to be all right."

"How are they on money?" John asked.

"They have health insurance," said Mrs. Smythe.

"See to it that the girl gets the proper treatment. Do it as low key as you can. Money is no object. If they run into trouble, contact me. If they need money, contact me."

"We will," said Mrs. Smythe. "Deborah is seeing Mrs. Lopez, a psychological counselor at the Catholic counseling center. Mrs. Lopez seems to be well qualified."

"That's good news," said John. "Do what you can to keep her attending counseling sessions, but stay in the background. Maybe some day we can see Deborah and get to know our grandchildren."

"John," Victoria asked after they had ended the phone call, "Is there any hope?"

"There's always hope, but you are going to have to change your feelings about Steven."

"NEVER! He's the cause of the problem!"

"Maybe you should see a psychological counselor."

"No, John! I'm not crazy!" Victoria burst into tears. "Steven's the cause of the problem, not me!"

She stomped out of the room crying.

"Congratulations, son," Hernando Cortez said as he shook Steven's hand. The graduation service was over, and Steve was in his cap and gown.

"You are the first of our family to graduate from a university. Where's Deborah?"

"Home, Dad. Juan's sick, but he'll be all right."

"Are you going to look for a better job?"

"I got a promotion at Fast Fred's. I'm in the central office now. There are two of us in accounting. We handle payroll, inventory, purchasing, and the records of our individual outlets. I might be able to get a better-paying job somewhere else, but we'd have to move. I'd like to stay here at least until Deb graduates. Then we'll see. The pay isn't the best, but Fast Fred's isn't a bad place to work. Nobody gets lavish salaries, and we do have benefits."

"You need to buy your own home, son. It doesn't pay to rent."

"We will, Dad, once we both get through school and can save money for the down payment."

X   X   X

"Hi," Betty Riggs said to Mrs. Wang. Betty was in the stockbroker's office. "Here are transaction orders for my account. Please give them to Mr. Tachonaka."

Betty handed the list to Mrs. Wang.

"I'll see that he gets this as soon as he gets off the phone. Do you want to wait?"

"Not today. Maybe some other time."

Mrs. Wang handed the list to Mr. Tachonaka as soon as he had completed his phone conversation, and he placed the orders.

"This might interest you," he said to Mrs. Wang. "Here are her buy and sell orders Mrs. Riggs had last month."

The secretary looked at the list.

"The stocks she bought all have gone up significantly in price. The ones she sold have all gone down after she sold them. She took a nice profit on each sale."

"She's buying more Clarke Industries," said Mrs. Wang.

"It's done quite well," said Mr. Tachonaka. "Clarke has bought another company in Europe and one in South America. He is also expanding his operations in the midwest. Maybe he'll buy a company here on the west coast."

"Does she ever sell short?"

"Never, and she doesn't buy on margin either. She doesn't do anything exotic, and she doesn't deal in options. She's made a bundle so far this year trading stocks. She has a good living just off of her dividends from Clarke Industries."

July, 1968

"The police were here this afternoon," Victoria said to her husband when he arrived home that evening.

"What did they want?"

"They wanted to see the house."

"What for?"

"Somebody told them about the secret entrance," Victoria said.

"We've made no secret of it," said John. "Did you show it to them?"

"I had to," said Victoria. "They had a search warrant. Then they asked where Mrs. Riggioletti was."

"What did you tell them?"

"I told them I didn't know. They think she's running the mob."

"That's ridiculous," said John. "We haven't heard from her since we bought the house."

"I told them to call her attorney," said Victoria. "They said they did. He told them she was in Sicily, but they don't believe him."

"Somebody is behind this," said John. "There's no need for them to bother us."

"I wish they'd leave us alone."

"I'll call the mayor in the morning," said John. "I'll put a stop to this nonsense. Betty Riggioletti wouldn't have sold this house if she were going to stay here and run the mob. There's another reason. I'm going to try to find out who's behind this and stop it."

"They asked about Betty Riggioletti's son. He was born in November of 1962. That's about the time Deborah's baby would have been born. I

115

figured it up. The baby would have been five going on six if it had lived."

"That's just a coincidence. Deborah's baby didn't have a head."

December, 1968

"Little Mike has made progress this past year," Mrs. Santiago said to Betty. This was a scheduled parent conference. "He will be ready for the first grade by next September."

"I'm glad I didn't try to start him last September," said Betty. "I want him to do well."

"He's barely six now. It would have been a mistake to start him early."

"I have enrolled him in a parochial school next year."

"Which one?" Mrs. Santiago asked.

"St. Benedict's."

"It's a good school," Mrs. Santiago said. "The students are mostly Mexican or part Mexican. The teachers are nuns. They're dedicated to their work. Sister Rosa Anita is the principal. I know her well.

"Our priest recommended the school. The students get individual attention."

"Here comes Mike."

SEVENTEEN

January, 1969

"Hi, Dad," said Steve. "Come in. I'm glad you could come by."

"Thanks," said Hernando Cortez. "I have a late Christmas present for Bianca and Juan."

"What is it?"

"I have a place for Bianca in St. Benedict's kindergarten starting a year from next September. Once she's in kindergarten, she will automatically advance into St. Benedict's elementary school."

"Wee appreciate this, Dad, but St. Benedict's is a parochial school. We don't have the money to send her there. You don't have it either."

"I'm paying for it, son. You're my only child. They are my only grandchildren. I want them to get a good start in school. I have a place reserved for Juan when he's old enough, too."

"Thanks, Dad, we appreciate this, but no hard feelings if you find it's too much to pay."

"I want the best for my grandchildren. St. Benedict's is the best school in Pacific City for Mexican children.

"Hi, Dad," Deborah said as she came inside. She was carrying a bag of groceries. "Please stay for supper."

"Well." Hernando Cortez hesitated. "I don't want to impose."

"We insist," said Steve.

"Let me help with the groceries," Hernando said.

117

X   X   X

Steve and Carlos were in the accounting office of Fast Fred's Hot Foods preparing to pay the company's December invoices.

"The mail's here," said Carlos.

"I'll see if anything came in today." Steve got up from his desk and went to the receptionist's desk.

As he looked through the mail, a financial magazine headline caught his eye.

"CLARKE INDUSTRIES BUYS SANCHOS CONSTRUCTION".

Steve stayed late that afternoon working on accounts payable records. When the others had left, he went into the various offices looking for the magazine. He found it and read the article.

According to the magazine, multimillionaire John Clarke, Chairman of the Board, CEO, and majority stockholder of Clarke Industries announced the purchase of Sanchos Construction, Inc., on the west coast. It would operate as a separate division. Its workers and management are mostly Mexican-Americans.

"We'll keep the present management," he said. "They're part of the reason we're buying the company."

"I won't tell Deborah about this," Steve said to himself. "Sooner or later, we'll have to face them. Dad does a lot of work for Sanchos. I wonder how this will affect him?"

June, 1969

"We're proud of you, Deb," said Steve. He was holding Bianca, and his father was holding Juan. Deborah was wearing her cap and gown. Her graduation ceremony was over, and she held her diploma from Pacific Coast University.

"We're both out of school now," Steve said to his father. "Maybe we can start saving to buy a house. That's our next goal."

"Are you looking for a job?" Hernando Cortez asked Deborah.

"Not now," she answered. "I'm going to stay home with the children until they're in school. I'm also going to keep Jess and Rosa while their mothers work. They're Juan's age."

X   X   X

"Mike, it's time to leave for school," Betty Riggs said. It was his first day in the first grade at St. Benedict's.

"But Mamma, I don't want to go!"

"You're all ready, Mike. We're on our way." His mother took his hand and led him out the front door to the car. "Today is a half day. School is over at noon. I'll pick you up then."

"I don't want to go to the new school. Why can't I stay at the old one?"

"You have outgrown it, Mike. You are a bigger boy now."

X   X   X

Betty Riggs picked up Mike at noon.

"How was school?" She asked on the way home.

"I didn't like it."

"Why not?"

"There were no toys to play with. I didn't know anybody. I had to sit at my desk and listen to the teacher. She talked like we were dumb. I already know my ABC's, and I can count. I want to go back to the old school."

"You are six now, Mike, almost seven. You've outgrown the old school. You have to go to the first grade. It's less play and more study."

"But I don't know anybody."

"You'll have to make new friends."

"But I don't know how."

"You can learn." Betty Riggs turned into their driveway. "I'll have lunch fixed soon."

X   X   X

"Bianca, let's do letters and numbers for Juan, Jess, and Rosa." Deborah was at home with the children. Steve was at work.

"A, B, C, D, E, F, G," Deborah sang with Bianca. "H, I, J, K, L, M, N."

She caught her breath momentarily and then continued. "O, P, Q, R, S, T, U."

Deborah paused to let Bianca catch up. Bianca had missed a few of the letters. "V, double U, X, Y, and Z."

119

"That's good." They clapped their hands. "Now let's do numbers."

"One, two, three, four, five, six, seven," they sang. "Eight, nine, ten, eleven, twelve." They paused momentarily.

"Thirteen, fourteen, fifteen, sixteen." They paused again. "Seventeen, eighteen, nineteen, twenty."

Bianca missed a few of the numbers, The three younger children looked on in silence.

"That's good." They clapped their hands. "Letters and numbers are important."

"Next year you will start kindergarten," Deborah said to Bianca. "Granddaddy has reserved a place for you at St. Benedict's."

Deborah had been preparing Bianca for school ever since she was two. Deborah had little in the way of teaching materials, only out-of-date books she borrowed from the public library and what she could buy at the bookstores. Bianca could count to twenty, she knew the alphabet, and she could identify the major colors and shapes. She also enjoyed watching children's programs on TV.

X   X   X

"Why are you crying, Mike?" Betty asked when she picked him up at school. "You have been here a month. You are doing well."

"They say you're not my mommy."

"Who says that?"

"The other kids at school."

"Then who am I if I'm not your mommy?"

"They say you're my granny."

"I'm your mommy, Mike. I was older than most mommys when you were born. The other kids are confused because I'm old enough to be your granny. Your granny is dead. She died before you were born. You can call me granny if you want to, but I'm still your mommy."

"You're my mommy! I don't care what they call you!" Tears came to his eyes, and he put his arms around her. "I don't care how old you are."

Betty took his hand and led him to the car. "We have to go home now. We can talk more later if you want to."

Victoria Clarke had returned from the country club. She came in the kitchen door and went straight to her husband's study where he was reading.

"John," she asked, "is the club inviting Dr. Crawford and his chink wife to join? The girls are talking about her today."

"He's on the list of people they're going to invite after the first of the year."

"What about HER?"

"If he is invited," her husband said, "she has to be included."

"But the Crawfords are mixed. The other minority couples aren't. The wives are the same as their husbands."

"The board voted to invite them. I don't have any objections."

"But, John, they have those two mixed boys. They're light mud-colored like her."

"The board voted to invite them," John Clarke repeated. "I don't object."

"What about his ex-wife? She's a member. She won't like it."

"Angel Crawford has no say in the matter."

"She says her two children aren't his."

"I don't believe that," John said. "They look too much like him."

"She says the two mud-colored boys aren't his, either. He can't have children. That's why she divorced him."

"I don't believe that," John repeated. "Those boys look like him, too."

"She keeps asking about Deborah," Victoria said.

"What do you tell her?"

"I don't tell her anything," Victoria said. "She scares me. Why does she keep asking?"

"I don't know," said John. "The next time she asks, tell her to ask me. I'll tell her it's none of her business. It's time for the news. I'll turn on the TV."

Victoria Clarke was sitting in the den when her husband got home that evening.

"John, it has been another year without Deborah. It will be another lonely Christmas."

"I don't know what to do about it," he answered. "What about the plans for our Christmas party?"

"Everything's set. We're doing the same thing as last year. Is Dr. Crawford bringing his chink wife?"

"They're coming."

"Why?"

"We have to invite him. He's the chief physician in obstetrics and gynecology at the hospital, and he's a past president of the state medical society. I don't have any problem with their coming. We're inviting the minority doctors this year."

"Why did he marry a chink?"

"He can marry whoever he wants."

"But they have those two boys. The girls at the club talk about her."

"They would talk about us if they knew about Deborah."

"John, what if we sent the children toys?"

"Deborah would only return them."

"It's Steven, John. Deborah would write to us if it weren't for Steven. I know she would."

"Blaming Steven isn't going to solve anything."

"Our grandchildren, John, we could change their last name to Clarke. We could give them American first names. Maybe they look enough like Deborah that no one would know they're half Mexican."

"I don't think that's a good idea."

"It's all Steven's fault. I don't know why he hates us so."

"Let's turn on the news. Ask the cook how long it will be before supper."

EIGHTEEN

January, 1970

"We have an invitation to join the country club," Charles Crawford said. He and Syndi were at home in the kitchen. She was fixing supper. "How do you feel about it?"

"Do we have to join?"

"No, we don't."

"Victoria Clarke barely tolerates me at her Christmas parties each year," Syndi said. "She goes out of her way to make me feel uncomfortable. She doesn't like it because my parents are Asian. Why are they inviting us to join?"

"The board opened the membership to minorities this year," said Charles. "They're afraid of a lawsuit if they don't. Several new minority doctors at the hospital have complained."

"The ladies' auxiliary at the club don't like it because I married you and because we had the boys. They have said some very hateful things to me. It's been hard, but I have tried to ignore it."

"They don't like anyone of mixed ancestry," said Charles.

"What about themselves?" Asked Syndi. "Three of them brag about being part American Indian. Nobody in this country is racially pure. They are no better than anyone else."

"They don't want to understand things that way," said Charles. "They set themselves up as standards and judge everyone else accordingly."

"We can join if we have to," said Syndi, "but I'll be uncomfortable going their social events. I refuse to be a member of the auxiliary."

"I don't want to join," said Charles, "but I wanted to make sure felt the same way before I declined membership."

Syndi smiled and gave her husband a big hug. "I love you, dear. You won't have to wash the dishes tonight. Go get the boys while I set the table."

February, 1970

John Clarke arrived home after ten o'clock that evening. He had attended the monthly country club board meeting.

"How did it go?" Victoria saw the expression on his face. Something was wrong. "What happened?"

"The Crawfords turned down membership in the club."

"Why?"

"Charles said they were too busy doing other things. He spends long hours with his medical practice. He serves on the National Obstetrics and Gynecology board. He doesn't have enough time for his family. Syndi helps him at work and tends to the boys."

"Where does he play golf?" Victoria asked.

"He doesn't, to my knowledge."

"What about the others the board invited?" Asked Victoria.

"They all accepted. The Crawfords were the only ones to decline. They were the ones the board wanted most."

"It's his chink wife. I don't know why she doesn't like us. The girls at the club have been nice to her. She must be ashamed of her two mud-colored boys. Do we have to invite them to any more of our Christmas parties?"

"We'll invite them. I don't want to hear any more of this. I'm tired. I'm going to bed." He went up the stairs to their bedroom.

Victoria stood there for a moment and then followed him.

"John, can we talk? It's about Steven."

"I don't want to hear it."

March, 1970

Sister Rosa Anita was in the hall when Betty Riggs came in with Mike.

124

"I have been watching for you," she said to Betty. "We have Mr. Ferrari, a graduate student from Pacific Coast University assisting us this month. He's majoring in psychology. He gave Mike an IQ test last week. He wants to talk to us about the results. He insists it's important. Do you mind staying?"

"No," Betty answered. "I can stay. Mike, you go on to your classroom."

"Yes, Mamma." Mike hurried down the hall to his room.

Sister Rosa Anita and Betty Riggs went into Sister Rosa Anita's office. Mr. Ferrari and Sister Anna Maria, Mike's regular first-grade teacher, were waiting there.

"This is Mrs. Riggs," the principal said, "Mike's mother."

"I'm sorry, ma'am," said Mr. Ferrari, "but your son has no business being in this school. His test scores are the lowest I've ever seen."

"There must be some mistake," Betty said. She was concerned.

"There's no mistake, ma'am."

"But he's passing," said Sister Anna Maria. "He's no star student, but he's passing."

Sister Rosa Anita came to attention.

"Here are his scores." Mr. Ferrari handed them to Mike's teacher. "He doesn't belong here. He must be badly mentally retarded."

A disturbed look came across Betty's face.

"We need to talk to Mike about this." Sister Rosa Anita turned to Mr. Ferrari. "You wait in the outer office. We need to talk to Mike without you being present."

Mr. Ferrari followed Sister Rosa Anita to the outer office. He sat down while she went to Mike's classroom. She returned with the boy and took him into the inner office.

"Mike," Sister Rosa Anita asked, "do you remember that man sitting in the other room?"

"Yes."

"Did he give you a test last week?" Asked Sister Rosa Anita.

"I talked with him last week. I didn't know it was a test."

"What did you talk about?"

"He asked me a bunch of stupid questions, and I gave him a bunch of stupid answers."

"Mike!" His mother said. "You didn't!"

"Yes, Mamma, I did. I had all that stuff in the old school. He wouldn't believe me when I told him the truth so I told him the biggest lies I could get him to swallow."

"That's one IQ test down the drain." Sister Rosa Anita laughed. "I can't wait to tell that know-it-all young man he's mistaken."

"Mike," his mother said. "I'm ashamed of you! Go tell him you're sorry!"

"Do I have to?"

"Yes, you have to."

Mike went into the outer office. "I'm sorry." He continued unconcerned out the door. Sister Anna Maria was behind him. She took his hand and led him back to his classroom.

April, 1970

Betty Riggs brought Mike to school a few minutes early. She stopped to talk to Sister Anna Maria.

"How's Mike doing?"

"He isn't setting the world on fire, but he seems to have a knack for numbers."

"Are they going to give him another IQ test?" Betty asked.

"Not any time soon."

"Is he getting along with the other children?

"He keeps to himself. Some of the kids in his class don't even know who he is. He's not a behavior problem. He has a few friends, but not many. What does he do at home?

"He likes to watch children's programs on TV," Betty said. "He has a tutor, Mrs. Cervera. She's a retired teacher who comes each evening. I bought her the same books Mike uses in school."

"I know her," Sister Anna Maria said. "She called me once or twice about his assignments."

"What about summer school?" Betty asked. "Would this help him?"

"It wouldn't hurt," Sister Anna Maria said. "He could review the past year and get a head start on the second grade."

"It would keep him in the habit of going to school."

"I'm glad you have joined the Concerned Parents' Association," said Sister Anna Maria.

"I want to do my part," answered Betty.

"The tuition is low because most of the Mexican children have poor parents."

"Does the Church help?" Betty asked.

"We get some help from the Bishop, but there's never enough money in the budget to fund all of the school's needs."

The first bell rang, and Sister Anna Maria turned to go to her classroom.

"Thanks for helping Mike," Betty said.

September, 1970

"Bianca," said Deborah, "are you ready for school? It's time for us to leave."

"It's early, Mamma."

"We have to drive Daddy to work first."

Bianca said nothing. It was her first day of school, and she wasn't sure she wanted to go. Holding Juan, her mother took her hand and led her out to the car.

After taking Steve to work, Deborah drove to St. Benedict's. With Juan in her arms, she led Bianca up the steps and inside. They found the kindergarten room and met Bianca's teacher.

"School's over at noon," Deborah said to Bianca. "I'll pick you up then. Have a good day."

Deborah returned to her car and then drove to the church-counseling center with Juan. She had a session scheduled with Mrs. Lopez.

X   X   X

"John," said Victoria. "It's the detective agency."

"I'll get on the extension in the den."

"Mr. Clarke," said Mrs. Smythe, "your granddaughter started Kindergarten at St. Benedict's school."

"Oh, no, John," Victoria said, "it's a Catholic school."

"It's their choice. Where did the tuition money come from?"

"Hernando Cortez made the arrangements. He has a place reserved for Juan when he's old enough. The tuition hasn't been paid yet. He's set up to begin making monthly payments next month."

"Is it a good school?"

"It's better than the public schools. The students get more individual attention. They're mostly Mexican and Asian."

"I want to pay the tuition for the whole year. We'll do it without anyone knowing where the money's coming from. I'll talk to my attorney about how best to do this."

"John!" Victoria protested. "It's a Catholic school!"

"Keep an eye on the situation." John Clarke ignored his wife's concern.

"John!" Victoria said after they had hung up the phone. "Not only do we have Mexican grandchildren, but they're growing up Catholic. They're going to school with Mexicans, Asians, and who knows what other trash. They're being taught by nuns! Our granddaughter might even grow up to be a nun! What if the girls at the club find this out! It's all Steven's fault! I hate him, John!" She began crying. "Why does he treat us this way?"

"I don't care if the girls at the club do find out. Blaming Steven isn't going to solve anything. Maybe some day you'll come to accept him. He's Deborah's husband."

"NEVER!" In tears, Victoria went upstairs to her room.

October, 1970

"Where's Mike?" Betty asked Sister Anna Susanna, his second-grade teacher. School was over, and Betty was there to take him home.

"He's in Sister Rosa Anita's office for fighting."

"I'd better find out what this is all about." Betty went to the principal's office.

"Mike's fast with his fists," Sister Rosa Anita said to Betty with Mike present. "He broke the other boy's nose. Mike will have to learn self control."

"Mamma, he called me a WOP!"

"Mike, you are almost eight years old," said his mother. "You shouldn't have hit him."

"But he's bigger than me. He called me a WOP!"

"You go to your room when we get home. You're going to have to learn not to hit people. Go get in the car!"

"I'll pay the boy's medical bills," Betty said to the mother superior as she was leaving the office. "See that he gets proper medical attention. I want him to be all right. I don't care who started the fight."

"I'm glad you feel that way," said Sister Rosa Anita. "His parents can't afford it."

"How's Mike doing in his school work?"

"He's slow, but he's making progress He's normally not a behavior problem.

"Thanks for helping out," Betty said as she turned to go.

X   X   X

Hernando Cortez went to his son's apartment one evening and knocked on the door.

"Steve," he said when Steve opened the door. "What do you know about Bianca's tuition?

"Nothing, Dad. You told us you were paying it. If you can't, we'll work out something. Come inside."

They went into the living room.

"I went to make the first payment, and they told me it had been paid for the entire year."

"We didn't pay it, Dad."

"They said it was paid by the Bishop's Discretionary Fund. Have you ever heard of them?"

"No, it sounds like a church charity."

"Did anyone say anything to you about this?"

"No, Dad. What about next year's tuition?"

"I don't know, son. I deposited the monthly payment into a savings account. I can do that each month. I'll have it next year with no trouble. I don't like us taking charity."

129

"Supper's almost ready," Deborah said as she came into the living room. "I set another plate. You're staying for supper. I'm not giving you a choice."

"Well, all right." Hernando laughed. "I'll stay."

NINETEEN

April, 1971

Steve and Deborah were sitting at the dining room table going over their finances that evening. The children were playing in the living room.

"We might have enough in savings to make a down-payment on a house," Steve said. "What do you think?"

"Our landlord raises the rent every July," Deborah said. "This would be a good time to move. Bianca will start the first grade this fall. Is your Dad still planning to pay the tuition?"

"He's prepared to do it now. What is the Bishop's Discretionary Fund going to do?"

"I don't know," said Deborah. "I don't know how they found out about us. St. Benedict's is better than the public schools. I hope Bianca can keep going there. I worry about that."

"Why don't you look in the newspaper to see what is being advertised? Then maybe we can contact a real estate agent?"

"I'll get a newspaper tomorrow morning," said Deborah. "I hope we find something we can afford. I'm tired of renting." Deborah looked at the clock. "It's bedtime. I'd better get the children ready for bed."

May, 1971

"Hello." John Clarke was at his office when his private line rang.

"Mr. Clarke, this is Mrs. Smythe at the detective agency. We have some news on Steve and Deborah."

"What is it?"

"There was a credit check placed on them by the Pacific Coast National Bank. We inquired and learned the kids are trying to buy a house in the suburbs of Pacific City. It's contingent on their getting a mortgage. It's a marginal situation."

"Stay on the line. I'm going to add Jim England."

John Clarke added Jim England, President of Atlantic National Bank, a subsidiary of Clarke Industries, to the conference call. Then they called the Pacific Coast National Bank.

"This is Jim England, President of Atlantic National Bank. I would like to speak to Gene Westbrook."

The call was transferred to Gene Westbrook's office.

"Hello, Jim, how are you?"

"Fine, John Clarke is on the line. We'd like to talk about one of your mortgage loan applications."

"Hello, John. Let me get them on the line."

"Mortgage loan department." A loan officer answered the phone.

"This is Gene Westbrook. Ok, Jim, go ahead."

"Take over, John."

"We're calling about the loan application of Steve and Deborah Cortez. What's its status?"

"I'll have to have my supervisor's approval before I can talk about it," said the Clerk.

"You have my approval," Gene Westbrook said. "Your supervisor's boss reports to me. What's its status?"

The mortgage loan officer got the file. He opened it and looked at the papers.

"Marginal at best," he said. "The house barely appraises for what they're buying it for. Their down payment is too low, and their income isn't enough. It's a risky loan. I don't think the loan committee will approve it. If they do, it will be at the highest interest rate we charge for mortgages. We're not sure his income is enough to make the payments. I won't recommend it. It's more than they can afford."

"Is the house in a good neighborhood?" Asked John Clarke.

"It's in a new subdivision. It's nice but definitely middle class."

"The status of that loan application is about to change," John Clarke said. "I'll personally guarantee that loan. Once the loan is made, I'll buy that loan and let you service it. Jim, you work out the details and get back to me. I want you to charge them your lowest interest rate. Will your loan committee do this?"

"Once you put up collateral," said the loan officer.

"You don't need collateral," said Gene Westbrook. "Everyone on the loan committee reports to me."

"There's one condition," said John Clarke.

"What's that?" Asked the loan officer.

"Steve and Deborah Cortez must not find out about my involvement. They must not know who owns the loan."

"We can handle that," said Gene Westbrook. "We can be ready to close within a week."

"Gene," said Jim England. "Get me a figure, and I'll wire you the money to cover this."

"You hear that," Gene Westbrook said to the loan officer. "I want everything worked out and all the numbers on my desk as soon as possible. This is top priority. Tell your supervisor if he has any problems with this, he is to contact me direct. Jim, I'll call you back with the numbers."

"Thanks, Gene," said Jim England.

"Thanks, Jim." Said John Clarke. "Keep me posted."

"Who are they," the loan officer asked Gene Westbrook after John Clarke and Jim England had hung up their phones.

"John Clarke is the CEO and Chairman of the Board of Clarke Industries. They bought out Sanchos Construction recently. They're expanding out here. We want their business."

X   X   X

"Steve, this is Jarvis Jenkins, your realtor." He called Steve at work. "Who do you know at the bank?"

"Nobody."

"Your loan has been approved. They're giving you the lowest rate they offer. You must know somebody."

"Huh?"

"They want to close Friday."

"Is this a joke?" Steve asked. "You told me it would take at least three weeks before we'd know if the loan would even go through. That was a week ago."

"The loan's gone through," the real estate agent said. "That's why I asked who you know at the bank. I made them check again to see if there was some mistake."

"What did they say?" Asked Steve.

"They said we're scheduled to close Friday morning. The paperwork's done. There's no mistake."

Steve called home after talking to Mr. Jenkins.

"Deb, our loan has apparently gone through. The bank wants to close Friday morning."

"What. I wasn't expecting to hear about it this quick."

"I wasn't either," Steve said. "If this is true, with Dad's help we can move in by the end of the month."

Steve put down the phone. He was puzzled. There was the Bishop's Discretionary Fund paying Bianca's tuition at St. Benedict's and now this. It seemed too good to be true.

Steve's thoughts were interrupted when Carlos came into the room.

"Do you have the month-end sales figures yet?"

"I'm almost finished. I'll have them in fifteen minutes."

X   X   X

"Thanks, Dad," Steve said after they had unloaded the last of their boxes. It was almost dark. "We're in before the first of the month, but you shouldn't have taken off from work."

"You saved a month's rent," Hernando Cortez said. "You gave me a place to stay until I could get on my feet. It's the least I could do."

"Deb and I will go back to the apartment tomorrow and finish cleaning up. The new people plan to move in the first of June. It will take a little time to get unpacked and settled, but the hard part is over."

"I'll get home now," Hernando said as he got into his pick-up truck. "I'm glad I could help. I have a house to stucco tomorrow."

"I cancelled our old telephone number," Steve said to Deborah after his father had left. "The new one's unlisted. Dad has it, and they have it at work. Nobody else has it yet. Our mail will be forwarded to a post office box. We'll see how long it takes for your folks to find out where we live."

"Let's get these dishes unpacked so I can cook supper. I don't want to think about my parents."

June, 1971

Chuck Crawford's high school graduation service was over. Still in his cap and gown, he was standing with his family in the school's football field where the service was held.

"Congratulations, Son," Charles Crawford said. Syndi, Jason, and Jeremy were by his side. "You have done well. Too bad you were beaten out for valedictorian."

"I ought to take you back to court," Angel said to Charles. She was standing behind their son. "His grades are too good. He's got a full scholarship, and you don't have to pay anything for his college."

"His scholarship doesn't pay for everything," said Charles. "Anyway, he's eighteen. I'll pay what I want to."

"I don't understand why he has to start at Midwest University this summer!" Angel said. "There are good schools close to home. Ellen went to Atlantic Coast University. He could have gone there, and he could have waited until fall like Ellen did."

"He's not Ellen. I wanted him to go to college on the west coast," Charles said. "If he starts in the summer, he'll have a head start on the others. Anyway, his scholarship doesn't begin until fall. I'm paying for the summer term, including out-of-state tuition."

"You're doing this to take him away from me."

"People aren't your property, Angel. For once, let the boy do what he wants."

"Where did you get the fifty thousand?"

"I won it playing poker."

"Maffi Riggioletti paid you, didn't he? Where did you get that baby? The butcher shop? What girl did they kill to get it?"

"Look, Angel, the divorce is over. The boy's Betty Riggioletti's baby. Cut the crap out."

"Where does Betty Riggioletti live?"

"I don't know. Ask her attorney."

"MUD CRAWFORD! YOU ARE LYING!"

"Stuff it, Angel. The divorce is over."

"I'M GOING TO RUIN YOU IF IT'S THE LAST THING I DO!" She took Chuck by the arm. "We're going home. He's not your real father, anyway."

"That's hogwash! Charles said. "GO EAT A CHOCOLATE-COVERED RAT!"

Angel glared at him as she led Chuck away.

September, 1971

"Bianca," said Deborah, "are you ready for school?" This was Bianca's first day in the first grade. Steve had already gone to work in the old car.

"I guess so, Mom."

"I'll pick you up at noon," Deborah said. She took Bianca's hand and led her out the door. "We get to ride in our new car."

"How was your first day?" Deborah said when she met Bianca at noon in front of the school.

"All right, I guess."

"Did you meet many new friends?"

"No, Mom, they were mostly the same kids from kindergarten. What's the Bishop's Discretionary Fund?"

"It's a church fund of some sort."

"Why are they paying my tuition?"

"I don't know why they selected you," Deborah said. "How did you find out?"

"I heard some of the teachers talking about it."

They reached the car and went home.

X   X   X

"Where's Mike," Betty asked his third grade teacher. "He's usually at the door waiting for me."

136

"He's been in detention since recess. He was in a fight."

"I'd better go to the office and find out what this is all about."

"I hate it, but I had to put him in detention," Sister Rosa Anita said to Betty in private. "Don't be too hard on him. He beat up the school bully. The boy is bigger and two years older than Mike. The bully started the fight and had it coming."

"Unfortunately, Mike is a fighter like his father."

Sister Rosa Anita and Betty went to get Mike.

"Mike, you have been fighting again. You know better than that."

"Yes, Mamma." He looked at the floor.

"Let's go to the car."

"Ok." Mike started for the car, and his mother followed.

X   X   X

"Steve," Deborah said as they were getting ready for bed. "I went to the doctor today. I'm three months' pregnant. I know we didn't plan it this way, but I want us to keep this baby."

"We didn't plan any of our children," said Steve. "This one is no different from Bianca and Juan. I want this baby, too. We have health insurance this time. You can go to a regular doctor. You don't have to go to the clinic."

"I'll still go to the clinic," said Deborah, "but I'll use one of the regular doctors."

"You seem so sad," said Steve.

"I don't want to lose the house," said Deborah. "I want our children to go to St. Benedict's. Bianca would be hurt if she has to drop out and go to the public schools. She likes the nuns. I don't see how we can make it."

"We've had tight times before. I'll talk to Dad He still wants to help. I wish I knew more about the Bishop's Discretionary Fund. I don't understand why they chose us. I know we can't seem to get ahead, but there are many families worse off than we are. We'll make it some day. Let's go to sleep."

TWENTY

January, 1972

Victoria Clarke came home late that afternoon from the country club. Her husband was sitting in the den reading a newspaper. The cook was in the kitchen preparing dinner.

"John, these new minority members act like they own the club," she said. "They don't show any respect for us older members."

"What happened?" John did not look up.

"It's Mrs. Rodriguez. She said we're no better than she is. I told her a thing or two."

"What did you say?" John Clarke did not take his eyes off of his newspaper.

"I told her we're not ordinary Clarks. We are Clarkes with an 'e'. We're related to the Queen, and you are fifth in line to be the Duke of Clarke."

"What did she say?"

"Nothing," Victoria said. "She just glared at me. She should be grateful we let minorities and foreigners join, but she's not. She wants to run the club."

"They may win a few seats on the board, but not many. They have a right to have a voice in the club's affairs."

"Why can't things be like they were? Why can't minorities and foreigners stay in their places? Why do we have to have them in the club?"

"Times are changing." John Clarke turned to the next page.

"It's that Steven. Deborah would write if it weren't for him. We have Mexican grandchildren. They're growing up Catholic. They are being taught by nuns! They're going to school with Mexicans, Asians, and who knows what other kind of trash. It's all Steven's fault. Why does he hate us so?"

Victoria burst into tears.

"You need to calm down, dear.

Victoria started upstairs to her room.

"Dinner's ready," the cook announced.

"It looks like I'm eating alone," John said to the cook.

X   X   X

"The baby's anencephalic," Charles said to Syndi. She and Charles were in the physicians' lounge after a delivery. "It didn't live long. I told the father, but I'll have to wait until the mother wakes up to tell her."

"It's too bad they didn't have an abortion," Syndi said.

"We didn't know," said Charles.

"Betty's baby was anencephalic," said Syndi, "until you gave her Mike."

"This is the first one we've had since then."

"Mike would be eight years old now, going on nine," Syndi said. "I wonder where he is in school?"

"I wish I could contact Betty to see how things are going," Charles said.

"Didn't she move to Pacific City?" Syndi asked.

"Dr. McCormick said he sent a copy of Mike's medical records out there, but I haven't been able to find her."

"Have you heard anything more about Deborah?" Syndi asked.

"No, I haven't," Charles said. "I don't believe she's in Europe like the Clarkes say."

"What happened to her boyfriend?" Syndi asked.

"Hernando said he's out west but didn't say where."

"Maybe Deborah ran off with him," Syndi suggested.

"That's possible," said Charles.

"What if they meet up with Betty Riggioletti and little Mike?" Syndi asked.

"That's not likely," said Charles, "but if they did, they'd have to figure things out before there would be a problem."

"Not if Angel finds them," said Syndi.

"Let's hope that never happens."

"Don't ever under underestimate her, Charles," said Syndi. "She's a wicked woman."

March, 1972

"The baby's on the way," Deborah said to Steve. He had just come home from work.

"How much time do we have?" He asked.

"Contractions started about two hours ago, but they're getting stronger."

"I'll take the children next door to Mrs. Morris. I'm glad she can keep them."

"Their things are by the door." said Deborah. "I'll get my bag and meet you at the car."

They arrived at the hospital without incident, and Steve took Deborah into the emergency room.

Steve entered the waiting room and went to a pay phone. He ordered a dozen roses for Deborah from a local florist and then sat down.

Steve noticed the January, 1972, issue of CLOCKE magazine on the table. The words 'THE ERA OF JOHN CLARKE' were at the top of the front cover. Below was the picture of Deborah's father. Steve picked up the magazine and began reading the cover story.

It was about Clarke Industries, a multinational company with branches in Europe, South America, and Asia. Its stock had doubled in price every two years since it went public in 1964. The company had a policy of rewarding its shareholders each year by paying twenty-five percent of its earnings in the form of dividends. It had recently split four-for-one and was still growing.

Yet, John Clarke was a private person. He rarely granted interviews, and when he did, he would not talk about himself or his family.

Clarke and his wife Victoria lived in a mansion formerly owned by a gangster, Maffi Riggioletti. The five-acre estate was surrounded by a tall brick wall, and there was a guard house at the entrance. Clarke's daughter, his only child, was reported to be in Europe.

"Congratulations, Mr. Cortez." A nurse interrupted his thoughts. "You have a baby girl. There were no complications. What are you going to name her?"

"Juanita Marie Cortez," Steve said as he rolled up the magazine to take with him. "When can I see Deb?"

"In a few minutes. She's in the recovery room now."

"I'm glad for an easy birth," Deborah said to Steve. "You even brought me roses."

"You get some sleep. I'll stop by later this morning."

Steve was uneasy as he drove home. He wanted to finish reading the magazine article. He hoped Deborah wouldn't notice it on a newsstand somewhere.

"Sooner or later Deborah will have to face them," he said to himself. "They know where we are."

X   X   X

"What was my daddy like?" Mike asked his mother. They were looking at the pictures in the family album.

"He was over fifty years old when you were born," Betty said. "This is your father when he was a boy." She pointed to a person in a picture. "This is his father, and this is his grandfather."

"Where did they come from?"

"They came from Sicily. It's part of Italy. Your father was born over here."

"You said daddy was a gangster. Why was he?"

"His father and his grandfather were gangsters before him. They grew up that way. It was their way of life. He didn't want you to grow up to be a gangster."

"Why do you still take 'THE GANGSTER CHRONICLE'?"

"I can keep up with your father's friends that way."

"Why is our last name shorter than his?" He pointed to the name 'Michael Thomas Riggioletti' written in the album.

141

"I had it changed when we moved here. Your father didn't want you to be known by his gangster name. Let's not tell other people about your father. They wouldn't understand. Let's not say we lived back east. Let that be our secret."

"Can I go back some day and see the house we lived in?" He was looking at a picture of the old Riggioletti mansion.

"Don't ever go there, Mike. Someone else owns it now. If the gangsters in the city found out who you were, they would kill you. They would think you were coming back to be a gangster like your father. You must never go back there!"

"I don't understand, Mamma. I'm not a gangster."

"Your father didn't want you to be a gangster like him. Don't ever go back there. They will kill you!"

X   X   X

John Clarke was home early that afternoon. He and his wife were getting ready to attend a country club dinner. The telephone rang, and Victoria answered it.

"John, it's the detective agency."

"I'll get on the other phone."

"You have another granddaughter," said Mrs. Smythe." Her name is Juanita Marie. She was born this morning."

"I think they could use American names," Victoria said.

"I think they named the first girl after her other grandmother," said John. "The boy was named after his other grandfather. This may be another family name."

"Why couldn't they name this one after me?" Victoria asked.

"Are they all right?" John asked. "How did things go?"

"Everything went fine."

"Keep us informed."

"Deborah's first baby would be nine years old if it had lived," Victoria said to John after they had hung up. "Too bad it didn't have a head."

"That's all in the past," John said.

"It's all Steven's fault," Victoria said. "I don't know why he hates us so."

142

"Blaming Steven isn't going to solve anything. Have you taken your medicine today?"

"No."

"I'll get it for you."

"John, do I have to? I don't like the doctor you take me to."

"You have to take your medicine. Let's get it done. We don't want to be late to the dinner. Please try to have a good time."

September, 1972

Steve was watching TV in the living room while Deborah was fixing supper. Bianca, Juan, and Juanita were in the living room with their father.

"I volunteered to help at the school today," Deborah said as she came from the kitchen. "Mrs. Lopez suggested it. She said I needed to get out of the house more."

"What about the children?"

"The school has a daycare for its staff. I can leave Juanita there when I work. There's no charge. Juanita is almost six months old now."

"What will you be doing?"

"I'll be a teacher's aide. I have a university degree. Most of the volunteers don't have any college. Some don't even have high school diplomas."

"It's fine with me," Steve said. "The Bishop's Discretionary Fund paid Bianca's tuition again this year. They picked up Juan's tuition for kindergarten without us asking. It's only fair for us to give something back."

"Supper is almost ready." Deborah went back into the kitchen. "Bianca, would you set the table?"

"Ok, Mom."

X   X   X

Betty Riggs stopped by the school office one afternoon on her way to get Mike.

143

"We're losing Mike's tutor," she said to Sister Rosa Anita. "She's moving to Gulf Coast City to live with her daughter. Do you know anyone who might be interested in tutoring Mike?"

"Why not Deborah Cortez? She's a volunteer. She has a teaching degree from Pacific Coast University. We plan to use her as a substitute teacher."

"How do I contact her?"

"I'll arrange for you to meet her one afternoon this week. She has three children, one is preschool, one started kindergarten this fall, and the oldest is in the second grade. The youngest stays in the daycare while she's here."

X   X   X

"Good morning," Sister Rosa Anita said. Deborah was on her way to the daycare with Juanita. She had already taken Juan to kindergarten. Bianca was going to her second grade class.

"I'll be back in a few minutes," Deborah answered.

"I have an interesting fourth-grader for you today," Sister Rosa Anita said when Deborah returned. "His name is Mike Riggs. He's a slow learner, but he responds well to one-on-one teaching. His mother helps in the office in the afternoons."

"I haven't met her yet," said Deborah.

"She's a member of the Concerned Parents Association. She's looking for a tutor to help Mike with his homework, and I recommended you."

"Let me get to know him first."

"Let's go observe his classroom."

"Good idea."

Deborah and Sister Rosa Anita went down the hall to Mike's room.

X   X   X

Betty Riggs went to St. Benedict's about one o'clock that afternoon to help in the office.

"Catch the phones for a minute, Betty," Sister Rosa Anita said. "The receptionist is out today. I'll be back in a moment." She went out of the office and down the hall.

144

Betty Riggs sat down at the receptionist's desk, and Deborah Cortez came into the office.

"I'm Deborah Cortez. Are you Betty Riggs.?"

"Yes, I am."

"Sister Rosa Anita told me about you."

"I have heard a lot about you. Mike is my son."

"He's an interesting boy."

"Would you be interested in tutoring him on a regular basis after school?"

"I would, but I don't know if we can arrange it. I have a daughter in the second grade, a son in kindergarten, and a daughter I leave in the daycare while I work. I have to take them home after school."

"If you could tutor him for an hour after school each day, I'll stay with your children in the daycare. I'm here anyway. I work in the office in the afternoons now. I'll still pay the full amount for tutoring."

"Can we use the daycare?"

Sister Rosa Anita says we can. We may have to share it with other parents, though."

"Let's see how it works out."

"Can we start tomorrow?"

"I'll ask my husband, but I'm sure he won't mind."

Sister Rosa Anita came back into the office. "Any calls?"

"None so far," Betty answered.

"I'd better get back to my classroom," said Deborah. "We can start tomorrow."

X   X   X

Betty was in the daycare at St. Bernard's after school with Deborah's children while she was tutoring Mike. Betty was changing Juanita's diaper, and Bianca was watching with interest.

"Bianca," Betty said, "you were once a little baby like Juanita, only you didn't have any big sisters to help."

Bianca was puzzled.

"You were your mother's first baby." Betty had noticed Bianca's puzzled facial expression. "You didn't have any older brothers and sisters. You were the first one born in your family."

"I was Mamma's second baby," said Bianca. "The first one died."

"I'm sorry," said Betty Riggs.

"Mamma still cries about it."

"Help me change Juanita's diaper," said Betty. "I'm sorry for your mother. I almost lost Mike. I can understand how she must feel."

When they were finished changing, she put Juanita down on the floor near Juan. He was playing with blocks.

"Let's read a story," Betty said to Bianca.

"Ok, what do we read?"

"Why not a story about a bear family?"

X   X   X

"How's Mike's tutoring working out?" Sister Rosa Anita asked Betty Riggs one afternoon. Betty was doing some bookkeeping in the school office.

"Deborah's good. She's well worth what I am paying her. What does her husband do?"

"I'm not sure. He works downtown."

"They must be a deserving family," said Betty. "The Bishop's Discretionary Fund paid Juan's and Bianca's tuition this year. I've never heard of that fund before."

"I didn't know the fund existed either until they called and sent the first payment," said Sister Rosa Anita. "It was for Bianca's first year. They plan to pay for Juanita when she starts school."

"Do they pay for other children?" Asked Betty.

"Not that I know of."

"The Bishop must know something," Betty said. "It may involve the baby Deborah lost."

"I didn't know she lost a baby," said Sister Rosa Anita.

"Bianca told me about it while I sat with them. She didn't understand the details. I'm sorry for Deborah. Mike is the only child I have. I almost lost him before he was born.

146

A Mexican couple came in with their pre-school-age daughter.

"May I help you?" Asked Sister Rosa Anita.

"We want to get our daughter on the waiting list."

X   X   X

"We don't have a granny," Bianca said to Betty Riggs one afternoon in the daycare room. "Will you be our granny?"

"I don't mind being your granny if it's all right with your mommy. You ask her when you get home. Let's read a book. Is there one about a granny on the shelf?"

"Mommy," Bianca said that night at home. "We don't have a granny. Can Mike's mommy be our granny?"

"It's all right if she doesn't mind. You should ask her first."

"I already did. She said she didn't mind, but I should ask you first."

"I'm glad you like her."

"She said something about me being the oldest, and how nice it was for me to help look after Juan and Juanita. I told her I wasn't the oldest. Our first baby died."

"Let's not talk about our first baby with others, not even granny. They might not understand. You can talk about it with me. You're our first baby now."

"Was our first baby a girl or a boy?"

Deborah hesitated to answer. She didn't want to say she didn't know. "A girl."

"What was her name?"

"She died before we could name her."

"Oh." Bianca could tell her mother didn't want to continue the conversation. "I won't talk about it, not even with granny."

TWENTY ONE

January, 1973

"I substituted for Sister Anna Maria in the first grade today," Deborah told Steve after supper. Their children were in their rooms doing homework. "She was ill. She'll probably be back tomorrow."

"How did it go?"

"Ok."

"It's good experience," said Steve. "I know the pay isn't much."

"I enjoy tutoring Mike," said Deborah. "The children like being with Mrs. Riggs in the daycare after school. She enjoys keeping them. Perhaps you can meet Mike and his mother sometime,"

"What does her husband do?"

"She's a widow. Mike's her only child. I heard her say he was her last chance to have a baby, and she almost lost him before he was born. I'll never forget how we lost our first baby. I can understand how she must feel."

"I would like to meet her," Steve said as he looked at his watch. "I'm going to see what's on TV. Maybe we can find a good movie."

May, 1973

John Clarke came home late from the office. Victoria met him at the door.

"John, it's those foreigners again," she said. "All they do is complain about the other members mistreat them. They act like they own the club."

148

"They have a right to have a voice in the club's affairs."

"A Puerto Rican dentist won the golf tournament. Puerto Ricans are worse than Mexicans. Why did they have to let him win?"

"They didn't let him win. He won fair and square."

"Why didn't one of the other members win it?"

"They could have, but they didn't."

"Why did they have to let a Puerto Rican become a dentist?"

"He has just as much right to become a dentist as anyone else."

"It's all Steven's fault, John." Tears filled Victoria's eyes. "Deborah doesn't write to us. She returns my letters unopened. Our grandchildren are Mexicans. They're growing up Catholic. They're being taught by nuns. They're going to school with Mexicans, Asians, and l sorts of trash. I don't know why Steven hates us so. What can we do?"

"I don't know what to do. I wish you would get control of yourself. Maybe your doctor needs to change your medication."

"John! Don't say that! I am in control of myself! I'm not the problem! It's Steven!" Mrs. Clark hurried up the stairs in tears. "It's all Steven's fault!"

X   X   X

"How's Mike doing?" Betty Riggs asked Sister Rosa Anita. They were in the office working. The school day was almost over. "Should I send him to Summer School?"

"I'd send him to summer camp instead. The change would do him good. The church has a good summer camp program."

"Mike has never been away from home very long. I'll check into it, thanks."

The school bell rang. Betty got up from her desk and put her work away. "I'll see you tomorrow afternoon."

Betty went down the hall to the daycare where Juan and Juanita were waiting for her. The other children were leaving with their parents. Mike came a few minutes later.

"Sister Rosa Anita suggested I send you to camp this summer. Do you want to go?"

"Yea!"

"I'll make arrangements for a week. Do you think you can be away from home that long?"

"I'll miss you, Mamma."

"I'll miss you, too, but it will be good for you to go."

Deborah Cortez came into the daycare with Bianca.

"I'll trade."

Leaving Bianca with Betty, she took Mike's hand, and they went to another room for tutoring.

X   X   X

"Mommy," Bianca said. Her mother was driving them home from school that afternoon. "How come Mike gets to go to summer camp and I don't?"

"You're only seven years old. Maybe when you are older."

"I'll be eight in November."

"Mike is ten. He'll be eleven in November."

"Will you teach Mike after school again next year?"

"You'll have to ask Granny," said Deborah. "It's up to her."

"Can we help her take Mike to camp? She said she didn't want to come back by herself."

"I'll ask her about that," said Deborah.

"I hope you teach Mike next year," said Bianca. "Juan, Juanita and I like having a granny."

"I'm glad you can have her for a granny." Deborah turned a corner.

"If she's our granny, who's Mike?"

"She's a pretend granny. If she were your real granny, Mike would be your uncle."

Deborah turned the car into their driveway and stopped.

"Uncle Mike! Wait 'til I call him that."

Bianca got out of the car and ran to the house.

"Mike, are you ready?" Betty was standing by the front door. "I have your things in the car."

"Yea, I guess." Mike was still in his bedroom.

"I'm taking Mrs. Cortez with us so I won't have to drive back by myself."

"Ok." Mike came through the living room to the front door. "Let's go."

Betty and Mike were soon on their way.

"Who did you say is going with us?" Mike asked.

"Mrs. Cortez and Bianca. I'm not sure about Juan and Juanita."

Deborah Cortez and all three children were waiting on their front porch. Bianca ran to the car as soon as it stopped in the driveway.

"She's more excited than Mike," Betty said.

"She's anxious to find out what summer camp is all about," Deborah answered.

They arrived at the camp about noon. The trip had taken four hours. Mike was slow about getting out, but Bianca was out of the car once it had stopped.

"I want to go to camp next year," Bianca said. "Can I stay now?"

"You didn't bring any clothes," her mother said. "Let's see if someone will show us around the camp."

X   X   X

"Mike will be surprised you and the kids came with me to pick him up," Betty Riggs said. In Betty's car, they were on the road leading to the camp.

"Bianca had to come."

"Granny," Bianca asked, "is Mommy going to teach Mike next year?"

"I certainly hope so," Betty answered.

"Good, we want to keep you as our granny."

"You can keep me as a granny whether your mother teaches Mike or not."

They arrived at the camp and parked in front of the office.

"Hi, mom," Mike came running out of the dining hall. "My stuff is over here. Can I come back next summer?"

"You must have had a good time."

"Yea, I want to stay a whole month. I want to take more stuff, too."

"That's a little ambitious. We'll see about next year."

"Granny, Mamma, can we stay and play?" Bianca didn't want to get back into the car."

"No," said Deborah. "We have to go home."

November, 1973

"Steve, can you keep the kids and little Mike on Thursday nights?" Deborah asked. They were eating supper. "Mike will bring toys to play with."

"I have toys in case he forgets his," Bianca said.

"What's happening on Thursday nights?" Steve asked.

"Betty and I want to run the concession stand at the basketball games this season. The profit goes to the school."

"I'll keep the kids," said Steve. "When does this start?"

"This Thursday."

"Why does Bianca call Betty Riggs granny?"

"Bianca doesn't have a grandmother, so she started calling Betty granny. Betty doesn't mind. She's not sensitive about her age. I don't see any harm in it. I hope you don't mind."

"I don't care."

"Ready for desert?"

X   X   X

"Hi, Betty," Deborah said. Betty and Mike were at the front door. "I'm almost ready. Come in."

"Where do you want Mike to play?" Asked Betty. Mike carried a wooden box of toys.

"Why not over there?" Deborah pointed to a corner in the living room. "He won't be in the way there if Steve wants to watch television."

152

Mike went to the corner and emptied his box on the floor. He sat down and began to play.

"I'm ready," Deborah said. "We're leaving, Steve."

After her mother left with Betty, Bianca came into the living room. She was holding two of her dolls. "Can I play, too?"

"I'm not a sissy," said Mike. "I don't play with dolls."

Bianca set her dolls on the floor and went to her room. She returned with a doll buggy and some doll clothes. She sat down near Mike and began playing with her dolls.

"What's that?" Bianca asked without looking up.

"It's an army tank with guns and things"

"I don't like army things."

"I don't like doll things. You play with your dolls, and I'll play with my tanks and trucks."

Steve came into the living room and turned on the TV. He was holding Juan. Juanita was playing in her playpen.

X   X   X

"How did things go?" Deborah asked when she and Betty returned from the basketball game.

"Mike played by himself all evening," Steve said. "He wasn't much trouble, but he wouldn't play with Bianca. He said he didn't like girl things. Bianca didn't like that. She told him she didn't like his toys. How did things go at the game?"

"We cleared almost five hundred dollars," said Deborah. "We put the money in the bank night deposit box on the way home."

"Did you have fun?" Betty Riggs asked Mike after they were in the car.

"Mamma," Mike asked. "Why do they have three children and we have only one?"

"That's the way things happened."

"Two of them are girls, poor Juan."

"Your attitude towards girls will change."

"It will?"

"It's past your bedtime. When we get home, you put on your pajamas."

153

TWENTY TWO

January, 1974

That evening, Betty sat down at her desk and began going through that day's mail.

"Mamma," Mike said as he came into his mother's office. "I'm eleven. Can I have an allowance? Alfredo gets one."

"You can if you earn it." Betty put down the magazine she was reading.

"How?"

"Yard work, house work, do dishes."

"Doing dishes is for girls. I'm not a sissy, but I'll work in the yard and do other things."

"You'll have to clean up your room and keep your toys picked up, too."

"Aw, Mamma!"

"It's time you learned to make up your bed and pick up after yourself."

"You mean, I have to?"

"You do if you want an allowance."

"Ok, I guess I'll do it, but I don't want to."

"What do you plan to do with your money, Mike?"

"Save it until I can buy stock like you do."

"You will have to save it for a long time to get enough to buy stock. You won't have any to buy candy and stuff."

"That long?"

"And you will need to learn the fundamentals of investing and how to study a company before you buy stock"

"Where do I learn all that stuff?"

"The school library and the public library are good places to start. I can help you."

"Can I invest in a professional baseball team?"

"Maybe."

"Can I buy the West Coast Bears some day?"

"We'll see."

Mike went to his room and got his baseball and bat. "I'm going outside. I'd like to buy stock in the Bears."

X   X   X

John Clarke was getting ready for a country club business meeting when his wife came home from a woman's auxiliary meeting at the club.

"John, if I told one of them we had Mexican grandchildren, she'd laugh in my face.

"Who is this?"

"Mrs. Rodriguez. I set her straight, today."

"What happened?"

"She called me Vicky. I told her I'M NOT VICKY, I'M VICTORIA!"

"What was this all about?"

"She constantly gripes about the way the club is being run. All she does is bitch."

"What did you say?"

"I told her if she didn't like it, she could start her own club."

"I hope you didn't tell her about Deborah."

"I didn't say anything about Deborah. She wouldn't understand. It's all Steven's fault. He won't let Deborah write to us. He makes her return my letters. Our grandchildren are Mexican. They're growing up Catholic. They're going to school with Mexicans, Asians, and all sorts of trash. I don't know why Steven hates us so. I don't know what to do."

"I don't know what to do, either."

155

"I hate him, John!" Mrs. Clarke burst into tears.

"Don't talk like that. He's Deborah's husband. He's the father of our grandchildren."

"I still hate him!" Crying, Victoria started up the stairs to her room.

"I wish you would get control of yourself. If you don't, I'll have to do something about it. Have you taken your medicine today?"

Victoria continued up the stairs without answering. She had a grim look on her face.

May, 1974

Deborah and the children were at the table having supper when Steve arrived home from work.

"Hard day?" Deborah got up from the table to greet him.

"Not too hard." Steve put down his briefcase. "Just long."

"Betty promised Mike if he made good grades in school this year, he could go to the West Coast Bears' opening baseball game next Saturday afternoon. He made the best grades ever. Would you be interested in taking him? Betty said she would buy the tickets."

"May I go, too?" Bianca did not give her father time to answer.

"You will have to ask granny," said Steve. "I'll be back in a minute." He went to the bathroom to wash his hands for supper.

Bianca got up from the table and ran to the telephone. Excited, she dialed Betty Riggs's number.

"Hello," Betty answered.

"Granny, can I go to the baseball game with Daddy and Mike?"

"If it's all right with your father." Betty laughed. "I'll buy you a ticket, too."

"It's ok with him. Thanks, Granny, see you tomorrow." Bianca hung up the phone. "I'm going!"

"I'll see Betty tomorrow," Deborah said to Steve. "I'll work things out with her. Do you want to take both Mike and Bianca?"

"Do I have a choice?" He laughed as he sat down at the table. "Pass the food. I'm hungry."

X   X   X

After the game, Steve and Bianca took Mike to his mother's and then went home.

"How was the game?" Deborah asked.

"The Bears won," said Steve.

"How did things go?"

"We had a good time. Mike spent most of the game telling Bianca about the players. I didn't realize he knew that much about baseball."

"He's smarter than you think," said Deborah. "He's good at math, too."

"The ticket-taker referred to Mike and Bianca as my children. When I told him Mike was only a friend, he said we looked like a family."

"Mike's not even Mexican." Deborah laughed.

"He does resemble Bianca," said Steve.

"Betty said he looks like his father. His father was Italian."

"It's just a coincidence," said Steve, "but Mike is about the age our first baby would have been. Maybe that's why we get along so well with him and his mother."

"Please, Steve, I'm trying to forget." Deborah began to cry. She turned to go to their bedroom but stopped. "I can't let that destroy me. I have got to get over it. I'm sorry, Steve. I have another appointment with Mrs. Lopez tomorrow."

"I'm sorry I mentioned it." He put his arms around her. "We have three beautiful children and each other."

"I love you Steve."

"I love you, Deb."

X   X   X

"John," Victoria said," it's Mrs. Smythe from the detective agency on the phone."

He was out in the yard practicing his golf swing.

"I'm coming."

He put his down his golf club as he came inside, and he picked up the phone.

157

"This is John Clarke."

"The school principal at St. Benedict's wrote the Bishop's Discretionary Fund and asked if we had money to send Bianca to church camp this summer. How do you feel about it?"

"If the cost is reasonable, we'll let her go."

"If we do it for her this year, we'll have to do it for the others."

"That's ok. Let me know how it works out. I'll get Jim England to advance the money."

"John," Victoria asked after they had hung up the phones. "Why do we send them to church camp? It's a Catholic Church camp! Why can't they come here and see us?"

She burst into tears. "It's all Steven's fault! He wouldn't let them come. He won't let Deborah write to us. He makes her return our letters. Our grandchildren are Mexican. They're growing up Catholic. They're going to school with Mexicans, Asians, and all sorts of trash. Why does Steven hate us so?"

"I don't know." John Clarke didn't want to talk about it.

"I HATE HIM!" Crying, Victoria Clarke hurried upstairs to her room.

Mrs. Smythe called later that afternoon, and John Clarke answered the phone.

"Mr. Clarke, Hernando Cortez has already paid for Bianca's summer camp. We'll stay out of it for now."

"Keep an eye on things and keep me informed. Thanks for calling back."

"John. Do you have Deborah's phone number?" Victoria asked. "I want to call Steven and GIVE HIM A PIECE OF MY MIND!"

"No, I don't. It's unlisted. Don't try to call them. You'll only make matters worse."

"Why don't we hire a hit man to kill Steven?"

"We're not going to kill anyone. I don't want to hear any more of this nonsense. I'm going to watch the news on TV."

He went into the den.

"JOHN! JOHN!"

He turned on the TV and did not answer her.

June, 1978

Ned smiled as he entered "THE GANGSTER CHRONICLE" business office. Ned was a hit man of noted reputation. He had gotten his start in Maffi Riggioletti's organization.

"I'm Ned," he said to the receptionist. "I have an appointment to see Rocky."

Rocky was the general manager, and he was standing in the doorway of his office.

"I'm Rocky. I've been expecting you."

"What's up?" Ned asked as he sat down in Rocky's office.

"We're an honest business," Rocky said as he closed the door.

Ned nervously looked around the room. He didn't like being in a closed room.

"We sell advertising and subscriptions." Rocky sat down at his desk. "Nobody has to advertise, nobody has to subscribe. We don't shake down nobody."

"What's the problem?" Ned asked. His eyes narrowed suspiciously.

"A federal marshal, Jimmy Moore."

"What's he doing?"

"He wants to know who our subscribers are, and he wants to put us out of business. He's been leaning on our advertisers."

"How long has he been bothering you?"

"Over a year," said Rocky. "We have a file on him. Here's a copy, including pictures." He handed a folder to Ned. "We've tried to get him to leave us alone, but he won't listen to reason."

Ned looked over the information in the file.

"We want him dead. We want his body found eventually, but not now."

"You want him to disappear. What about his buddies?"

"It'll be a message to them. They'll leave us alone."

"Ok, we'll do it," Ned said. He held up the man's picture. "Bennett and Rigsby will help me."

Early the next evening, Bennett drove Jimmy Moore's car to the airport and parked it in the long-term parking area. Ned and Rigsby were behind him in Rigsby's car. Bennett took off his plastic gloves as he got into the back seat of Rigsby's car, and they left the airport. No fingerprints were left behind.

"Where to?" Asked Rigsby. He was driving.

"The cemetery," Ned said. "Do you know of a better place to hide a body?"

Once inside the gate, following Ned's directions, Rigsby drove to the back of the cemetery and parked near a backhoe.

"That's convenient," said Bennett, referring to the backhoe.

"They dug a grave near the front entrance this morning," said Ned. "They'll plant somebody tomorrow. Meanwhile, we'll plant Jimmy Moore tonight."

Using a key on his key ring, Ned started the backhoe. He drove it to a gravesite a short distance away, and he dug a grave three feet deep.

Rigsby and Bennett took Jimmy Moore's bullet-riddled body out of the trunk of Rigsby's car and dropped it into the hole. Then Ned covered it with dirt.

"A professional job," Rigsby said as he looked at the filled grave. "Couldn't do better myself."

"Remind me to order a tombstone," Ned said when he got into the car.

Ned was in Rocky's office the next afternoon.

"The job's done."

"You don't waste time."

"He stayed late in his office yesterday. We got him in the parking lot. We took him to a convenient place in the country and wasted him. Nobody saw anything."

"Where did you hide the body?"

"In the cemetery. We paid for a tombstone this morning, a cheap one. It's to be delivered to the gravesite next week."

"Why a tombstone?"

"To keep it from being noticed," said Ned. "A grave without a tombstone in a cemetery soon becomes conspicuous. The cops won't be able to trace a thing."

"He's been reported missing," said Rocky. "The cops have already been here. His car was found at the airport."

"What did you tell them?"

"Maybe he took a trip."

"It will take a while for them to find him," Ned said. "Where's our money?"

"Just a minute," Rocky said as he got up from his desk. "I'll have to get it. We don't keep cash in the office."

While Rocky was gone, Ned noticed a list of names and addresses on Rocky's desk. It was the subscribers to THE GANGSTER CHRONICLE. Curious, he went down the list looking at the names.

"Betty Riggs," he said to himself when he reached her name. "She's at a post office box at Ocean Spray. I wonder if she's Betty Riggioletti. I'll check it out when someone makes it worth my while."

He wrote the name and address down in his small notebook.

Hearing Rocky coming back, he quickly sat down.

"Here's your money," Rocky said as he handed Ned a small briefcase.

"Thanks," Ned said. "Glad to do business with you."

October, 1974

Betty was in the daycare at St. Benedict's after school with Bianca, Juan, and Juanita. Deborah came in with Mike after his tutoring session was over.

"I'm having my will revised," Betty said to Deborah. "I'm leaving everything to Mike, of course, but I have a problem."

"What is it?"

"I have no family other than Mike. If something happened to me before he was grown, would you and Steve be his guardians?"

"I'll have to ask Steve, but I would be glad to do it. Would you be willing to look after our children if something happened to us? I don't think we have a will."

"Yes, I would." Betty smiled. "After all, I'm their granny."

"Steve's father would do the best he could, but he's an older man. I don't want to hurt his feelings, but you would be more suitable for younger children. I'll have to talk to Steve."

"I would be willing to help in any way I could."

"I'll talk to Steve about it." Deborah turned to the children. "Are you ready to go home?"

161

"We're having fun, Mamma," Bianca said. "Granny's reading to us."

"Mike and I are going home," said Betty. "I'll see you tomorrow afternoon. We'll read the rest of the book then."

X   X   X

John Clarke was in his office when he received a call on his private line. It was Stan at the bank.

"George Benny's forming a new company," he said. "Would you be interested in getting in on it?"

"I might. What are the details?"

"He's buying a near-bankrupt fast-food chain on the west coast for almost nothing. The new name will be 'Benny's'. He's keeping twenty-five percent of the stock. The rest he's selling for more capital. He's giving his friends a chance to get in on it at a buck a share before he goes public."

"It sounds interesting. Send what you have to my home."

"It's on the way. You should get it in a day or two."

X   X   X

"Stan, this is John Clarke." He was calling from home two days later. "I got your stuff on Benny's today. It's a gamble. I'll go as much as George has. I'll buy twenty-five percent at a buck a share."

"I'm in it for a thousand shares," Stan said. "It could go big."

"According to what you sent me, George plans to close and sell the outlets in the low-income areas and the minority locations. He's going to modernize the rest and build in new locations."

"He wants outlets only where the money is. That's his philosophy. We'll make a bundle."

"John," Victoria said after he had finished his call with Stan. "I thought the call might be from the detective agency. I listened in the den. Where is this new company?"

"On the west coast. Its headquarters will be in Pacific City."

"Why do you want this stock? You are not out there to look after the company."

"To make money."

162

"Is that all? Deborah is out there. Steven works at a fast food place. Does he work for this company?"

"No, but if he loses his job, I might be able to help him get a job at Benny's."

"Why do you want to help him, John? It's all Steven's fault."

"I don't want to talk about it."

"If Steven loses his job, Deborah might come home."

"I'd be surprised if she did."

"I want to see my grandchildren." Victoria turned and went to the front door.

"Where are you going?"

"Out in the yard." She opened the door and went outside.

Trying to act unconcerned, John turned on the TV.

TWENTY THREE

June, 1975

"Congratulations, Chuck," Charles Crawford said. Midwest University's graduation ceremony was over. It had been held at the football field. Chuck was still in his cap and gown. Syndi, Jason, and Jeremy were there, too.

"You have done well," said Syndi.

"I appreciate your flying out here for this," Chuck said as they began walking to the parking lot.

"I'm glad you got admitted to the Medical School at Atlantic Coast University," Charles said, "but it's too close to home. I hope you can get out west for a while."

"You were right when you said things are different here, but I didn't have much time to explore the territory. I'll have even less time in medical school."

"What about your mother?" Charles said. "I'm not surprised she didn't come."

"I don't see her much. She has a new boyfriend. He takes her places."

"I'm surprised she hasn't remarried," said Charles.

"It's more fun to keep them on the string. She wants me to come home every weekend when I'm at medical school. I told her I need my time for studying. I'll see her during vacation, though."

"She still sends me a dozen dead roses every year."

"I heard you were being considered for Surgeon General."

164

"I withdrew my name for that. I don't want to move to Washington and be involved in politics."

They reached the rental car Charles had picked up at the airport.

"We'll pick you up tomorrow morning," Charles said. Chuck was going to fly home with them.

Charles, Syndi, Jason, and Jeremy got into the car. Chuck watched as they drove away to their motel. Then he left to spend his last night at the dormitory.

"When I look at our boys," Syndi said as they drove away, "I often think of little Mike."

"He should be twelve years old," Charles said. "He was born just after we were married."

"I hope he's doing well," Syndi said. "Maybe we can see him some day."

"I'm not going to try to find him as long as Angel is in the picture," Charles said. "Here's the motel."

X   X   X

"John," Victoria said. She had just come home from the country club. "I feel like a has-been. I'm disgusted."

"What's this all about?"

"Mrs. Rodriguez wants to be president of the women's auxiliary. She thinks we ought to speak out for minority rights. Most of the girls don't come to the meetings any more. They don't like her loud mouth."

"The club isn't a political organization."

"She thinks because she's Puerto Rican, she has the right to run things. If we don't like it, we're discriminating. I don't understand why she can't stay in her place. Why do we have to let her run things?"

"We don't," said John. "She has the right to her opinions, but she doesn't have the right to take over. We're still members of the club. She's not the majority.

"She thinks she is!"

"Supper's almost ready," the cook said.

John turned and went into the den. "I'll eat in here. I'm going to watch the news."

165

September, 1975

Deborah Cortez had been home with the children for about an hour when Steve turned into the driveway..

"Mommy," said Bianca, "I need to ask you and daddy to sign this." She handed her mother a permission form from the school. "I want to try out for cheerleader."

"It's all right with me. I'll ask your father. He's coming inside."

Steve came in the back door.

"Steve, do you mind if Bianca tries out for cheerleader?"

"I don't care. I didn't realize they had cheerleaders in the fifth grade. Does she have a chance?"

"They have a hard time finding enough girls because they also have a girls' basketball team."

"Who would she cheer for, the boys' team or the girls' team?"

"Both."

"Who do they play against?"

"Fifth grade teams at other schools. This is the first year St. Benedict's has had elementary school teams. Betty and I can take her to the games. The Concerned Parents' Association will be running the concession stand."

X   X   X

"Granny, I made cheerleader!" Bianca said to Betty the next afternoon after school. She was late getting to the daycare because of the try-outs.

"You'll need a uniform. I asked your mom about it. May I buy it for you as an early birthday present?

"Thanks, Granny." Bianca was excited. "Thanks a lot."

"What's wrong with her?" Mike asked. His tutoring session was over, and he had overheard only the end of the conversation.

"I'm a cheerleader!"

"Why would you want to be that?"

"It's fun!"

"Not to me, I'm a seventh grade boy."

166

"Mike!" Betty said, "don't talk like that. We're going to get her a uniform as soon as her mother gets here. Tell her you are sorry!"

Reluctantly, Mike turned to Bianca. "I'm sorry."

X   X   X

"Congratulations, Betty," Sister Rosa Anita and Betty were alone in the school office.

Betty looked up from her secretarial work.

"You have been elected President of the Concerned Parents' Association."

"I was embarrassed. I didn't run for the office."

"It's an honor. Over the years, you and Deborah have raised a lot of money for the school. Your efforts are much appreciated."

"Thank you, I want a good school for my son."

"Most of our students are Mexicans or Asians. Their parents are uneducated and can barely afford the tuition. I'm glad you feel the way you do,"

X   X   X

"I'm sorry about the front windows," Sister Rosa Anita said. She met Betty on St. Benedict's front steps that morning. Students and their parents stared at the smashed windows as they arrived. "We barely got the broken glass cleaned up before school."

"What happened?" Betty had brought Mike to school that morning and had planned to stay to prepare fund-raising letters for the Concerned Parents' Association.

"Vandalism. It happened sometime last night. I called the police, but they haven't come yet."

"Is the damage covered by insurance?"

"Our insurance doesn't cover vandalism unless it's fire or theft. Nothing was stolen, and the building wasn't burned." She lowered her head.

"What will it cost to fix the damage?"

"Henry Martinez looked at it this morning. He said he could get it fixed for ten thousand dollars. That's a cut rate, but it's money we don't have."

167

Betty stayed in the office while Sister Rosa Anita went with the policemen to inspect the damage.

The telephone rang.

"St. Benedict's," Betty answered.

"Hey, Sister, we heard your windows got smashed last night. You wouldn't want that to happen again, would you?"

"Who is this?" Betty answered.

"We sell insurance, insurance it won't happen again."

"What do you mean?"

"You pay us, and your building is safe. You don't, and the next time it will be worse."

"What do you want?"

"A thousand a week, CASH. That's cheap."

"That's ridiculous! We don't have that kind of money."

"Think it over, Sister."

"I would have to talk to other people here. Who are you?"

"You get the money. We'll call back."

"When?"

"Before noon."

"What is your number? I'll call you as soon as I know something."

"The caller hung up without leaving his number.

"It's Jimmy Garcia's gang," Sister Rosa Anita said after Betty had told her about the call. They were alone in the office.

"The police are afraid of them," Sister Rosa Anita continued. "I don't know what to do. They might hurt our children."

"Let me handle this," Betty said.

"Can you do it?"

"I did this sort of thing when my husband was alive. What do you know about them?"

"Not much," the Nun said. "They have never bothered the Church before. They're into gambling and prostitution"

It was almost noon when someone from Jimmy Garcia's gang called back. Betty answered the phone. She was alone in the office.

"Thought it over, Sister?"

"When can I meet with Jimmy Garcia?" Betty asked firmly.

"It won't change anything. Got the money?"

"I want to talk with Jimmy!"

"You're not serious?"

"I'm serious. I want to meet with Jimmy tonight!"

"I'll ask him."

Betty waited for an answer.

"Jimmy says he'll meet you at eleven at the Star Inn Bar on Fifth Avenue South. Ask for Jimmy and be alone! BRING THE MONEY!"

"I'll find the bar. I'll be there, alone." Betty hung up the phone.

"I'm going outside for a moment," Betty said after Sister Rosa Anita had returned. "I need some fresh air." Betty didn't tell her about the second call.

Once outside, Betty went to the convent behind the school. She knew all of the Sisters would be gone. She opened the door with a key she had borrowed from the school office and entered the building.

She found several clean habits folded on a shelf in the laundry. Betty picked up one and then put it back.

"Too small."

She looked at another and another until she found one her size.

"This will do."

She put it into a paper sack and took it with her out of the convent. Locking the sack inside her car, she went back to the office.

X   X   X

At eleven that evening, a "nun" entered the Star Inn Bar. She carried a violin case. A band was playing soft music, and couples were dining and dancing. Many stared at her wondering why a nun would be there and why she would be carrying a violin case.

"Where's Jimmy Garcia?"

"He's in the conference room at the end of the hall." The waiter was puzzled. "He's been expecting you."

The "nun" went down the hall and entered the room. As her eyes became accustomed to the dim light, she saw five men sitting at a table near the back. They were smoking, drinking, and playing cards. One was obviously intoxicated. There were three pistols on the table.

"Who's Jimmy Garcia?"

"Well, Sister, you made it. I'm Jimmy. I didn't think you would show. Gimme the money!"

"What's the violin for?" Another one asked. "Do you have the money in that case?"

The "nun" put the violin case on the table.

"I'm going to play you a lullaby."

She opened it, pulled out a tommy gun, and started shooting.

"Sorry, this is the only language your kind understands."

The men did not have time to grab their guns.

She put the tommy gun back inside the case and closed it.

"Once you have it, you never lose your touch."

She went out into the hall with her violin case and back to the bar. The music had stopped. The people had heard the shots and wondered what had happened.

The "nun" put the case on the counter beside the cash register and opened it. She picked up the tommy gun and cleared off the bar with bullets.

The musicians, patrons, and waiters dropped to the floor.

One by one, she cleared off the tops of all of the tables. She shot the pictures off of the walls. She turned back to the bar and smashed the bottles of liquor and empty glasses on the shelves behind it. Then, as an afterthought, she shot out the lights.

The "nun" put the tommy gun back into the violin case and closed it. She left a note by the cash register as she turned to go.

"Some day, I'll donate this tommy gun to the new Gangster's Hall of Fame," she said to herself as she left the restaurant, "but not now."

When she was gone, the cashier took the note to a window and opened the curtain. Using the dim glow from a streetlight to see, he read the note aloud.

"You owe St. Benedict's School twenty grand in cash to cover broken windows and other damage. Leave a tip for luck. Pay up or we will be back! Don't let it happen again! Don't talk to the police!"

170

It was signed, "The Sisterhood".

X   X   X

Betty was in the school office the next afternoon with Sister Rosa Anita when a police detective arrived.

"Jimmy Garcia won't be bothering you any more," he said. "He was murdered last night."

"What happened?" Sister Rosa Anita asked.

Betty listened intently but said nothing.

"Jimmy and four of his men were gunned down in the conference room at the Star Inn Bar."

"Who did it?"

"Witnesses said the killer was dressed as a nun. He carried a tommy gun inside a violin case. He went to the conference room where Jimmy and his men were waiting and shot them. Then he came out and shot up the bar."

"I don't believe a nun would do anything like that," said Sister Rosa Anita.

"We don't either," said the policeman. "We're certain it was a man dressed as a nun to throw us off. It may have been done by a rival gang trying to expand their territory."

"Do you have organized crime here?" Betty asked.

"Yes, but not like they do on the east coast. The trigger man was probably an import. The FBI says no one out here is that good with a tommy gun."

"What do you mean?" Betty asked.

"He was good enough to clean off the bar and tabletops without hitting any of the patrons. He even got all of the liquor bottles and empty glasses on the shelves behind the bar. There were over forty people in that room. It's remarkable nobody was hit. The guy had to be good."

"How much money did he get?" Sister Rosa Anita asked.

"He left the cash register alone," said the police officer. "Robbery was not the motive. That's why we think it was gang-related."

"Do you have any suspects?" Asked Betty.

171

"The FBI could only come up with one person who was that good with a tommy gun, but he's been dead for some ten years."

"Who is that?" Asked Sister Rosa Anita.

"An east-coast gangster named Michael Thomas Riggioletti."

Betty remained calm.

"His wife and son moved away soon after his death. We don't think she's in organized crime any more. We still think it's a man."

"What do the patrons say?" Asked Sister Rosa Anita.

"Nobody at the Star Inn will talk. We can't get a good description. All they'll say is that he wore a nun's outfit and carried his tommy gun in a violin case."

"I'm sorry," said Sister Rosa Anita. "I don't want anyone killed, not even Jimmy Garcia."

"It wasn't much of a loss," said the police officer. "We're better off without that hoodlum. We'll let you know if we learn anything else."

"God blessed us in another way," Sister Rosa Anita said to Betty after the police had gone. "This morning, I found twenty-five thousand dollars in cash in a grocery sack in front of my office door. It's locked in my desk." She opened the desk and showed the money to Betty. "This note came with the money."

"Sorry, Sister, our mistake. We left a tip for luck. It won't happen again."

"Did you tell the police?" Betty asked.

"No, I didn't They would take the money. We'll use the anonymous donation to fix the broken windows and to pay for other school needs. God performs his wonders in mysterious ways."

TWENTY FOUR

January, 1976

"Mrs. Rodriguez brought her grandchildren to the club this afternoon," Victoria said. She and her husband were watching the news in their den that evening. "They're nothing but little rats!"

"She doesn't think so," said John.

"I don't see how anybody could be proud of them. They're small, dark, and filthy. They acted uncivilized."

"They're probably typical Puerto Rican children."

"John, I would like to see Deborah and our grandchildren. I hope they don't behave like little rats."

"I would like to see them, too."

"All we have is the pictures secretly taken by the private detective agency."

"At least we know they're all right."

"It's all Steven's fault. I hate him. We're paying their school tuition, and his father's getting the credit."

"As far as they know, the Bishop's Discretionary Fund is paying the tuition."

"The catholic bishop shouldn't get credit for it. Why don't we tell them the truth?"

"I want our grandchildren to get a good education. Deborah wouldn't take the money if she knew where it was coming from."

"Why not!"

"She's stubborn like you."

"It's all Steven's fault. He has no right to do this to us. I want to see Deborah and our grandchildren."

"Maybe we can some day." John got up from his chair. "I'm going to the kitchen to see if supper is ready."

"SOME DAY I'M GOING TO SEE OUR GRANDCHILDREN!" Victoria screamed as she ran upstairs to her room.

March, 1976

"John, it's disgusting!" Victoria had come home from the club.

"What's that?" John was tired after a hard day at the office.

"The way George Benny chases after Angel Crawford. It's utterly despicable!"

"But his wife died two or three years ago." John Clarke sat down in an easy chair and looked through his mail.

"She'd roll over in her grave if she knew how he's misbehaving."

"He's over sixty years old, and Angel Crawford is no spring chicken."

"She's under fifty! They're worse than teenagers. There are plenty of girls his age available. He doesn't have to chase after her!"

"I don't like it either, but they're adults. I can't stop them. I don't run their lives."

"His children are upset, and the girls at the club are talking. It's a scandal!" Victoria went into the kitchen.

John Clarke put down the mail. "I don't want to hear any more about it. I have more important things to think about." He turned on the TV. "It's time for network news."

May, 1976

"Hello," Betty Riggs answered the telephone at home one evening. Mike was in his room playing.

"This is Andrew Walker." It was her attorney on the east coast.

"Andrew, this is a surprise. I haven't spoken to you since I moved out here."

"Angel Crawford has been trying to find you for a long time. She's Dr. Charles Crawford's ex-wife. I haven't given her your address. Nobody here has picked up on your name change."

"What does she want?"

"She's still trying to dig up dirt on her ex-husband."

"What does she want to know?"

"I don't know. It has something to do with the birth of your son. That's been almost fourteen years ago. It doesn't make sense."

"I have a new life now. My son is all I have. Dr. Crawford saved him for me. Little Mike is doing well, and he is making passing grades in school. I'm not interested in helping her make trouble for Dr. Crawford. Please don't tell her where I am."

"I won't, but she's persistent. She may find you. She thinks you are out west somewhere. The word is she and George Benny are going to be married in Las Vegas next month. They might show up out there. Be careful."

"Thanks for the warning. I won't help her."

June, 1976

"The whole club is talking," Victoria said. She was outside on the deck at the Clarke home. It was Saturday afternoon, and she had just come home from a luncheon at the country club.

"What's this?" John asked impatiently. He was practicing putting on his practice green near the deck.

"George Benny and Angel Crawford got married in Las Vegas yesterday."

"I knew they had plans." He hit the ball with his putter, and it barely missed the hole. "They're going out to the west coast to see first hand how our fast food chain is doing." He walked up to the flag.

"He should have married a girl his own age."

"They're adults." John tapped the ball into the hole. "I can't do anything about it." He picked up the ball.

"She has to be after his money."

"George has always had an interest in younger women. I quit going to conventions with him years ago because of that."

"What do you mean?"

"Each night he always had a pick-up with him in his room."

"That's shameful. Did his wife know?"

"She couldn't help but know."

"She should have divorced him and taken every dime he had."

"The mail's here." He went inside. "It's on the hall table. There wasn't much for me."

"I'll bet it's all junk." Victoria followed him inside.

"I'm going to watch the news."

X   X   X

"We've made good progress at Benny's," George Benny said over the phone. He had called John Clarke from Pacific City. "It's better than I thought it would be."

"Have you been to many of our outlets?" John asked.

"Angel and I have visited all of them except Ocean Spray. We'll go there tomorrow. Our places have been renovated and look new."

"How does the bottom line look?"

"We've turned the business around," said George. "We're making a profit at all of our locations. Our earnings are paying down debt and will fund most of our future expansion."

"I haven't kept up with the stock prices," said John.

"Benny's opened a three dollars and twenty-five cents a share this morning. It has more than tripled in value since you bought it," George said. "It will double again in the next two or three years."

"What have you done out there?"

"We closed and sold all of the outlets in the non-white areas. We've renovated the others. They look new. We're planning to open a few new ones next year."

"Who's our competition?" John Clarke asked.

"Mom-and Pop outfits mostly."

"What about Fast Fred's I hear they're going big."

"That company's mostly in non-white areas," George said. "It was started by Fred Gonzales. He's Mexican. We sold a few of the outlets we closed to them."

"How are they doing?" John asked.

"They operate on a shoestring. There's no money behind them."

"Are they much competition?" John asked. "You seem to know a lot about them."

"They don't compete with us except in Ocean Spray and Pacific City," George said. "We will go head-to-head with them in a few years but only when we expand back into non-white areas."

"Will we have non-white employees then?"

" Not in management," George answered.

"How can we expand into non-white areas against Fast Fred's without having non-white employees in management?" John asked.

"We're going to buy them out when we're stronger," said George. "We can hurt them whenever we want to. A couple of bad quarters will get them to sell. We can buy up their stock for a song and then hit it big. We can work that out later."

"How are you going to do it?" John asked. "We won't have enough cash."

"We'll probably issue more stock," said George Benny.

"Are we going to offer them a stock swap?"

"We'll buy the stock ourselves and use the money to buy them out. We can keep our management that way. We'll have control."

"How do you keep up with the day-to-day operations?" John Clarke asked.

"George, Jr., is running Benny's for me. He's done a great job. He's also keeping an eye on Fast Fred's. When we buy them out, we'll keep the non-white employees in the outlets, but not those in management."

"How has the new Mrs. Benny enjoyed the trip?"

"Fine, so far," George said. "She's checked the phone books everywhere we stopped. She's looking for Betty Riggioletti, the gangster's wife. You bought the house from her after her husband was murdered."

"Has she found her?" John Clarke asked.

"Not yet. She's certain Betty Riggioletti is out here somewhere. Do you know where she is?"

"No," answered John Clarke. "Why is Angel trying to find her?"

"She wants to interview her for an article. It must be important. It's almost an obsession."

"John," Victoria Clarke said after George Benny had hung up the phone. "I listened in on the call. I hope Benny's buys Fast Fred's because Steven will be out of a job. Then maybe Deborah will come home. She can bring her children. We'll change their last name to Clarke and give them American first names. They'll look enough like Deborah that nobody will know they're half Mexican."

"Steven will have a job," John answered. "I'll see to that."

"But John!" Victoria burst into tears. "It's all Steven's fault! Why does he hate us so? Why can't we see Deborah and the grandchildren?" She stomped out of the room.

"Why? John, why?" She burst into tears.

"Times have changed."

"No, they haven't! She shouted from the stairs. "It's all Steven's fault! I HATE HIM!" She fled to her room.

X   X   X

"This is our last Benny's," George Benny said as he and Angel drove into the parking lot of the Ocean Spray Benny's.

"It looks like the rest of them," said Angel. She had become bored with the business aspect of the trip. "What was its bottom line?"

"It's in the last report," said George. "I don't remember the specifics."

They went inside, and George introduced himself and his wife to Mr. Morrison, the manager.

"Do you have a local phone book?" Angel asked. "I'm trying to find a friend." She showed no interest in the facility.

"Yes, we do." Mr. Morrison handed her a phone book.

Angel looked for the Riggioletti name. She didn't find it, but an interesting listing caught her eye.

"Riggs, Betty".

Angel hesitated for a moment and then started to write down the number and address.

"No, it couldn't be." She closed the phone book and handed it back to the manager. "No luck here."

August, 1976

Charles Crawford was in his office that evening with Syndi when his private line rang.

"Hello."

"MUD CRAWFORD! WHERE DID YOU GET THAT BABY?"

"Angel!" He wasn't expecting this call. He turned on the speaker so Syndi could listen, but he continued to speak through the receiver. "Congratulations, I heard you got married."

"Don't get your hopes up! Your name is still MUD CRAWFORD." Angel laughed wickedly.

"What about your new husband?" Charles said.

"Where's Betty Riggioletti and her baby?" Angel demanded.

"I don't know," Charles answered. "The boy isn't a baby any more."

"Who does he look like?" Asked Angel. "I bet he doesn't look like Maffi!"

"Betty thought he did."

"Where is she?" Angel demanded.

"She moved to Sicily. She's staying with Maffi's people."

"That's a laugh!" Angel said.

"Go eat a chocolate rat!" Charles said.

"I'll get you yet, MUD CRAWFORD." Angel slammed down the phone.

"I guess it was wishful thinking," said Syndi. "I hoped her getting married meant she was going to leave us alone."

"No such luck."

179

TWENTY FIVE

March, 1977

"What's wrong with Bianca?" Steve asked. "I called her to supper, but she didn't come."

"She's in her room feeling sorry for herself," Deborah said.

"What happened?"

"An eighth-grade boy looked at her today. Then she found out he had an eighth-grade girl friend. It broke her heart."

"I didn't realize she was that interested in boys yet. She's only in the sixth grade. Didn't she have a crush on Mike?"

"He doesn't care. He's not interested in girls yet."

X   X   X

"Mike," his mother said. "I found this in your room."

She was holding up a copy of 'NUDE' magazine. On the cover was a picture of an unclothed young woman with large breasts sitting in a seductive pose. The caption read: "LOOK AT THE TITS ON HER!"

"All women have breasts, Mike, unless they've been surgically removed. The quality of a woman isn't determined by the size of her breasts. It's what's above the neck, inside the head, that counts. She's got to be the right kind of person there. That's what matters."

"It's Bobby's magazine. He loaned it to me."

"Give it back to Bobby." Betty handed it back to Mike. "There are certain things it is best to leave alone. They get you into trouble. This magazine is one of them. Leave this kind of literature alone."

"Yes, Mama." Mike took the magazine from his mother. "I'll give it back to Bobby."

December, 1977

Parked in front of St. Benedict's school, Victoria Clarke sat patiently in the driver's seat of her rented car. Nervously, she glanced at a picture of her grandchildren as she waited for classes to be dismissed.

Looking up, she saw children coming out of the front door, and she got out of the car. Holding the picture, she went up the steps and inside the school. She stood by the door and watched the children in the hallway as they went by.

She saw Bianca and Juan coming down the hall on their way to the day care, and she approached them.

"Bianca, Juan, I'm your grandmother, Deborah's mother."

"Help! Help! Help! Run for it!" Bianca grabbed her brother's hand, and they Juan fled down the hallway towards the day care.

Victoria started after them. "I won't hurt you! I'm your grandmother!"

"Help! Help! Help!" The children ran faster.

A nun stopped them "What's wrong?"

"Save us! She's a wicked witch!" Bianca pointed at Victoria. "She's after us! She'll murder us!"

"Calm down," said the nun. She could see the children were badly scared. "You're safe. We won't let anyone hurt you."

Horrified, Victoria watched as the nun tried to calm the two children.

"Who are you?" The nun asked. "I don't know you."

"I'm their grandmother," Victoria answered. "Their mother is my daughter. I don't understand this. I've never hurt anyone. I won't hurt them. I've never been allowed to see them. They're my only grandchildren. I want to know them and have them know me. I'm not a wicked witch."

The two children broke away from the nun and ran screaming to the day care.

"Granny, save us! She'll murder us!"

"You'd better leave," said the nun. "I don't know what's going on here, but the children are afraid of you. Perhaps I should call the police."

Victoria broke into tears as she turned away. She hurried to the front door as the nun went to see about the children. She went down the steps to her car. Still in tears, she got in the car, started the engine, and drove away.

X   X   X

"What's this murder business all about?" Betty asked Deborah when she came to see about her children.

"A strange woman tried to pick them up in the hall," Deborah said. "She said she knew them. Sister Rosa Anita has called the police."

"I have tried my best to calm them down," said Betty, "but they're still scared. Perhaps you had better take them home now. It won't hurt Mike to miss a day of tutoring."

"Thanks, Betty, but let me call Steve first. He's at work."

Deborah went into the office while Betty stayed in the day care with the children.

"Steve," Deborah said over the telephone. She was alone in the office. "Someone tried to pick up Bianca and Juan here at school this afternoon. It sounds like mother. It scared the life out of them. Sister has called the police. If it's mother, she may go to the house."

"I'll get home as soon as I can," said Steve, "but I have to work late. Can you go somewhere else until I can get home?"

"I don't know. I'll call your father. Maybe I can go to his house."

"Be careful. I'll see you when I can get home."

Deborah returned to the day care.

"Thanks, Betty. I'd take the children home now, but I'm scared. Steve will have to work late tonight. I may try to call his father."

"Why don't you bring them to my house?" asked Betty. "We're going home in a few minutes. You'll be safe there. You can even spend the night if it would help."

"It would help, thanks. I'll call Steve and tell him where we're going. We'll stay there tonight."

X   X   X

The housekeeper met John Clarke at the door. He could tell she was upset. It was after dark, and he had arrived home from the airport.

"Mr. Clarke, Mrs. Clarke said she would be back some time tonight."

"Where did she go?"

"She said she was going to get Deborah and the grandchildren and bring them home. I tried to stop her. I had no way to contact you."

"She knew you wouldn't be able to reach me." John Clarke was angry. "I was flying home from London. When did she leave?"

"She went to the airport early this morning. I don't know when her flight left."

"I'd better contact the detective agency. There's no telling what she's done."

John Clarke went to the phone and called the detective agency.

"It's too late," Mrs. Smythe told him. "She caused a disturbance at the school. She tried to pick up Bianca and Juan. Our west coast people picked up on it, and ran interference. Deborah didn't tell the police that it was her mother. We're sure Deborah knew who it was. The police think the person is still out there."

"Where is she now?"

"We got her on a flight home. A lady from the agency is with her to make sure she stays on the plane. It's flight 256, and it lands here in an hour."

X   X   X

John was waiting at the airport when the plane landed. He met Victoria at the gate. She was crying. The lady detective went to check on her return flight.

"John, it was horrible! The children ran away from me. They called me a wicked witch. They said I would murder them. A nun called the police. I had to leave. It was awful. I wouldn't hurt them. They're my grandchildren."

"You shouldn't have gone without telling me first. You almost landed in jail."

"It's all Steven's fault. We have Mexican grandchildren. He's poisoned them against us. They're growing up Catholic. They're going to school with Mexicans, Asians, and who knows what other trash. I hate him, John. What can we do?"

183

"I don't know." They reached the car, and he opened the door for her.

"I'm so upset! Do we have to have the Christmas party this year?"

"It's too late to call it off. I'm still chairman of the hospital board."

"I can't face people this year, Dr. Crawford's chink wife, Mrs. Rodriguez, and those foreigners. I feel like I'm going to have a breakdown."

John went around to the driver's side of the car and got in behind the wheel.

"I'll call your doctor."

"No, John, I don't want him to know about this. Take me home."

"I'll call him anyway. I'm taking you to the hospital."

"Don't, John, please don't! It's been an awful day."

"I'm going to talk to the doctor about hiring a live-in nurse."

"Don't, John. They'll find out at the club."

"I don't care. I've got to do something."

Victoria was in tears. "Please don't do this to me, John. Please don't."

"I've made up my mind. We're going to the hospital."

X   X   X

"Ned, I'm surprised to see you after all these years," Betty said when she answered her doorbell. She had known Ned as a minor mob figure before Maffi had been killed. She sensed he was up to no good. "What brings you here?"

"You're a hard lady to find."

"How did you find me?"

"I have my ways."

"Who sent you?"

"Angel Crawford Benny hired me to find you. She figured you were out here somewhere."

"Does she know I have shortened my name?"

"Not yet."

"Does she know where I live?"

"Not yet."

"Who have you told?"

"Nobody yet."

"Why did you come to me?"

"Some of the mob want you and your son dead."

"Who?"

"Rigsby and Bennett."

"What about Tonio?"

"They're after Tonio, but he still has the upper hand."

"What do you want?"

"Fifty grand will keep my mouth shut."

"What happens if I don't have it?"

"I tell where you are."

"My son is due home any minute. I don't want him to hear us talk. Can we go out back?"

"I want the money now."

"I'll have to have time to get it. I don't keep that kind of money at the house."

"How soon can you have it?"

"Let me get different shoes and a coat. We can talk better out back."

Betty Riggs went into her bedroom. The door was open, and Ned could watch her every move. She changed out of her slippers into shoes and put on a heavy jacket with an inside pocket. She slipped a pistol out of her purse without Ned seeing her and hid it in the inside pocket. Then she and Ned went out the back door and through the gate to the beech.

"You have a nice view," he said.

"Thanks, let's go down to the water's edge."

"Is it always this noisy?"

"It's the waves. The ocean is never still. No one can overhear us now."

"How soon can you have the money?"

Nervous, Ned sensed danger. He reached for his gun.

Betty pulled out her pistol and fired a single shot. Ned fell to the ground dead.

"Sorry, Ned. You know how I feel about blackmail. High tide will carry you out to sea."

Leaving the body where it lay, she picked up his gun and went back into the house to make a long-distance call before Mike came home.

"Tonio, this is Betty Riggioletti."

"I haven't heard from you for ages. How are you?"

"I'm fine. I'm giving you a hot tip on the horses. Waste Rigsby and Bennett. They're after you."

"Who told you?"

"Ned, but that was before he decided to take a swim in the Pacific Ocean. He'll not be a problem any more. Take care of Rigsby and Bennett before they get you."

"Thanks for the tip."

"I can't talk now. I've got to go." Betty hung up the phone. She saw Mike coming up the sidewalk, and she went to open the door for him."

TWENTY SIX

January, 1978

Angel looked for Rigsby's car as she drove down a seldom-traveled side street in the older part of the city. It was almost dark. She saw it parked on the left side of the street as she approached Bayside Boulevard.

The light was red. As she waited for the light to change, Bennett and Rigsby got out of Rigsby's car. They opened the back doors of her four-door sedan and got inside. Unknown to Angel and her passengers, a third gangster was watching from the bushes.

"I hear Ned's dead." The light changed and Angel turned right at the boulevard.. "When did it happen?"

"A couple of weeks ago," said Rigsby.

The man came out of the bushes as Angel's car disappeared out of sight. He carried a small cardboard box with two electrical wires extending from it. He opened the hood of Rigsby's car. Using a flashlight, he attached one wire to the starter and the other to the battery ground. Then he set the box beside the breather. Looking around cautiously, he closed the hood and disappeared into the night.

"Who killed Ned?" Angel asked as she drove down the boulevard.

"We don't know," said Bennett. "Somebody shot him and dumped his body into the ocean. It washed ashore on the beach at Pacific City."

"What was he doing on the west coast?" Angel turned right on a side street.

"He may have had somebody to waste out there," said Rigsby. "We figure they wasted him instead. It's a hazard of the trade."

"Have you found out anything on Betty Riggioletti?" Angel asked as she made another right turn. "Ned was looking for her. Maybe she wasted him."

"Maybe," said Bennett. "Mouse has been inside her attorney's office a dozen times. Her file isn't kept there."

"Mouse is good at it," said Rigsby. "He can go into a place and get out without anyone ever knowing he's been there."

"Where are the records kept?" Angel asked.

"We don't know," said Bennett.

"I can't find out anything about Deborah Clarke either." Angel made another right turn. "Nobody at the club knows where she is. They're all afraid of her father. Did you dig up any dirt on my step-children?"

"It's all here." Rigsby handed her a packet of papers. "There's a ton of dirt on George, Jr. The other two are clean."

"Why don't you let us waste that ex-husband of yours?" Asked Bennett. "We'll be reasonable. He must be a pain."

"I will," Angel said, "but I want his name to be MUD first." Angel pulled up at the stoplight where she had picked up the two men. "I want to see 'MUD CRAWFORD' on his tombstone."

"On one job we borrowed a backhoe at the cemetery," said Bennett. "We dug a grave some two or three feet deep. We dumped the guy into the grave and covered him up."

"Yeah," said Rigsby. "We even had a tombstone delivered. It had his name and date of death on it."

"The guy was missing for six months before somebody noticed the tombstone," said Bennett. "The grass was green on his grave when they dug up his bones."

"That's too good for Mud Crawford." Angel laughed. "I want something more humiliating. He must die in disgrace."

"We'll be back in touch," Rigsby said as they got out of the car.

"Give my regards to Mouse," Angel said as she drove away.

Rigsby and Bennett went to their car. Rigsby got in behind the steering wheel, and Bennett on the passenger's side.

Rigsby turned the ignition key to start the vehicle. The car exploded and burst into flames. The two hoodlums were killed instantly.

The police and fire department were called, and local television crews were soon on the scene.

Tonio was in his back-room office at the bar and grill. His phone rang, and he answered it. "Hello."

"Rigsby and Bennett are wasted," said the hit man. "They went BOOM! Like we planned. It will be on the ten o'clock news."

"Thanks, pal. You made them a good example for the others. Job well done. Your money is waiting."

X X X

Victoria Clarke got out of her Rolls Royce in the parking lot of Mallory's Pawnshop. Determined, she went inside and up to the gun counter. She set her purse on the counter and pointed to a pistol inside the glass showcase. "That's the one I want, the thirty-eight special."

The clerk got the gun out of the case.

"Show me how to work the safety."

"This one doesn't have a safety," said the clerk.

"Let me have a box of bullets, too, those more powerful ones. Help me load it, please."

Victoria watched the clerk handle the gun with great interest. He put five bullets in the chambers.

Yes, ma'am," the clerk said as she paid for the gun and bullets with cash. "I left the first chamber empty. It's a safety precaution in case the trigger gets pulled accidentally. You have to pull the trigger twice for it to fire the first time."

"I'm going to kill a varmint."

Victoria put the gun and bullets in her purse and left the store.

"Dime to a dollar says she shoots her husband," the clerk said to his assistant. "He's probably seeing a younger woman."

"She plans to shoot somebody. Should we call the police?"

"Nah, we don't know nothing. It's none of our business what she bought that gun for."

In the parking lot, Victoria took the gun out of her purse and looked at it.

"This will fix Steven! Then Deborah will come home."

189

Mrs. Clarke drove home and parked the Rolls Royce in the driveway. She paused momentarily at the back door before entering to see if any of the servants were near. Seeing no one, she went inside.

"Where can I hide this so that John won't find it?" She mumbled to herself. She had both hands on her purse.

"There's a secret hideaway in this closet."

She opened the hall closet door and looked for the hidden compartment. Finding it, she put the gun and bullets inside.

"John will never think to look there."

She closed the compartment and went out into the hall.

"It won't be murder. It's all Steven's fault. He's the cause of the trouble. We have Mexican grandchildren. He's poisoned them against us. They're growing up Catholic. They're going to school with Mexicans, Asians, and who knows what other trash. I HATE HIM!"

She paused momentarily before going into the kitchen.

"After I kill him, Deborah will come home. I know she will. We'll give the children American first names. We'll change their last name to Clarke. They look like Deborah. No one will know they're half Mexican. Deborah will come home. I know she will."

Mrs. Clarke stopped in the kitchen. She heard someone coming.

"There you are." It was her nurse. "I heard you talking. What were you saying?"

"None of your business!"

"You forgot to take your medicine this morning," the nurse said. "I have it here for you."

June, 1978

Charles Crawford was in his office late that afternoon completing paperwork when his private line rang.

"Hello," he answered.

"You never told me where the fifty thousand came from."

Syndi entered the office while her husband was on the phone. He turned on the speaker so she could hear the conversation. He continued to speak through the receiver.

"The divorce is over, Angel."

"Where did Betty Riggioletti move to?"

"I don't know. Betty Riggioletti was not involved in our divorce."

"Where did you get that baby?" Angel continued her interrogation.

"The divorce is over."

"I want to see who that baby looks like."

"He's not a baby any more."

"Where's Deborah Clarke?"

"I don't know. Deborah Clarke was not involved in our divorce."

"Maffi Riggioletti paid you that fifty thousand, didn't he?" Angel's voice was growing tense.

"Maffi Riggioletti was not involved in our divorce."

"How much did you pay the Clarkes for that baby?" Angel demanded.

"The divorce is over. I have work to do."

"You switched those babies, didn't you? You're a marked man, MUD CRAWFORD!"

"Go eat a chocolate rat!" He hung up the phone and shut off the speaker.

"A chocolate rat?" Asked Syndi.

"She likes chocolates."

"What's she trying to do?"

"She's trying to discredit me. She knows I'm going to be appointed to the National Medical Association's board of directors."

"She's close to figuring things out," Syndi said. "What happens if she does?"

"She can't prove anything." Charles said.

"Deborah was mad about losing her baby."

"I'm sorry for Deborah," Charles said, "but if we didn't do what we did, her father would have taken her to the butcher shop. They would have killed her and the baby. We didn't kill anyone. I've got to get this paperwork done. We can talk later."

"Ok," said Syndi. "I'm just worried about what Angel might do."

"I'm not! We'll deal with that if and when the time comes. I'm sorry I didn't hire Maffi Riggioletti's hit man back then. I'm tired of Angel's crap."

"So am I."

September, 1978

Betty Riggs was taking Mike home from school.

"Mom, the coach asked me to consider going out for the school's boxing team. What do you think?"

"I'll let you decide. I don't think it's a good idea. You're in too many fights as it is. You'll have to keep good grades in school to be on the team."

"I'm trying to do that, anyway, Mamma. I'd rather get an after-school job instead."

"That's a better idea. School's important, but you'll get a different kind of education on the job. Do you have any places in mind?"

"There's a Fast Fred's here in Ocean Spray. I might try there."

"Do they hire students under sixteen?"

"I'll be sixteen in November. I'm in the tenth grade. Benito works there. He's not sixteen yet."

"There's a Benny's Fast Foods here, too. You might try both places."

"That's a good idea. Can I go down to Fast Fred's tomorrow and apply? They are my first choice. Then I'll try Benny's."

"You'll need a copy of your school transcript to take with you. It will be a good experience to go to both places."

Betty turned on the street where they lived and pulled into their driveway.

"I'll tell Deborah Cortez," she said. "Her husband works for Fast Fred's. They'll be interested in knowing."

X   X   X

"How did your job interviews go?" Deborah asked Mike. It was after school, and they were beginning a tutoring session. "Your mother told me about it."

"I got the job at Fast Fred's."

"What about Benny's?"

192

"The manager was a Mr. Morrison. He wouldn't hire me. He didn't say why. He asked if I were Mexican. He was rude about it. I told him my father was Italian. He talked to me like I was dirt. I don't like him. I'm glad I'm not working for Benny's."

"I hope you like working for Fast Fred's."

"Fast Fred's is more friendly. They don't care that my father was Italian. I'm glad I got the job there."

"When do you start?"

"Saturday morning, but I have to go through training for a couple of weeks."

"I'll tell Steve. He'll be proud of you. Let's look at your school assignments."

X   X   X

Bianca came out of her room for supper. She was in the eighth grade.

"My homework's done, Mamma," she said. "Mike's got a job at Fast Fred's. He'll be working with Clarene."

"Who's Clarene?" Steve asked.

"She's a girl in Mike's class," said Deborah. "It's all right, Bianca. She's just a friend."

"No, she isn't! When can I get a job at Fast Fred's?"

"You have to be sixteen," said Steve.

"Mike isn't."

"He's almost sixteen," said Deborah.

"I'm almost thirteen."

"You'll have to wait three years," said Steve.

"When does he work?" Asked Deborah.

"From seven to nine weekday evenings," said Bianca, "and one to nine on Saturday afternoons."

"If I can arrange it with granny," said Deborah, "I'll take you, Juan, and Juanita to Ocean Spray next Saturday. We'll visit granny, and we'll stop by Fast Fred's and see Mike."

"Mike will be working," said Steve. "He can't spend much time visiting."

"We won't visit," said Deborah. "I'll treat the kids to ice cream cones, and we'll say 'hi'. We won't stay long. Is everyone ready for desert?"

X   X   X

Deborah Cortez and her three children entered Fast Fred's at Ocean Spray the next Saturday afternoon. Clarene was at the counter.

"Can I help you?"

"Three vanilla ice cream cones, please," Deborah said.

"Coming up," Clarene filled the cones at the machine and put a twirl at the top of each one."

As Clarene was finishing the last cone, Mike came out from the kitchen.

"Let me have their ticket," he said to Clarene. "They're friends of mine. Mom told me they were coming. The treat's on me."

"Thanks, Mike," Deborah said.

"I have to go back to the kitchen," said Mike. "I'm working there today. Have a good time. I'm glad you came by."

"Clarene seems like a nice girl," Deborah said to Bianca when they were outside.

"No, she isn't!"

TWENTY SEVEN

June, 1979

"Congratulations, Chuck," Charles Crawford said. Syndi, Jason, and Jeremy were at his side. They were attending Chuck's graduation ceremony at the Atlantic Coast University Medical School. He had graduated with honors. They were leaving the auditorium and were on their way home.

"I'm proud of you, son. I'm sorry your mother didn't come. I know she's proud of you, too."

"She and George Benny are on a Caribbean Cruise."

"What are your plans now?" His father asked.

"I have accepted an internship at Deep South University Hospital. It's a two-year deal. I start the first of July."

"They have a good medical school. I'm glad it's in a different part of the country."

"I had to, Dad. Mom called me every weekend wanting me to come home. When I went home, she'd be gone the whole time."

"Perhaps you can take your residency on the west coast. I want you to go out west and see what that part of the world is like."

"I know, Dad. We'll see,"

September, 1979

"Mike, you have worked at Fast Fred's a full year," Lee Gonzales said. He was the store manager. "You have done well. After you have been here a year, you can buy stock in Fast Fred's under the employee stock option program. If you do, the company matches your contribution. We hope you will consider it."

"What do the others do?" Asked Mike. He had not heard of this plan before.

"Most students don't participate because they have to work here at least five years before the company match is vested. They don't make that much money anyway."

"What's the deal?"

"The company will match up to five percent of what you make. You can contribute up to five percent more, but the company won't match the second five percent."

"What happens if I choose to participate and then decide not to stay for five years?"

"You get your money back or the stock it purchased plus any dividends on that stock. You don't lose anything. If you stay five years, you get all of the stock, including the match, and the dividends will have bought more stock.

"Let's say I go to college at Pacific Coast University. Could I work at one of our units in Pacific City?"

"You can, and your time will count towards your five years."

"Do I have to work full time?"

"The company encourages its employees to continue their education. You don't have to be full time if you are at least a three-quarter time student."

"I'll sign up."

"Take these papers home. Your mother will have to give her permission. You're not of legal age. If she has questions, please have her call me."

"Thanks, I'll take them home tonight."

X   X   X

"Mike," Betty Riggs said. "I looked over these papers. What do you want to do?"

"I think it's a good idea, Mamma. I could have three years in by the time I finish high school. I could transfer to a Fast Fred's in Pacific City if I

196

go there to college. I'll get stock at a reduced price because the company matches what I put in up to five percent of my pay."

"I'll sign it for you. It will be a good learning experience. You'll take a greater interest in your job, and you'll also learn more about investing."

"Thanks, Mom."

November, 1979

Early that Saturday evening in Pacific City, George Benny, Jr., drove into the parking lot of the Classy Brass Motel with his father.

"I've been expecting you." Angel smiled as she watched from a parked car. Unaware of her presence, her husband and his son went to the motel office.

"When it comes to cheating, Charles," Angel said to herself, "George doesn't hold a candle to you."

She had seen this all before. This time she was recording what she saw with a movie camera equipped with a long-distance night lens. She was grim as she watched the two men come out of the office and go to their suite.

"You stay first class."

Two Mexican ladies of the evening drove into the motel parking lot about thirty minutes later. They got out of their car and went to George Benny's suite. They knocked softly, and George let them in.

Angel waited patiently for about two hours until the two women came out. She got pictures of them leaving the motel room, going to their car, and driving away.

She followed them in her car to an all-night Mexican bar. She concealed a small tape recorder under her blouse and went inside.

Angel paused momentarily while her eyes became accustomed to the dim light. The women were sitting alone at a corner table. She waited while they had a few drinks, and then she went to their table.

"How did it go tonight, girls?"

"Who are you?" One of them asked. "Somebody's wife?"

Angel laughed momentarily before speaking. "I'm a feature writer doing a story about, shall I say, the motel business. Would you tell me about it? No names, please. You're anonymous."

"We gotta have drinks to settle our nerves after that pair," the second one said. "They were that bad."

"Do you go there often?"

"As often as they'll pay us," the first one said.

"How much did they pay you?"

"Ten brand new hundred dollar bills, five each," the second one said. "They paid for the room and gave us each another hundred dollars as a tip for an extra good time."

"Six hundred bucks apiece," said Angel.

"Not bad for a night's work," said the first one.

"Are they any fun?"

"They're a scream," said the second one.

"What about the old man?"

"Honey," said the first one, "he's not only over the hill, he's down the side of the Grand Canyon clear to the bottom of the Colorado River. It's that bad."

"Would you tell him that?"

"No way," said the first one." He's the one who pays us. We tell him he's a mean firecracker. We say his love muscle is out of this world."

Angel laughed again.

"The young guy's a tightwad," said the second one.

"What about him?"

"He's no better than the old man," said the second one.

"You mean he's over the hill, too?" Angel laughed.

"Honey," the second one continued, "he don't do nothing right. He goes wild when I hit my buttons like this." She ran her hand up and down the blouse buttons between her full-figured breasts. "He does it all in his imagination."

"If it's that bad, why do you go back?"

"We got mouths to feed," said the first one, "and no husbands to help. Can't make money like this any other way."

"And no taxes, too," said the second one. "It's a scream."

"What about their wives?"

"The old guy says his wife's a bitch," said the first one. "She must be getting old. He says her boobs sag."

Angel forced herself to laugh.

"The son doesn't talk about his wife," said the second one. "She's lost interest."

"Do you blame her?"

"No."

"You're Mexican. They're white. Does that matter?"

"Not to us, honey," said the first one. "A white man's dollar spends the same as a Mexican man's dollar."

"Latin's like satin," said the second one. "We know how to please a man better than the white girls do. Once he's gone Latin, he'll never see a white girl again."

Angel laughed to herself as she left the bar. "George, they're no competition. I'll be the sweetest wife you could ever want. You'll not know about this UNTIL I CHOOSE TO TELL YOU!"

X   X   X

George and Angel Benny were in a conference room at the law offices of Bingham, Jackson, and Shyes going over legal papers necessary for a complex business transaction.

"Let me look at them again," George said to Fred Shyes after he had finished. "I want to make sure everything's right."

"When you're through,' Shyes said, "take them to the secretary in the front office, and she'll notarize your signatures. She'll make the copies after everyone has signed. If you have any changes or further questions, she'll call me out of my meeting." Then he left the room to take care of another client.

While George was going over the legal papers, Angel slipped the signature page of another legal document out of the folder she was carrying.

"I'm finished," George said, finally. "It's all there. They did a good job."

Angel picked up the papers, and they went into the front office. The secretary, a receptionist, and a file clerk were at their desks busy with their work.

"We sign here," Angel said as George signed the first one in front of the secretary.

"And here." He signed the second one, and she added her signature to both documents.

The secretary paused from her typing enough to notarize the signatures and did not examine the documents. Angel watched her with interest.

"One more signature," Angel said to George. "Sign here."

George signed without looking at the page. It was the one Angel had taken out of her folder.

"This one requires two witnesses," Angel said after the secretary had notarized it. "I'll get the receptionist and the file clerk to be the witnesses."

The receptionist and the file clerk signed as witnesses without looking at the document page and continued on with their work.

"Let me put them together," Angel said, and she took all of the papers to a nearby table. She slipped the one page back into her folder while the others were not looking.

"Here are the official copies," Angel said to the secretary. "The pages are in order."

"I'll copy them tomorrow after everyone else has signed," the secretary said. "I'll mail your copies to you."

"It's important that this deal go through before the end of the year," George said.

"It will close tomorrow," said the secretary.

"We'll make a bundle," George said to Angel as they left the attorney's office.

"Will you be home for supper?" Angel asked.

"I may be late. I need to go to the office. I must call George, Jr., and see how things are going there." He got into his car to return to his office.

Angel laughed to herself as she got into her car with her folder.

"George, Jr., have I got a surprise for you!"

TWENTY EIGHT

January, 1980

"Mamma." Mike was home early. It was Saturday afternoon, and he had gotten off from work at two o'clock. He had driven his mother's car that day.

"I stopped at a Benny's Fast Foods place in Pacific City to check it out. I didn't tell them I worked at Fast Fred's."

"What did you find out?" Betty was at her desk in her office.

"Here's their advertisement showing the location of their outlets." Mike handed her the map. "They're circled in blue. I marked where the Fast Fred places are in red."

"They serve different areas," Betty said as she looked at the map.

"If these two companies were to merge," Mike said, "only one outlet would have to be closed. We could use Fast Fred's central office and eliminate Benny's. Food and kitchen supplies could be purchased in larger quantities at better prices, and we could eliminate one of the two warehouses. The combined company would be much more profitable than either one separately."

"Mike," said his mother, "you amaze me. I haven't spent much time studying small companies, but this is an interesting situation. I'll get all the information I can about these companies. Find out what you can, but don't tell anyone about your idea."

"I will, Mamma, and I won't tell anyone."

February, 1980

"Mike," Betty said one evening when he got home from work, "I have financial reports and other information on Benny's Fast Foods and on Fast Fred's Hot Foods in my office. You may want to look at them."

"Sure, Mamma."

They went into her office and sat down. Betty picked up the papers, and they looked at them together.

"Fast Fred's has less debt," she pointed out. "It pays a dividend. Benny's is larger, but it doesn't pay a dividend. Benny's has more outlets. The management of Fast Fred's is mainly Mexican. Most of its locations are in non-white neighborhoods, and it has mostly non-white employees."

Betty paused for a moment, and then continued.

"Benny's management is primarily from the east coast. They're all white, but they do employ a few non-whites in lower-paying jobs. Their outlets are all in predominantly white areas."

"We came from the east coast," said Mike, "so how come I got hired at Fast Fred's instead of Benny's?"

"Fast Fred's appears to be more open in their hiring practices than Benny's. Fast Fred's doesn't discriminate. It's friendly to its employees. It has an employee stock purchase program. Benny's appears to discriminate against minorities in its hiring, and employees can't purchase stock through the company."

"How do you buy Benny's stock?" Mike asked.

"Benny's sells on the Pacific Coast Stock Exchange. Fast Fred's can be bought through our broker, Mr. Tachonaka, over the counter."

"What do you think, Mamma?"

"Benny's stock is currently selling for ten dollars a share, and Fast Fred's is selling for twelve dollars a share. The price/earnings ratios and other ratios are similar for the two companies. Neither company is overpriced. According to my estimates, if Fast Fred's and Benny's merged, each Fast Fred's share would increase in value to about twenty-five dollars a share. Each Benny's share would be worth perhaps twenty dollars a share."

"That's double!"

"It's a gamble, but I'm going to suggest we begin buying Benny's at ten dollars a share and Fast Fred's at twelve dollars a share. We don't need to be in a hurry, and we don't want anyone to figure out what we're doing.

202

It may take a few years for things to happen. Sooner or later, somebody will try to put these two companies together."

"I'll keep buying Fast Fred's shares through the employee stock purchase program, too."

"Don't tell anyone about this. Silence is important."

"That's a good idea, Mamma. I'll keep it a secret."

September, 1980

It was in the early afternoon. Victoria Clarke came in with the day's mail.

"John, the detective agency sent these pictures of Deborah, Steven, and the grandchildren. How did they get them?"

"With a long-distance lens. It's done without them knowing they're being photographed."

"What can we do to get Deborah back?"

"I don't know. What about Steven and the children?"

"I hate him. He's turned our grandchildren against us. They're Mexican! They're growing up Catholic! They're going to school with Mexicans, Asians, and who knows what other trash!"

"There's nothing I can do. We'll have to wait."

"We've got to do something!"

"I'll have my broker find out about Fast Fred's Hot Foods. That's the company Steven works for. Maybe I can buy stock in it. Maybe I can do something that way to help them."

"That Steven!" Said Victoria. "Why do you want to help him?"

"I want him to keep his job. I don't like what George Benny and his son are doing out there. Times are changing. We need to have minorities in management."

"Steven's the cause of the trouble! I don't know why he hates us so. I want Deborah back! I want to see my grandchildren!"

"I want to see them, too, but stomping Steven into the dust isn't going to accomplish anything."

"I hate him!" Victoria ran to the stairs. "John! Why do you help him?" She ran up the stairs to her room.

Ignoring Victoria, John Clarke went to the telephone and called his broker.

"Stan, find out all you can about Fast Fred's Hot Foods. Its home office is in Pacific City."

"It may take a few days to get the information. It's an over-the-counter stock."

"Send it to me whenever you can." John Clarke ended the conversation and began reading his newspaper."

X   X   X

"I got the information you sent on Fast Fred's Hot Foods." John Clarke was in his study at home talking with Stan, his broker, over the phone.

"You own a similar stock out there, Benny's"

"I own twenty-five percent of that company," said John. "I bought the stock before it went public."

"Fast Fred's is a competitor. You can buy shares of it over the counter. It's not listed on a national or regional exchange like Benny's. Its price spread was fourteen to fourteen and a quarter yesterday. The company's making money, but the stock's not hot. It's fully priced. It's a stable company, but there are better buys on the market."

"Buy a thousand shares of Fast Fred's at fourteen to fourteen and a half."

"We may have to buy that many shares in pieces. There's not a lot of it available. It's mostly owned by Mexicans."

"Buy every share you can in that price range, but don't go higher. Don't stop at a thousand. I may go up later, but not now. Buy it in a street name. Let's keep the Clarke name out of this. I don't want George Benny or the Fast Fred's people to find out what I'm doing. I don't want people at my office to know what I'm doing, either."

"What are you trying to do, John?" Victoria asked after he had hung up the phone.

"I don't know, but I don't want to scare Deborah or Steven."

"I don't know why you're concerned about Steven. He's the source of the trouble. Maybe if you scared him, he'd let Deborah come home. I don't know why he hates us so."

Victoria turned and went out of the study. Once in the hall, she burst into tears.

John got up from his desk and went to her.

"Have you taken your medicine today?"

"Why do I have to take that stuff? It tastes awful."

"I'll ring for your nurse."

October, 1980

"This is John Clarke." He was calling Stan, his stockbroker, from his study at home. "I got your report on Fast Fred's Hot Foods. According to your figures, I own over twenty percent of the company. You've done a good job."

"They had a down quarter, but it doesn't look serious."

"Raise the price to fifteen. Let's see how much more we can get. Tell the other brokers we're not going higher. Don't tell them how much we own. I'm not a threat to management. Keep everything in a street name. Let's don't make this look like a big thing."

"Good luck on whatever you are trying to do. I'll place the order."

"What is this all about?" Overhearing John on the phone, Victoria had come into the study. Her nurse followed her into the room.

"I don't want my grandchildren to grow up in poverty."

"Oh," Victoria said as she turned away. "They don't have to live in poverty. They can live here. We'll give them American first names. We'll change their last name to Clarke. They look like Deborah. No one will know they're half Mexican."

Victoria's nurse followed her out of the study and into the kitchen.

X   X   X

"Steve," said Carlos. They were at their desks at the Fast Fred's business office. "We went into the market to buy stock for our employee stock purchase program. There wasn't much out there, and it was at fifteen and a half. That's high!"

"What's the problem?"

"According to our broker, someone's bought twenty-five percent of the company."

"Who?"

205

"It's some broker on the east coast. He maybe connected to Benny's."

"Who owns the rest of our stock?" Steve asked.

"An investment company with an Ocean Spray post office address owns twenty five percent through a local brokerage firm. They've left us alone so far. They purchased our stock nine or ten months ago. They haven't been as aggressive in their buying as the east-coast broker."

"What about the other fifty percent?" Asked Steve.

"Fred Gonzales owns five percent. His son Lee owns five percent. The other forty percent is owned by various small investors. Many are employees or former employees."

"What's happening?"

"I don't know," Carlos said, "but I don't like it. Benny's may be planning something. They don't like Mexicans. We could lose our jobs."

"Do you own any Fast Fred's stock?"

"I bought some through the employee stock purchase plan, and I inherited a few shares from my dad. I don't own much. How about you?"

"I've been in school at Pacific Coast University," Steve said. "We've had kids, and we've bought a house. Things have been tight for us. We haven't had any money to buy stock."

"If Benny's takes us over," Carlos said, "we'll lose our jobs. They'll change all our locations to Benny's."

"What can we do about it?"

"Not much, I guess."

"I don't think Fred will let that happen," said Steve.

"I hope you're right."

X   X   X

"Mike," said Betty. It was late, and he had come home from work. "I thought you'd be interested. Fast Fred's stock is at sixteen, an all-time high. Somebody else may be accumulating it. Its earnings don't justify that price. Have you heard anything?"

"No, Mamma, what should we do?"

"Benny's stock hasn't moved much. We'll buy more of it Somebody may be getting ready to put the companies together."

"What happens if it doesn't involve Benny's?"

"Who else might be buying the stock?"

"I don't know."

"That's a chance we'll have to take. I'll call the broker in the morning. Do you have any homework left to do?"

"I did it all at school."

December, 1980

"Fast Fred's stock has moved up to seventeen," George Benny said to his son over the phone. "One of the national stock exchanges is talking about listing it. It's like they struck oil or something. What's going on out there?"

"I don't know. The stock is overpriced. Its earnings aren't any better than ours. It should come down several points after this quarter's results."

"Something's happening. I don't want Fast Fred's to get away from us."

"Are any of the advisory services recommending it?" George, Jr., asked.

"Not that I know about. Do you think someone at Fast Fred's is bidding up the price? Maybe they're getting ready to dump the stock."

"Nobody at Fast Fred's has that kind of money," George, Jr., said. "I don't know what's happening."

"Try to find out."

"I'll ask around."

TWENTY NINE

May, 1981

"Can Bianca get a job at one of our outlets?" Steve asked Carlos. They were in the Fast Fred's business office. "She's almost sixteen and in the tenth grade."

"The new Fast Fred's near the St. Benedict's school needs people. Her hours would have to be limited until she's sixteen, though."

"Who would she work under?"

"Benito. He transferred there from Ocean Spray."

"I don't want him to know her father works for Fast Fred's. She doesn't need to get special treatment."

"He doesn't have to know where her father works. Send her down to apply. She'll have no trouble getting a job. They're short of help."

"Thanks, Carlos."

X   X   X

"What are your plans now?" Charles Crawford asked. Chuck was at home after finishing his internship at Deep South University Hospital, and they were sitting outside on the patio.

"I have applied for a residency program in medical genetics under Teigemeyer. He's at the Pacific Coast University Medical School. It's a new three-year program."

"What happens if you don't get accepted?"

"I sent out other applications, but Teigemeyer's my first choice."

"When will you know?"

"The funding doesn't start until July. They'll decide by the first of June. The other programs I applied to don't start until September."

"I know some people out there. I'll see what I can find out."

"Thanks, Dad. Ellen and Bob just drove up. I'll go help them bring in their stuff. Are you coming?"

"No, I'll go inside. I've got some business to tend to."

Charles went inside to his study while Chuck went to greet his sister and her husband. Charles placed a call to Dr. Bernard Benz, a long-time friend and Dean of the College of Medicine at Pacific Coast University.

"Barney, this is Charles Crawford."

"Glad to hear from you, Charles."

"I'm asking a favor."

"What is it?"

"Charles, Jr., has applied for a residency out there. His MD is from Atlantic Coast University. His internship was at Deep South University Hospital. He wants to study medical genetics under Teigemeyer. Anything you could do would be appreciated."

"The program's new. Let me get his application. It's here in the office." The Dean put down the phone and went into the next room. He came back with Chuck's application file, looked at it, and then picked up the phone.

"There aren't many applications. He's better qualified than the others. He'll be accepted. Teigemeyer owes me a favor."

"Thanks, Barney."

X   X   X

"Clarene, would you go to the senior prom with me?" Mike asked. It was closing time at Fast Fred's, and they were getting off work.

"I can't. It's my parents."

"Don't they like me?"

"They think you're a nice boy, but you're not Chinese."

"This is America. That doesn't matter."

209

"It does to them. They're from the old country. They want me to marry a Chinese boy. I can't date any boy who isn't Chinese. They would be greatly offended. I'm sorry. I don't want to hurt your feelings. Please ask someone else."

"I'll try." Mike was hurt by the rejection.

"Mike, I hope we can still be friends."

"We can."

X   X   X

"Mike, what's wrong?" Betty asked when Mike got home. "You look so sad."

"I asked Clarene to the Senior Prom, and she turned me down."

"Did she have another date?"

"She said her parents wouldn't let her date any boy who isn't Chinese. I don't think she's going."

"Let's see if we can find someone else."

"I don't know anybody else to ask."

"How about Bianca? She's a bit young, though. I'm not sure her parents would let her go."

"She'd probably turn me down, too."

"Do you mind if I call Deborah and ask?"

"I guess you can." Mike was unenthusiastic. "I'll go to my room and get ready for bed. I'm tired."

Betty went to the phone and called Deborah. "Mike asked Clarene to the senior prom, and she turned him down. She said her parents would object. They won't let her date any boy who isn't Chinese. I want him to go to the prom. He hasn't dated so far. I know Bianca's a bit young for this, but would you and Steve mind if Mike asked her to the prom?"

"We wouldn't, and she'd love to go."

"I'll try to get Mike to give her a call."

"She's in her room doing homework."

Betty waited nervously until Mike came out of his room.

"Deborah and Steve don't mind if you call Bianca. Why don't you call her now? She's at home."

210

"I'll give it a try," Mike said reluctantly. "What's her number?"

"Here it is." Betty wrote it down for him.

Mike went to the phone and nervously dialed the number.

"Hello," Deborah answered the phone.

"Is Bianca there?"

"Yes, she's in her room. I'll get her."

"Hello," Bianca said.

"Bianca, this is Mike. Would you go to the senior prom with me?"

"Sure." She could hardly believe her ears.

"You will!" He was surprised she accepted. "I'll pick you up at six. Do you know the day?"

"Yes!" She didn't, but she would find out.

"Thanks, see you then."

"Bye." She stood there with the phone in her hand. She didn't know what else to say.

"Mom!" Mike was excited as he hung up the phone. "She accepted!"

X   X   X

Mike was nervous that evening as he went to pick up Bianca. Driving his mother's car, he watched his speed carefully. He got off the freeway and finished the drive to her house.

"Hi," Deborah said as she opened the door. "Come on in. Bianca's almost ready."

Mike was stunned when he saw her in her black and red lace gown. Distinctly Latin, it had been made by two of Deborah's Mexican friends. The bodice had puffed black lace sleeves that barely stayed on her shoulders and a high neckline. The black lace ran down to her waist where a red lace ruffle extended to her knees. From there, a black lace ruffle dropped to almost the floor. Bianca's hair was pulled back and held in place with red combs that had belonged to her grandmother, Bianca Maria Cortez.

Unsure of himself, he escorted her to the car, and they were on their way.

X   X   X

The lights were out when Mike and Bianca returned after the prom, but Deborah was in the living room waiting. Mike opened the car door for Bianca and took her to the door. She opened it with her key and stepped inside.

"Goodnight," she said.

"Goodnight," he answered.

She waited there as he turned and went down the steps. She watched him go to the car and drive away. Still in a cloud, she closed the door and started to go to her room.

"How did things go?" Her mother asked as she turned on the light. Then Steve came into the room.

Bianca was startled. She hadn't realized her parents were up.

"It was wonderful! The music was so exciting. We danced almost every dance together."

"I'm glad you enjoyed it," said Steve. "Now we all can go to bed."

June, 1981

"Dad!" Chuck entered the hallway as his father came in the back door. "I have been accepted to study under Teigemeyer at Pacific Coast University. The letter's here in today's mail."

"Congratulations, son." Charles was home after making his evening rounds.

"Three years from now, I can be board-certified and have a PhD in medical genetics."

"Do you plan to teach in a medical school?"

"I might, but I won't make that decision now. I want to fly out there next week to get an apartment. I want to get familiar with the campus before the program starts."

"I think you'll like Teigemeyer." Charles turned toward the doorway to the kitchen. Syndi was standing there listening. "Is supper ready?"

"It's ready."

"I'll go wash my hands," said Chuck.

"We'll be out there sometime," Charles said to Syndi. "Maybe we can find Betty Riggioletti and little Mike."

"If they are out there," said Syndi.

212

August, 1981

Betty was at home alone in her office reading a financial newspaper when the chest pains began. At first she thought it was indigestion. She had eaten supper about an hour earlier. She stood up for a moment, and the pain became worse. She went to the front door and opened it. Returning to her desk, she sat down. Exhausted, she called for an ambulance.

"I don't know what's happening," she said slowly. "The pain is severe. It might be serious. The front door is open. Come on in."

"Conscious, Betty was still sitting at her desk when the ambulance arrived. The attendants helped her to the stretcher. She could not speak. She handed one of them a note. "Please call Deborah Cortez." It gave Deborah's phone number.

The attendants carried Betty out to the ambulance and took her to Pacific Coast University Hospital.

"It's a heart attack," the emergency room physician said. "Let's get her to the coronary care unit."

The ambulance attendant called Deborah from the hospital emergency room. "We carried Betty Riggs to University Hospital. It may be serious. She gave us your number to call."

"Thank you," said Deborah. "I'll call her son, and then I'll come."

"It's a heart attack," the heart specialist told Deborah and Mike at the hospital. "We have her in the coronary care unit. She's on oxygen. She's stable for now. We'll have to wait until tomorrow morning before we can assess the situation."

"Can we see her?" Deborah asked.

"Just for a few minutes," said the doctor. "One at a time, though, and not for long."

Mike," said Deborah, "you go first."

September, 1981

Mike was at home eating breakfast when the phone rang. His mother was still asleep.

"Hello."

"Are you ready?" Deborah asked. It was freshman orientation day at Pacific Coast University. "Steve and I want to help."

213

"I can handle it," said Mike.

"Do you know what classes you will be taking?"

"Mostly required courses. I'm starting off with a major in business."

"What about your job at Fast Fred's?"

"I transferred to the Fast Fred's near the university. I'm taking a light load at school and working nights and weekends. I'll be moving to the dorm."

"Will your mother be all right by herself?"

"The doctor says she'll do fine. She needs to take it easy. I'll go home when I can. I'll call her every night."

"Give us a tour of the campus when you're settled. Bianca is anxious to see what college life is all about."

November, 1981

Charles Crawford was late in getting to the office that morning.

"There was a break-in at Memorial Hospital last night," he said to Syndi. "The police questioned everybody."

"What was taken?"

"The only thing missing is a vial of a new heart drug. It's still experimental. In very small doses, it prevents heart attacks. In larger amounts, it causes fatal ones."

"Who knew the hospital had the drug?" Syndi asked.

"It was common knowledge among the staff."

"What have they found out?"

"So far, they're looking for clues. They think it was an inside job. Who is my first patient today?"

"Mrs. Yamazaki."

"Let's get started."

December, 1981

"George," Angel met him at the door. "Would you like to watch a movie tonight?" She seemed to be in a pleasant mood. "Supper isn't quite ready."

"I guess." He was tired and irritable from a hard day at the office. He sat down in his easy chair in the den.

Angel put a cassette into the VCR. She went behind her husband's chair and started the film with the remote control.

As the film reached the beginning, Angel took a hypodermic syringe out of her apron pocket and uncapped it. Quickly, she jabbed the needle into the back of George's shoulder and injected the contents.

"Ow! That hurt! What was that for?" He was angry.

She had the needle withdrawn, capped, and back into her pocket before he could see what had caused the pain.

The picture and sound came on. George saw himself and his son enter the office of the Classy Brass Motel. Sensing what the film was about, he got to his feet and faced Angel.

"What is the meaning of this!" Mad, he was holding his sore shoulder.

"My boobs sag! That's what you told them! I'm getting old! I should have pushed you overboard last summer when we were on that cruise!" Angel turned and walked away. "Latin is satin. Once he's gone Latin, he'll never see a white girl again! Is that true, George?"

Fear jumped across George's face, then severe pain. He clutched his chest. "YOU POISONED ME!" He fell to the floor.

"You had it coming, you dirty old fool."

The pain was severe. He groaned, and then it was over.

Laughing, Angel rewound the cartridge, took it out of the VCR, and changed the TV to a news program.

"This might come in handy later," she said as she put the cartridge back into its box. "George, Jr., hasn't seen it yet."

She smiled as she took the box to her bedroom and locked it inside a filing cabinet. "I'll get this out of here later."

Then returning to her husband, she picked up his arm and felt for a pulse. Not finding one, she went to the phone to call an ambulance.

X   X   X

"Your husband's dead," the emergency room physician told her. "It looks like a heart attack. Did he have a history of heart problems?"

"Not to my knowledge," Angel said. She was pretending to be a very concerned spouse. "I'd better call his children."

215

"George," she said to George, Jr., over the phone. "I'm sorry to call you at work. I'm at Memorial Hospital. Your father collapsed in the den about an hour ago while watching the news. I called the ambulance. He was dead when we got here, a heart attack. I'm sorry. There was nothing I could do."

"I'll come as soon as I can."

"I'll call your brother and your sister. I'll make arrangements for your father's funeral. He said he wanted to be cremated. His ashes will be at a memorial service."

"He never told us anything about being cremated."

"That's what he told me. I'll schedule the service after I talk to your brother and your sister."

George, Jr., was in a state of shock when he hung up the phone. Pausing for a few minutes, he looked up the phone number of a friend in his address book and called long distance.

"Harvey, this is George Benny, Jr. Are you still with the DA's office?"

"Yes, I am."

"I need a favor bad. My dad died about an hour ago, apparently of a heart attack. My stepmother wants to burn up the body. Something's wrong. Dad hadn't had heart trouble before."

"Where's the body?"

"It should still be at Memorial Hospital."

"I'll put a hold on it. The hospital will refrigerate the body until we can look at it. If things look suspicious, we'll do an autopsy."

"Thanks, I owe you one. Something's not right about this."

X   X   X

"Mrs. Benny," the funeral director called her the next morning. "We can schedule the memorial service any time, but the medical examiner won't be through with the autopsy for three days. We can't cremate your husband until after they release the body."

"I didn't know anything about an autopsy. I didn't authorize it. George wanted his body cremated immediately."

"We can't cremate it until they release it to us."

"I'll call the hospital." Angry, she hung up the phone.

Then she dialed the hospital administrator's number.

"This is Mrs. Benny. You have my husband's body. I want you to release it to the funeral home. We're trying to arrange the funeral services."

"We can't. The DA's office wants an autopsy."

"I haven't authorized an autopsy. The funeral service was scheduled for tomorrow. His children are from out of town. I don't want to inconvenience them."

"The DA's office had the body examined by a forensic expert. He found a suspicious puncture in the back of your husband's shoulder. They ordered an autopsy."

"What are they saying?"

"They're saying nothing until after the examination."

"How can I get the body released?"

"You'll have to get a court order. By the time you get it, they'll be through with the autopsy. I'm sorry."

Angry, Angel hung up the phone. "I'd better get certain things out of this house!"

X   X   X

"Mrs. Benny," the police detective said. He was at her front door the next morning. "They finished the autopsy on your husband last night. Your husband was murdered. Did you do it?"

"Murdered!" She looked at the officer as in disbelief. "They said he had a heart attack. Are you charging me with murder?"

"Not yet, but we're taking you in for questioning."

"This is a frame!"

"We also have a warrant to search your house."

"This is an outrage! My ex-husband's behind this! It's either him or my stepchildren. I'll not answer any questions until I talk with my attorney."

"Come with me. We're going down town."

THIRTY

January, 1982

"Do we have to go to George Benny's funeral?" Victoria asked. She and her husband were sitting in their den watching the news on TV. "They burned up his body last week."

"We have to go," said John. "Your doctor's appointment is in the morning. The services are in the afternoon."

"But George isn't going to be there. They burned him up."

"It's a memorial service," John said. "His ashes will be there in an urn."

"Why did they have to burn up his body?" Victoria said. "That's so disrespectful."

"You'll have to ask Angel Benny that."

"Why couldn't the service be held when he died?"

"They had an autopsy," her husband said.

"Didn't she murder him?" Victoria asked. "They ought to burn her up."

"She was arrested, but her case hasn't come up for trial."

"Will she be there?" Victoria asked.

"She's out on bail."

"What about his money?" Victoria asked.

"Angel says she has a will leaving everything to her."

"But she killed him!" Victoria said.

"Murders can't inherit," said her husband, "but she has to be convicted first."

"She'll spend it all before the trial."

"She can't," John said. "The children are fighting it. George's attorney has an earlier will leaving everything to his three children. The probate court named George, Jr., as the administrator. The estate can't be settled until Angel's murder charge is resolved."

"It's too bad we couldn't burn up Steven. He's the cause of our problem. Deborah would write to us if it weren't for him. We have Mexican grandchildren. They're growing up Catholic. They're being taught by nuns! They're going to school with Mexicans, Asians, and who knows what other trash. It's all Steven's fault. Why does he hate us so?" Victoria burst into tears.

"We're not going to burn up anybody."

X   X   X

"Ralph, this is Charles Crawford." He was calling from his office. "I need an appointment. It's Angel again."

"What's she up to?"

"She's trying to involve me in the death of her second husband, George Benny. She says I'm part of a plot to frame her for murder."

"I read about his death in the papers. Wasn't Angel charged with his murder?"

"That doesn't stop her from trying to involve me."

"Have you been formally charged with anything?"

"No, but the police want me to take a lie detector test."

"Don't say anything. Don't agree to anything. Everything goes through me. If they ask you questions, send them to me."

"I haven't told them anything so far," Charles said.

"How do you feel about a lie detector test?"

"I'll take one if it's honest and properly administered. I have nothing to hide. Angel will frame me if she can."

"I'll stay late. Can you be here before five?"

"I'll be there by four if I can."

John Clarke entered the law offices of Hamilton, Stuart, and York. "Bill is expecting me."

"He's waiting for you." The receptionist got up from her desk and escorted him back to Mr. Hamilton's office.

"Hi, John." The attorney got to his feet. "We've got all of the papers filed. Are you ready?"

"I want to get this over with."

"Let's go. The limousine is waiting."

They went into the parking garage and got into the law firm's limousine. The driver took them to the courthouse steps and let them out. Silently, they went up the steps and into the building. Taking the elevator, they got out on the third floor and entered the courtroom. Court was in session, and they took their seats on the third row.

"I hate this," John whispered to Bill.

Their case was called, and they went before the judge.

"Everything is here," Judge Murphy said. "The court-appointed psychologist has made his report. He agrees with your doctor. They say your wife is psychotic and suffers from serious personality defects. She's not responsible for her behavior. While she hasn't hurt anyone so far, she is potentially dangerous and needs to be confined."

"Mr. Clarke wants her declared insane," said Bill Hamilton. "He wishes to be appointed her guardian with that authority passing to me if he becomes unable to carry out that responsibility."

"What are your plans, Mr. Clarke?" The judge asked.

"I don't want her in an institution. I want her to spend the rest of her life in the style she is accustomed to. Our home is private. It is surrounded by a high wall. There is a gate at the driveway. We have registered nurses there around the clock to tend to her. She rarely leaves the house, and when she does, her nurses accompany her."

"Has anyone told her what is happening?" The judge asked.

"She doesn't know," said Mr. Hamilton. "She wouldn't understand."

"What about the expense of all of this?" The judge asked.

"Their assets were placed in a trust several years ago," said Mr. Hamilton. "Mr. Clarke controls the trust, and if he becomes unable to manage the trust, that authority passes to me."

"Mrs. Victoria Clarke is hereby declared insane. John Clarke is appointed her legal guardian with that responsibility automatically passing to Bill Hamilton if John becomes unable to serve. Mr. Hamilton, prepare the order, and I will sign it."

"Thank you, your honor. I will prepare the order."

"I'm sorry I had to do it," John said to Bill as they were leaving the courtroom.

"You didn't have a choice."

"I'm glad it's over."

November, 1982

"Mr. Shyes can see you now," the receptionist said to George Benny, Jr. "He's in his office."

George was at the law office of Bingham, Jackson, and Shyes. Fred Shyes had sent for him in regard to negotiations involving his father's estate. He put down the magazine he had been trying to read and went down the hall to Mr. Shyes' office.

"Hi, George," Mr. Shyes greeted him. "Come inside my office. It's bad news time."

George went inside and sat down. The attorney closed the door. He went to his desk and sat down. He took off his glasses and looked at his client in a stern manner.

"George, I have spent the last two weeks in discussions with Angel's lawyer and the district attorney's office."

"I don't want to plea bargain," George interrupted. "I want my step-mother in the electric chair."

"I understand how you feel, but it isn't that easy. Angel and her lawyer have agreed to a compromise. In exchange for all charges being dropped, she'll agree to take only one-fourth of your father's estate. That will leave you, your brother, and your sister with a fourth each instead of a third. I think you should accept it."

"She shouldn't get a dime! Murderers can't inherit!"

"The DA's office doesn't have a chance of convicting her, and they know it. The only evidence they have is circumstantial. If this goes to trial and the jury turns her loose, she gets everything. You three get nothing."

"Her will's a fake. Dad would never sign something like that."

"I agree there's something wrong with the will, but his signature is authentic. It wasn't forged. My secretary notarized it, and my receptionist and my file clerk witnessed it. Their signatures weren't forged either. I don't understand how this happened since we didn't prepare the will, but it did."

"Who prepared it?"

"The will was typed on your father's old typewriter. His secretary says she didn't type it."

"Angel wrote it, then."

"She says he did it. Her lawyer says it doesn't matter who typed it. The signatures are all authentic. Your father was of sound mind when he signed it. That's what counts, and the judge will agree. If the jury turns her loose, she gets everything."

"What about the puncture in dad's shoulder?"

"The DA can't prove Angel did it. Somebody else could have done it."

"Who?"

"She says her ex-husband did it while the body was at the hospital before the district Attorney' office had the body examined."

"Did they find the vial of that heart drug that was stolen from the hospital? It's the same drug they found in dad's body."

"They haven't found anything to connect Angel to that missing vial. She says her ex-husband could have stolen it. She says she didn't kill your father."

"That's a lie!"

"According to her theory, you found out about the will, and you and Dr. Crawford tried to get her blamed for your father's death."

"That's ridiculous! Crawford and I passed lie detector tests. She wouldn't take one."

"Results of lie detector tests aren't admissible in a murder trial."

"Do you believe she's innocent?" George, Jr., asked.

"No. I believe she did it and so does the DA's office. Convincing a jury is a different matter."

"And you're saying we should turn her loose?"

"If this case goes to trial, she plans to make it a circus. She'll say you arranged for prostitutes to be in your father's motel room every time he

222

went to Pacific City. She has some of it on videotape. She says you were trying to destroy their marriage."

"She killed him! Why can't they put her in the electric chair?"

"You were a playboy in your younger years. You ran around with wild women and experimented with drugs. This didn't stop when you got married."

"I quit using drugs."

"She's got pictures, motel records, all sorts of things to blackmail you with. She's threatening to make this public. If your wife ever finds out, she could sue you for divorce and take everything you've got. It's that bad."

"But Angel murdered my father!"

"Your best bet is to accept her offer and drop the charges."

"She's getting too much!"

"She thinks the DA has a stronger case than it has. That's why she's willing to compromise. Her first offer was that she get half. We got them to reduce it to a fourth. She's not going lower. This is your best deal."

"I want her in the electric chair!"

"You won't get that. If this case goes to court, she'll be acquitted. The DA's office has done a lot of bluffing trying to get more evidence. They haven't been able to find enough to convict her. They won't bring this case to trial. They'll drop the charges if you don't accept this offer."

"In other words, I don't have any choice."

"That's the extent of it. It's the best of a bad deal." Mr. Shyes got up from his desk.

"I'll have to think about it. I don't like it." George, Jr., stood up.

"I'll contact your brother and your sister, but I wanted to talk to you first." Mr. Shyes came around the desk and went to the door. "I understand how you feel, but I think you had better accept this compromise. Let's talk about this again tomorrow."

They shook hands, and George left the office in an angry mood.

"I'm glad I could catch you in town," John Clarke said. He was treating George Benny to lunch at the Golden Garden. "I didn't want to talk about this over the phone."

"What is it?"

"Why did they turn your step-mother loose?"

"She's guilty," said George. "They didn't have enough evidence to convict her."

The waiter came with their orders, and they started eating.

"What about your father's estate?"

"We compromised. My brother, my sister, and I each get a fourth. Angel gets a fourth."

"She shouldn't get anything."

"I agree," said George. "It was either this or she gets everything."

"Who gets the Benny's stock?"

"As administrator, I'm offering Angel her portion in cash. My brother and my sister don't care. I want the Benny's stock."

"Do you want to sell any of it?" John asked.

"No, I plan to keep it."

"If you have to sell it, please let me know."

"If you bought it," George said, "that would give you fifty percent ownership. I'd still want to be CEO."

"I don't want to run the company. I have no plans to move to the west coast."

"If you want to sell your interest," George said, "I'll buy you out."

"Do you have the money?"

"I'd try to raise it."

"What do you plan to do with Benny's," John asked.

"I want to expand it."

"How?"

"By buying Fast Fred's Hot Foods."

"That was your father's plan. How is that going to help?"

"Fast Fred's is strong in minority areas," George said. "Benny's is strong in white areas. There would be considerable cost savings. We wouldn't need Fast Fred's business office. Ours could handle things for the combined company. We'd need only one warehouse instead of two. We could buy in larger quantities and get lower prices."

"Benny's doesn't have the money to buy out Fast Fred's," John said. "Are you planning a stock swap?"

"NO way! Mexicans own most of their stock. We'd have to keep some Mexicans in management. It would dilute my holdings. I want total control."

"How do you plan to do that?"

"I don't know," said George.

"Between us," John said, "we control Benny's."

"That's right."

"If I want to sell, I'll give you first chance. If you want to sell, you'll give me first chance. Is that a deal?"

"It's a deal," said George.

THIRTY ONE

June, 1983

"Congratulations," Steve said.

Bianca was wearing her cap and gown and holding her high school diploma. They were in the St. Benedict's football field after the commencement ceremony.

"Hold it," her mother said as she snapped Bianca's picture. Juan and Juanita were standing beside their mother. "Mike has a treat waiting for us at Fast Fred's. He's at the hospital visiting his mother."

"How's Granny doing?" Asked Bianca.

"She'll be home in a few days. The doctor says she's recovering. It was another heart attack. The doctor told us she probably won't live more than two or three years. She has a weak heart."

"I'm sorry," said Bianca.

"We are, too," said Deborah. "Mike's taking it hard."

"Does she know?" Bianca asked.

"I don't think they've told her yet."

September, 1983

"Well, my little granddaughter is going to college," Betty Riggs said. She was resting in a chair in her living room. Her live-in nurse was in the kitchen. Deborah and Bianca were visiting her. "What are you planning to study?"

"Nursing," said Bianca. "I'll be living at home."

"Will you be working?"

"I am working at the Fast Fred's near the university with Mike. My hours are in the evenings and on week-ends like Mike."

X   X   X

John Clarke glanced at his watch as he left his office. It was almost ten o'clock. He had stayed late that evening to review a bid Clarke Construction was preparing for a commercial building project. The construction unit of Clarke Industries had always been his favorite.

Tired, he closed his office door and headed to the elevator. He thought about the project as he rode down to his car. Yes, he was confident they would get the job.

Clarke drove his Rolls Royce out of the parking garage and turned left into the main street. Stopping at a red light, he set the radio to a local news station and turned it on.

He heard police sirens in the distance as he entered the boulevard. The sounds were coming closer and closer. He could see the flashing lights of police cars fast approaching.

The radio announcer said a high-speed chase was in the opposite lanes. The car the police were after was on the other side of the median. He relaxed. This would not involve him.

But as the fleeing car approached, it cut across the median and skidded out of control. The police were in hot pursuit.

The car headed straight towards Clarke's car. He swerved to the right trying to avoid a collision. The oncoming car hit his Rolls Royce in the driver's door, and the Clarke car rolled over several times before coming to rest in the ditch.

Out of control, the fleeing car flipped over on its roof and slid down the highway until it came to a stop.

Police were everywhere. Ambulances arrived, but it was too late. The occupants of both cars were dead.

"Poor guy," one of the police officers told a news reporter. "Clarke never had a chance."

"Who was in the other car?" The reporter asked.

"Three men. Their car was stolen. We're trying to identify them now. They robbed an armored truck of more than a million dollars earlier this afternoon. The money was inside of the car."

X   X   X

Deborah and her children finished supper early that evening. They didn't wait for Steve. He was working late at the office.

The children took their plates to the kitchen and went to their rooms to do homework. Deborah cleared the table and washed the dishes. Finished in the kitchen, she went into the living room and sat down to watch a movie on television.

The phone rang, and she answered it.

"Deborah, this is your mother! Don't hang up!"

Deborah was stunned. She was not prepared for this.

"Your father was killed in an automobile accident less than an hour ago! You must come home!"

"How did you get my number? It's unlisted!"

"Your father's dead. You must come home!"

"Leave me alone!" Tears filled her eyes. "You killed my baby! You wouldn't even tell me whether it was a boy or a girl!"

"I don't know whether it was a boy or a girl. I never saw it. That's been a long time ago. Can't you forget? Your father's dead!"

"I can't forget! I've tried!"

"I quit going to the club several years ago. Your father insisted. I'm your mother! I need you now! I have a big, empty house. With your father gone, you're all I got! You must come home!"

"My home is here! My husband and children are here! I'm not going to leave my husband and children to go back to you!" Deborah was crying.

"You can bring the children. We'll give them American first names. We'll change their last name to Clarke. No one will know they are half Mexican."

"Steve's their father!" Deborah was regaining her composure. "I'm not going to leave him. You killed my first baby because Steve was its father. Are you going to kill my other children? Steve is their father, too. Are you going to kill him?"

"Deborah! That's ridiculous! I'm your mother! I haven't killed anybody! Your baby didn't have a head! You must come home! I need you!"

"Leave me alone! You killed my baby! I'm not coming home!" Deborah hung up the phone and burst into tears.

"Who was that?" Steve asked as he came through the front door.

"Mother called. My father's dead. She wants me to leave you and move back in with her. Why can't she leave us alone? I hope she doesn't try to come here."

"What happened?" Steve asked.

"I don't know. I don't want to know. I don't want their money. I want her to leave us alone!"

"Maybe you should call the counseling service and arrange for an appointment for tomorrow," said Steve.

"Mrs. Lopez says I must learn to forgive," Deborah said. "I'm trying, but it's hard to forgive someone who isn't sorry. I'll see how I feel in the morning."

X   X   X

"I went to John Clarke's funeral this afternoon," Charles Crawford said to Syndi. They were in the kitchen. Syndi was preparing supper. "Deborah wasn't there. Have you heard anything about her?"

"I haven't heard anything in years."

"Her disappearance has always puzzled me. She may have been unstable like her mother."

"I still think she ran away with her boyfriend," Syndi said. "She didn't go to Europe like her mother said."

"I don't know."

"Did you ever find out where Betty Riggioletti is?" Syndi asked.

"I understand she wanted to get away from Maffi's enemies," Charles said. "Little Mike must be grown by now. I lost contact with them when they moved to the west coast."

"Was Angel at the funeral?" Syndi asked.

"She was there. She asked about Deborah, but Mrs. Clarke wouldn't talk to her."

"Does Mrs. Clarke know where Deborah is?" Syndi asked.

"I don't know." Charles said.

"How's she taking things?"

"Not well. She's under medical care. An RN is with her around the clock."

"Who is handling things?" Syndi asked. "She's not able to do it."

"John left his attorney, Bill Hamilton, in control of everything. I don't know any of the details."

"It bothers me that Deborah wasn't at the funeral," Syndi said.

"I wish John Clarke would have been more reasonable about the baby," Charles said.

"I agree," said Syndi, "but I'm sure Betty's been a good mother."

X   X   X

"I'm glad you could come," Victoria Clarke said to her minister. It was the day after the funeral. She met him at the front door, and they went into the living room.

"I can't stay long," he said. "What is it you wanted to talk about?"

"You asked about Deborah. I'll explain. She returns my letters unopened, and she won't talk to me over the telephone. She wouldn't come to her father's funeral."

"Why?" The minister asked.

"It's over a problem she had while she was in high school."

"Was it a school problem?"

"She had an abortion. It was for her own good. She says we killed her baby. The doctor said it didn't have a head. It wouldn't have lived very long anyway."

"What happened?" The minister was uneasy.

"We wanted her to marry better. After high school, she ran away with the same boy and married him. She has had three babies since then and could have had more if she wanted them. Why does she miss the first one so much? It would have died anyway. She doesn't want to have anything to do with me. I don't understand. With John gone, she's all I have."

"What happened after she left?"

"We sold the house and bought this one. It's great for parties, but it's so lonely for me by myself. John and I kept most of the rooms closed off.

Deborah and her family could move here. There would be plenty of room."

"Maybe her husband likes his job," said the minister.

"He doesn't have to work. John left enough money. It's in a trust for her. All I get is enough to live on. When I'm gone, she gets it all."

"Was that in his will?"

"John put everything we owned in a trust, even the house. He tricked me into signing the papers."

"Did he leave anything to charity? Did he leave anything to the church?"

"Everything goes to her. John even bought her twenty-five percent of the company her husband works for, Fast Fred's Hot Foods. It's in the trust."

"Do they know about this?"

"Not yet."

"It's a shame he didn't leave anything to the church." The minister got to his feet.

"How do I get Deborah back?"

"Don't threaten. You'll only drive the wedge deeper. You won't win them back by causing them trouble."

"What can I do?"

"Pray for them. I have to go now."

"Thank you for coming. I had to tell somebody." Victoria was in tears.

"I hope things work out. I'll pray for you."

December, 1983

"Are you John Clarke's attorney?" George Benny asked. He was in Bill Hamilton's law office. "I'm back east on business, and this is the address I have."

"Yes, I'm the attorney for the Clarke trust."

"I'm George Benny. My father started Benny's. John Clarke owned twenty-five percent of the stock. I'd like to buy his shares."

"The stock's not for sale. John left specific instructions."

"When will it be sold?"

"The trust provides for Mrs. Clarke for the rest of her life. After her death, it goes to their daughter. That's public information. The daughter can decide what she wants to do with it then. I can't tell you any more than that."

"Who is the daughter, and where is she?"

"I won't tell you that."

"I want to talk with her about it."

"You'll have to wait. She can't sell it now anyway."

"Wait how long?"

"It depends on how long Mrs. Clarke lives. That could be a long time." The attorney got up from his chair and started toward the door. "I make those decisions as long as Mrs. Clarke is alive. Glad to meet you, Mr. Benny. I'm sorry I can't give you more time." He held the door open for George Benny to leave.

"I still want to buy the stock," George said as he was leaving.

"Right now, it's not for sale."

THIRTY TWO

April, 1984

"George, Jr., I came to get the Benny's stock," Angel said. They were alone in his office at Benny's Fast Foods. She had come unannounced.

"I thought we agreed. You would get cash."

"I changed my mind."

"Why?" George asked.

"John Clarke is dead. He owned twenty-five percent of Benny's."

"What does that have to do with it?" George asked.

"After his wife dies, his daughter will get it. She'll have to come out of hiding."

"I don't understand."

"I've been trying to find her for years," Angel said.

"Then you don't really want the stock?"

"I still have the video!" Angel said.

"What video?" George answered.

"The one of you and your father meeting those whores at the Classy Brass Motel. I'm sure you remember it. I have tons of dirt on you."

"What do you mean?"

"You know what I mean. We've been through this before. You've seen it all."

"You'll have to spell it out."

"If I give it to your wife, she'll have grounds to divorce you and take every cent you've got. I own you."

"But I need this stock to protect my job. I'm the CEO of Benny's."

"You don't run Benny's, Mrs. Kerrick does."

"Mrs. Kerrick is my secretary, not my mamma."

"She's old enough to be your mamma. She's got more business sense in the tip end of her little finger than you do in your entire body."

"I'm the CEO, not Mrs. Kerrick."

"My price is Deborah Clarke, the name she uses, her address, her phone number, and everything you can find out about her."

"But we've got to settle the estate!"

"YOU KNOW WHAT I WANT AND WHAT I WILL DO IF I DON'T GET IT!" Angel stomped out of his office and slammed the door behind her.

X   X   X

"Angel," George said over the phone. He was calling from his east coast attorney's office. "I'm calling from Mr. Shyes' office. He's my attorney. We sold all of the Benny's stock today. There was a buyer at the market price. We'll all get cash. We're settling the estate next week whether you like it or not!"

"You can't do that! You can't sell that stock without court approval. I want it or I tell your wife everything!"

"Look, Angel, I can't find Deborah Clarke. The Clarke trust people won't tell me where she is."

"Who's running the Clarke trust?" Angel asked.

"Bill Hamilton of Hamilton, Stuart, and York."

"Hamilton, Stuart, and York? A law firm?" Angel asked as she wrote down the name.

"I talked to Mr. Shyes about your attempt to blackmail me, and I followed his advice. I told my wife everything. She doesn't want a divorce. If you make any of that stuff public, I'll sue you for everything you've got."

"I'll see my lawyer about this!"

"It's too late. I've already transferred the stock. The judge approved the sale this morning. If you want Benny's stock, you can buy it on the open market. It's a listed stock."

"I'LL GET YOU FOR THIS!" Angel slammed down the phone. George smiled as he hung up the phone. "We'd better keep that stock out of sight until she cools off."

"Once the estate is settled," Mr. Shyes said, "we'll transfer the stock back to you. She can't do anything then. We'll be discrete about it."

"That was the last obstacle," George said.

"We'll settle the estate next week," said Mr. Shyes. "Since everyone is getting cash, there's nothing left to fight about."

"Angel will get her money," said George. "I'll ask my brother and my sister if they will let me transfer theirs into a money market account. We can use it to buy out Fast Fred's Hot Foods and merge it with Benny's."

X   X   X

After hanging up on George Benny, Angel took her purse. She looked up a telephone number and dialed it.

"Bugsy's Bar and Grill."

"Is Mouse there?" Angel asked. It was his favorite hangout.

"Who's calling?"

"Angel Benny."

"I'll see if he's here."

"Hello, Babe," Mouse answered a few minutes later. "What's up?"

"This is Angel Benny. I have a job for you. We need to talk about it somewhere."

"What is it, Babe?"

"I need some information. It's in a law office, Hamilton, Stuart, and York, When can we talk about it?"

"How about tonight, Babe? I'll be here at eleven."

"See you, Mouse."

"See ya, Babe. I like it green."

X   X   X

Angel hurried as she entered the city park. She saw Mouse sitting alone on a park bench, and she sat down beside him.

"Did you find anything?"

"I got it, Babe. Deborah Clarke Cortez is her name. I found her address, her phone number, and a few other goodies. It's all here in this envelope."

He handed her a sealed manila envelope.

"I copied everything," Mouse continued. "They'll never know I was there."

"Anything on Betty Riggioletti?" Angel asked.

"No luck, Babe. Nary a trace."

"Thanks." Angel handed him a white envelope with his pay. "I'd better be going. I may need you again."

"Thanks, Babe." Mouse counted the hundred-dollar bills. "Call me any time. I like it green"

May, 1984

"Dad." Chuck Crawford had called from his apartment at Pacific Coast University. "I passed the board exams. I'm now certified in medical genetics."

"What's next?" Charles Crawford was sitting in his living room.

"I am going to stay here to head up a research team. We've got a new federal grant. It's good for three years. It's an interesting project."

"When will you complete your PhD?" Charles asked.

"Probably next year," Chuck answered. "All I lack is my thesis. I'm doing the research now."

"You'll have an MD, a PhD in medical genetics, and be board certified. That will be quite an accomplishment. There aren't many in the country with those credentials."

"I'll have a regular faculty position here when the grant runs out. Teigemeyer is retiring then."

"Don't stay if you don't get the position," Charles said.

"I won't," said Chuck. "I'll have no trouble finding something at another medical school."

It was late that evening. Mike and Bianca had worked at the Fast Fred's near the campus until closing time. They talked as Mike drove her home. He stopped in the driveway and turned to her.

"Will you marry me?"

Bianca was stunned. Was she dreaming? She wasn't expecting this. He had been her dream ever since she was a little girl.

"Yes," she said, "but I want to finish school. I'm only a sophomore. I'm sure my parents would want this."

"I love you." He put his arms around her and kissed her. "We both need to finish school."

"I love you." She put her arms around him and kissed him.

"Do you work tomorrow afternoon?" He asked. "Can we get a ring then?"

"My last class is at two." Bianca smiled. "I don't work until five."

"I'll meet you at two." He held her close. "I love you, Bianca."

"I love you, Mike."

"What will your parents say?" Mike said as he walked her to the door.

"They'll want me to finish school. What about your mom?"

"She'd be relieved. She doesn't think I'll ever get married. She'll be glad it's to you. I hope we can get married while she's still alive."

"Good night."

X   X   X

"Hi, Mom," Bianca said. Mike had brought her home for a moment before taking her to work. "See my ring! Mike and I are engaged!"

"I don't object to you marrying Mike," Deborah said as she looked at the ring, "bit I want you to finish school."

"What will Dad say?"

"He'll say the same thing. You should tell Betty as soon as you can."

"What will she say?"

"She'll be delighted, but she'll want you to finish school, too."

X   X   X

"Chuck, this is Syndi," She was calling from a telephone booth at Memorial Hospital.

"What's up? You sound worried." He was at his apartment that morning getting ready to go to the medical genetics laboratory.

"I'm at Memorial Hospital. I delayed calling because I didn't want to wake you. Your Dad has been sick. He went in for tests yesterday. They found cancer, and it has spread. They say he has about two years to live, three at most."

"Should I come home now?"

"It's almost Christmas. You can wait until then, but I did think you should know. I'm sorry. Please don't tell your mother anything. She'll only make trouble."

"I won't. I'll be home for Christmas."

THIRTY THREE

March, 1985

It was Monday morning, and George Benny had just arrived at his office at Benny's Fast Foods.

"Did you see Sunday's paper?" George asked Mrs. Kerrick as he took off his coat.

"What's so important?" Mrs. Kerrick was at her desk.

"Fred Gonzales plans to retire after Fast Fred's annual stockholders' meeting in June." George handed her the business section of the newspaper. She put it down on her desk and continued on her work.

"He's the founder of Fast Fred's," George said. "He's their CEO and board chairman. Two members of his board also plan to retire. They're all past seventy. Fred feels it's time for younger people to take over."

"So what's happening?" Mrs. Kerrick did not look up.

"If we buy Fast Fred's, it needs to be now before they select a new CEO and replace the board members."

"We're not ready," Mrs. Kerrick picked up the newspaper and looked at the article with concern. "We don't have the cash to buy them out. They're not bothering us. Why don't we leave them alone?"

"We'll never have an opportunity like this again. My brother and my sister are backing us with their part of Dad's estate. I'm holding their money in a money-market account. I've been waiting for Fast Fred's stock to go down, but it hasn't. We're going to buy out Fast Fred's for cash."

"What about our people?" Mrs. Kerrick asked. "Who'll lose their jobs?"

239

"Nobody. We'll be the surviving company. I don't want any minorities in management. Get Fred Gonzales on the phone."

Mrs. Kerrick looked up the number and placed the call.

"Fred, this is George Benny at Benny's Fast Foods."

"What brings you to the west coast?" Fred Gonzales was uneasy. The Bennys had not been nice to him before. He had never been on a first-name basis with them.

"That was my father. He passed away over a year ago."

"I'm sorry." Fred was even more uncomfortable. The younger George Benny had been more hateful than his father.

"Now that you're retiring, we want to buy Fast Fred's. You've done a terrific job. It will be a great deal for your stockholders."

"I can't sell it." Fred closed his eyes and shook his head in disapproval. "Our board would have to meet, and we'd have to consider our shareholders and employees."

"What about your stock?" George asked. "You're retiring. At twenty-five dollars a share, you'll be making a nice profit."

"My stock's not for sale."

"We'll offer your stockholders twenty-five dollars a share. It's a great deal at current prices. They'd be getting a premium of six dollars a share over Friday's close."

"You can submit it to our board, but they'll turn you down." Fred was concerned.

"How much do you want?" George asked.

"We're not going to sell at any price."

"Why not?" George Benny asked. "It's in the best interest of your shareholders."

"I didn't build this company for you to take it over."

"Then it will be a hostile takeover. Your stockholders will see things my way. It's in the bag!"

"You can submit it to our board."

"I want to submit it in person."

"We're not going to have a disturbance at our board meeting. They would through you out."

"I want a list of your stockholders," said George. "Your annual stockholders' meeting is in June. I'll go straight to them! To hell with your board!"

"They'll turn you down."

"We'll see about that!"

"Those damn Mexicans," George said to Mrs. Kerrick after he had hung up the phone. "They want the moon."

X   X   X

"Benny's wants to buy us out," Fred Gonzales said to Carlos and Steve. They were in Fast Fred's central office. "They're offering twenty-five dollars a share."

"Are you going to sell?" Steve asked.

"I'm seventy two years old," said Fred. "It's time for me to retire. I'll talk to the other two retiring board members. If they agree, we'll stay on until this fight is over."

"What will it mean for us if their buy-out goes through?" Asked Steve.

"We lose our jobs," said Carlos.

"What can we do to stop it?" Asked Steve.

"It would have to be approved by the board of directors or by the stockholders," said Fred. "There isn't a board meeting scheduled before our annual stockholders' meeting in June."

"What does that mean?" Asked Carlos.

"They can go to the stockholders for approval, or they can try to buy a majority of the shares."

X   X   X

"Fred," George Benny said over the phone, "I have the proposal ready. It's being typed now. When can I submit it?"

"I talked with our attorney about this. He said we can call a meeting of our board and let them vote on it. They'll turn you down cold."

"When can I present it to them?"

"You send me your proposal. Then I'll see about calling a meeting to consider it."

"When is the meeting? It will have to be quick."

"I'll have to have the proposal first. We have to have something to consider. I'm sure the board members will want to study it."

"But I want to present it in person. It's a great deal for your stockholders."

"I'll ask them if they want you to come."

"I want a list of your stockholders. We'll go directly to them."

"You'll have to submit that request in writing."

X   X   X

"Carlos and Steve, Fred wants you," Fred's secretary said. They were at the central office of Fast Fred's Hot Foods.

"We're coming."

Steve and Carlos went into Fred's office and sat down.

"Here's the Benny proposal," Fred said. They're offering twenty-five dollars a share for all of Fast Fred's common stock."

"Let's see it," said Carlos.

Carlos and Steve looked over the document.

"What cards does Benny hold?" Asked Steve.

"I don't know," said Fred. "He wants a list of our stockholders. He says he's going directly to them."

"What can we do?" Asked Carlos

"I have a list of the stockholders here," said Fred.

"How many shares does Benny control?" Asked Steve.

"I don't know," said Fred.

"How many will be on our side?" Asked Carlos.

"We can count on fifteen percent to support us," said Fred. "I'm not sure about the rest."

"That's not enough," Steve said as he looked down the list.

"Some are in brokerage house names," said Fred. "A local broker holds twenty-five percent for the Ocean Spray Investment Company. I don't know who they are. A broker on the east coast holds twenty-five percent. I don't know who owns those shares either. They may be in Benny's

242

pocket. The rest is owned by employees, former employees, and the general public."

"What will we do?" Carlos asked.

"I can submit their proposal to the board at a called meeting," said Fred. "They'll turn it down. Then he'll take it to our annual meeting."

"When would it be voted on?" Asked Steve.

"The stockholders' meeting is on June 4th at seven o'clock," Fred said. "I can't stall it later than that. Meanwhile, we need to get as many proxies as we can, even if it means buy the shares."

X   X   X

"Fast Fred's having a stockholders' meeting on June 4th," George Benny said to Mrs. Kerrick. He had just arrived at the office. "He's sending us a list of his stockholders."

"What are you going to do?" Mrs. Kerrick asked.

"I don't know." He went to his desk and sat down. "Somehow, we're going to turn this to our advantage."

"How?"

"We're going to make our offer public. We're offering twenty-five dollars a share for each and every share of Fast Fred's we can buy. Their stockholders will see things our way."

X   X   X

Angel Crawford Benny hurried from the plane at the Pacific City airport. It was almost dark. Inside the airport, she got her bag.

"Charles Crawford, your name is MUD!" She said to herself.

She took a cab to her hotel. She laughed wickedly as she rode the elevator to her room.

"MUD CRAWFORD!"

The next morning, she took a cab to the office of the Nightingale Detective Agency.

"I'm Angel Benny. I have an appointment."

"We've been expecting you, How can we be of service?"

243

"I want you to find out everything you can about Deborah Clarke Cortez. Everything I know about her is in this file." She handed the file to the detective. "I'm also looking for a Betty Riggioletti. I think she's out here somewhere, but I don't know where. Everything I know about her is in this second file."

"We'll get on this right away."

"Here is your advance." Angel gave him a check. "I know it's on an east-coast bank, but it's good."

"We're not worried."

"My flight leaves in an hour. You can call me at home."

"We'll contact you as soon as we find out something."

THIRTY FOUR

May 1, 1985

"Hey, Mike!"

Mike and Bianca were walking across the Pacific Coast University campus when David approached. He was a friend.

"Do you and Bianca want to earn some extra money?"

"Sure, what's up?"

"They need two people down at the medical genetics lab to serve as controls in an experiment."

"What kind of experiment?"

"It's a genetics experiment. All they want is blood samples and a little information. It's a quick way to make fifty bucks apiece."

"What about it, Bianca?" Mike asked.

"Sure, we could use a hundred bucks."

"Go down to the genetics lab and ask for Chuck Crawford," David said. "He's a research doctor. Tell him I sent you. He'll want to copy your student IDs."

X   X   X

"Dr. Crawford, please."

Mike and Bianca were at the genetics lab.

"I'm Dr. Crawford."

"David sent us to see you," said Mike. "He said you need two people to serve as controls in an experiment. He said you would pay fifty bucks each."

"You'll have to fill out some papers. We'll need a blood sample and some information. I'll need to copy your student Ids."

May 3, 1985

"Hey, David!" Chuck Crawford saw David at the cafeteria. "That couple you sent were bummers. I wanted them unrelated. You screwed up the whole test."

"They are unrelated. They're engaged. Did you see that rock on her hand?"

"The test results show them to be brother and sister."

"Are you sure your technician didn't mix up the blood samples?"

"She hasn't done it before. You get that couple down to the lab for a retest. We're going to find out what happened."

"I'll try."

May 4, 1985

"Hey Mike, can you and Bianca go by the genetics lab?"

David had found them at Fast Fred's.

"What's up?"

"They screwed up the tests at the lab. They need another set of blood samples."

"Do we get another fifty bucks each?"

"I don't think so. Do it as a favor to me. Crawford's hot. He thinks I gave him a bummer. Go as soon as you can. Help me straighten things out with him. He thinks you're brother and sister. They screwed up the samples."

"We'll go now."

May 7, 1985

Chuck Crawford found Mike and Bianca studying at the library.

"What gives with you two? You're supposed to be unrelated!"

"We are," answered Mike.

"Not according to these tests." He showed them the results. "I took the samples myself and ran the tests. They weren't screwed up. The results are the same as the first time. They're what I would expect from a brother and sister. What's going on?"

"We're not brother and sister," said Mike. "We're not even related My father's dead. He's Italian. My mom lives in Ocean Spray. Her folks live here in Pacific City. Her dad's Mexican."

"Look, kids, this is serious business. We got a million-dollar research project involved in the outcome of these tests. Do you have birth certificates?"

"Yes, I do," said Mike.

"Can I see it?"

"It's at home," said Mike. "I can get it for you this week end."

"I can get one," said Bianca, "but I don't know whether my folks have a copy at home. Why don't you try the admissions office? They have the names of our parents."

"I'll do that," Dr. Crawford said. "Meanwhile, you get your birth certificates and bring them to me Monday. I want to make copies."

May 14, 1985

It was Monday morning, and Steve and Deborah came to the lab with Bianca.

"Are you Dr. Crawford," Steve asked.

"Yes, I am."

"I'm Bianca's father. Deborah is her mother." Steve pointed to Deborah. "Our daughter is very upset. Mike is her fiancé, not her brother. They're not related. His father is dead. We know his mother well. There's some mistake."

"I'm Bianca's mother. You look familiar. Have I seen you before?"

"Not that I know of," answered Chuck Crawford. "My test results aren't personal. There's some mistake somewhere. I'm just trying to find it."

"Here's my birth certificate," said Mike. He had just entered the lab. "And here's an official copy of a court order changing my last name to Riggs."

"I see you were born on the east coast," said the doctor. "That's where I grew up."

"So did we," Deborah said as she looked at the birth certificate. "I remember who your father was, Maffi Riggioletti. He was a mobster."

"He was murdered soon after I was born. My mother changed our last name and moved here before I was two years old. She didn't want me to be part of the mob."

"I know that Dr. Crawford, too," Deborah said as she noticed the name of the doctor on Mike's birth certificate.

"You look like him," she said to Chuck Crawford. "He murdered our first baby."

She burst into tears.

"Do you know that Dr. Crawford?" Steve asked. "Are you related?"

"He's my father," said Chuck Crawford. "What happened?"

"We weren't married then," Steve said. "We were in our junior year of high school. Deborah got pregnant. We hid it as long as we could. Her folks were mad when they found out. They didn't want her to marry me. I'm Mexican, and my father is a brick mason. They were high society. They didn't want her to have the baby. They took her to your father. He put her in the hospital, he said to run tests. When she woke up, he had caused her to have a miscarriage. He said the baby didn't have a head. We didn't believe it."

"He murdered our baby!" Deborah sobbed.

"We're not going to go through this any more," said Steve. "Deborah, let's go."

Steve and Deborah turned to go.

"Wait a minute," Chuck Crawford said. "I don't know anything about this. There's something wrong. When did this happen? What year?"

"We left the east coast in June of 1963," said Steve, "a few days after graduating from high school. This was before then, perhaps in July or August of 1962."

"Mike was born in November of 1962," said Chuck Crawford.

"What are you saying?" Steve asked.

248

"I don't know what happened," said Chuck, "but there's too much here to be a coincidence."

"We'd better leave," said Steve. "I'm sorry we came."

"Please, I don't like this matter either," said Chuck. "I'm going home Wednesday for a few days. I'm going to find out. I'll get in touch with you as soon as I get back. I want to get to the bottom of this."

"I wish you would," said Steve.

Deborah continued to cry.

"Let's go, Deb."

May 16, 1985

Syndi was waiting for Chuck at the airport.

"Hi, Syndi, how's Dad?"

"The local medical association honored him at their meeting last week."

"How's the boys?"

"They haven't come home from school yet."

"How are they doing?

"Jason is thinking about medical school. Jeremy is thinking about engineering."

"Heard from Ellen?"

"She and her husband plan to be here tonight with their kids."

They got his baggage and went to Syndi's car.

"I've run into something," Chuck said as they got into her car. "It's puzzling. Maybe you can help me find an answer."

"What is it?" Syndi backed out of the parking place and drove toward an exit. Chuck waited until they were almost out of the airport before continuing.

"Something may have happened the year Dad and Mom got a divorce. You married Dad then. Do you remember a Deborah Clarke and a Betty Riggioletti?"

Syndi drove up the ramp on to the freeway. She did not answer.

Chuck handed her copies of Mike's and Bianca's birth certificates. Syndi glanced at the certificates, and her face became grim.

249

"Betty Riggioletti's son Mike is engaged to marry Deborah's daughter Bianca," said Chuck. "My genetic tests show Mike and Bianca to be brother and sister. There's too much here to be a coincidence."

"What do they say?" Syndi asked.

"According to Deborah's story, she became pregnant when she was a junior in high school. She wasn't married then. She hid her pregnancy as long as she could. Her parents didn't find out until she was in her fifth or sixth month."

Chuck paused momentarily before continuing.

"This was July, 1962, the summer before her senior year. Her folks were mad and didn't want her to have the baby. They didn't like Steve, the baby's father. He was Mexican, and his family didn't have social status."

Chuck waited for a moment, but Syndi did not respond.

"Deborah's parents took her to Dad. He admitted her to the hospital, supposedly for tests. When Deborah woke up, she found out she had miscarried. Dad showed her an x-ray of a baby that didn't have a head and told her it was hers. She thinks her parents paid Dad to get rid of the baby."

Syndi's face was pale.

"Deborah and Steve ran off after their high school graduation in June, 1963, and got married." Chuck continued. "They had Bianca and two more children."

Steve paused again.

"According to birth certificates, Mike Riggioletti was born in November, 1962. Dad delivered him by cesarean. My genetics tests show Mike and Bianca to be brother and sister. The probability of error is less than one percent."

"If he weren't involved," said Syndi, "your father would be proud of you. Does your mother know anything about this?"

"No, she doesn't."

"What else do you know?"

"I told you everything."

"How do they feel about it?"

"The boy refuses to believe it. The girl and her parents are confused and upset."

"I have been bothered about it ever since it happened," Syndi said. "Your mother told your father she'd give him a divorce if he came up with fifty thousand dollars more than what he had offered her. She wouldn't back down. He didn't have the money."

"That must be the fifty thousand mother keeps referring to."

"Deborah's father was John Clarke. You may remember him. He was the Chairman of the Board of Memorial Hospital where all this took place. He threatened to ruin your father if he didn't give Deborah an abortion. Clarke threatened to take Deborah to the butcher shop had your father not done what he did."

"I remember that place," said Chuck. "The authorities finally closed that place down when I was a senior in high school."

"They should have closed it down long before then."

"As I recall," Chuck said, "three or four girls died that year after getting abortions. The operators were sent to prison."

"Betty Riggioletti was carrying an anencephalic baby," Syndi continued. "Her husband was a gangster. He couldn't accept the fact that his baby wasn't going to be normal. He threatened to kill your father if Betty didn't have a normal baby."

"I remember Maffi Riggioletti's funeral," said Chuck. "I think the Clarkes bought his house."

"Lab tests showed Deborah Clarke's baby was compatible with Betty Riggioletti. Your father took the healthy baby from Deborah and used it to replace the abnormal one inside Betty Riggioletti."

"That's a remarkable medical accomplishment."

"He told Deborah the anencephalic baby was hers. He got everything documented to protect himself. He even got Deborah's signature on a consent form. Betty's new baby went to term and was born by Cesarean."

"He did everything but change the baby's genes."

"What's going to happen?" Syndi asked.

"I don't know," Chuck answered. "Did Betty Riggioletti ever know the baby she had wasn't really hers?"

"Your father told her he had to operate on her unborn baby. She didn't know about the switch."

"I don't know how this is going to turn out."

"I think you'd better talk to your father, but let me tell him first."

251

X   X   X

"The official medical records are so old they have probably been discarded." Charles Crawford said to his son. They were sitting in his study. "I kept a private notebook. It tells what happened from a medical perspective."

Charles Crawford got up from his chair. He went to the closet and took down a box from the top shelf.

"Here it is." He handed the notebook to his son. "I have private notes about other interesting cases here, too. I was getting ready to throw them all away. I have no interest in keeping them any more."

Charles Crawford looked at some of the other notebooks momentarily before returning them to the box.

"It's all there. You can look it over, but I want the book left here. It doesn't need to be made public."

"I don't care about the others," said Chuck, "but don't throw this book away, at least until this case is resolved."

"Look it over. If you have any medical questions, I'll try to answer them, but I don't want you to tell your mother anything about this."

"I won't talk to Mom," said Chuck, "but I don't know what to say to Deborah and to Mike."

"Tell them the truth. I'll take the consequences."

THIRTY FIVE

May 21, 1985

"Is everyone here?" Asked Chuck Crawford. "I don't see Bianca. She should be in on this."

They were in the conference room at the genetics lab.

"She's taking an exam," said Steve. "Tell us what you found out."

"I know it wasn't right," Chuck said to Deborah as they sat down at a table. "Your parents decided you were going to have an abortion. If my father didn't do it, they were going to take you to the butcher shop."

Deborah looked at the floor.

"The law closed that place down a few years later. About a third of the girls who had abortions there either died or were permanently injured. Dad knew that, and didn't want that to happen to you. You were at high risk because you were too far along for normal abortion techniques."

"What happened?" Deborah did not look up.

"Once you were under anesthesia, he gave you a shot causing you to have a miscarriage. He took your normal baby and put it inside Betty Riggioletti, exchanging it for hers. Her baby was the one with no head. She carried your baby to term and gave birth to Mike."

"Are you saying I'm Mike's mother?" Deborah looked up at Chuck Crawford seemingly in disbelief.

"Betty Riggioletti was never told about the swap. Her pregnancy had been a troubled one. Dad told her he had to operate on her unborn baby to save its life."

"And he gave her my baby instead," Deborah said.

"I have never heard of anything like this before." Steve stood up.

"I haven't either," said Chuck.

"If I'm Mike's mother, who's going to tell Betty?" Deborah turned to Mike.

"Nobody's going to tell her anything!" Mike stood up. "I don't want her to know anything about this! She has a bad heart. It will kill her! She doesn't have long to live as it is!"

"Am I your mother?" Deborah asked.

"She's my mother! She always will be, I don't care what anybody says."

"I didn't give you away!" Deborah was in tears. "I didn't abandon you! You were stolen from me! I thought they killed you! I'm your mother!"

"NO! YOU'RE NOT!"

"If I can't be your mother, then let me be your aunt! I've got to be something to you!"

"I don't believe this," said Steve. "This must be someone's idea of a cruel joke."

"Let's all calm down," said Chuck Crawford. "We'll never solve things this way."

"Perhaps it would help if we went back to where it happened," said Steve. He was trying to comfort Deborah.

"Mamma told me never to go back there," said Mike. "My father was a gangster. My life would be in danger. I'm going to see our lawyer. I want to find out what my rights are. I don't believe this is happening."

"Perhaps we should see one, too," said Steve. "We need to talk to Bianca."

"I have to go to a seminar this afternoon," said Chuck Crawford. "Let's meet back here tomorrow morning and talk this over. Maybe we can come up with a peaceful resolution. I'm sorry I uncovered this."

"I am, too," said Steve.

X   X   X

Mike went to his mother's attorney that afternoon and explained what had happened.

"I don't care what that doctor says," the lawyer told him. "You were born the son of Maffi and Betty Riggioletti. Your mother had her last name

254

and yours changed to Riggs after your father was killed. Bianca is the daughter of Steve and Deborah Cortez. There are birth certificates to that effect.

The lawyer paused.

"The law is more than biology. There's nothing in the law to prevent you and Bianca from getting married. Even if that doctor is right, he's not going into court to stop you. Your mother gave birth to you. She cared for you during your tender years. Her relationship to you was that of mother and son. No judge is going to deny that."

"I may have to tell Mamma something if Bianca calls off the wedding. She loves Bianca."

"Your mother put everything in your name when you were small. She kept a life estate."

"How much is there?" Mike asked.

"Several million dollars, I'm not sure."

"Mamma told me not to tell people what I'm worth. Money doesn't make a person."

"Does Bianca and her family know about the money?"

"I'm not sure what they know. Mamma didn't discuss our business with other people."

"Do they have money?" The attorney asked.

"I don't think so. Bianca's father works in the main office of Fast Fred's Hot Foods. He's an accountant."

"Do you have any other family? Any cousins? Anybody that might try to claim your mother's money?"

"Not that I know of. It's Mamma and me. After she's gone, I'm alone."

"If you were under age at the time of your mother's death, she wanted Steve and Deborah to be your guardians. It's in her will."

"I didn't know that," Mike said.

"What if they prove to be your biological parents? Wouldn't you be marrying your sister?"

"I don't know." Mike looked down at the floor.

"If this is right, after your mother is gone, would you consider adopting them as your parents? Bianca could be your sister."

"Mamma will always be Mamma. They can't replace her."

"You are of legal age. Nobody can force you to accept them, but think about it. Don't do anything hasty. You don't have to make any decisions now."

"I won't do anything until after Mamma's gone. She's my Mamma. I don't care what anyone says. Nobody can replace her. After she's gone, I feel I want to get as far away from all of this as I can."

X   X   X

That same afternoon, Steve and Deborah went to see Mrs. Lopez at the counseling center, and they told her about their meetings with Chuck Crawford.

"This is a strange twist," the counselor said. "We've talked about the loss of your first baby for many years. Now you are being told he's alive and you've known him since he was in elementary school.

"We would not have made it without the money Betty Riggs paid Deborah for tutoring Mike," Steve said. "I don't think Betty knew any of this."

"She's been the best friend I've ever had." Deborah burst into tears. "But how do I get my son back?"

"You can't force yourself on him," the counselor said. "Mike is of legal age. Even if a court declared you to be his mother, he could choose to have nothing to do with you. How do you want him to feel towards Betty?"

Deborah remembered how she had rejected her parents. She didn't want him to reject her.

"His mother is seriously ill," Mrs. Lopez continued. "She probably won't live long. Perhaps when she's gone, you might have a chance at a relationship with him, but not now."

"What would a court decide?" Asked Steve.

"I don't know, but there's no way you can win by forcing the question."

"Can we prosecute the doctor who did this?" Deborah asked. "He didn't even have the decency to tell us whether it was a boy or a girl. Could I sue him for everything he's worth?"

"You could," said Mrs. Lopez, "but after twenty-two years, it would be a hard case to win. The official medical records have probably been discarded. An opposing attorney can always say you gave your baby away. What would you accomplish if you did win? It won't get your son back. He's not going to renounce the lady who raised him. I don't think

256

this matter is best solved by litigation. It can only be settled by forgiveness."

"But he stole my baby!" Deborah continued to cry.

"What he did may not have been right, but in your heart, you must forgive him. Going to court won't give you satisfaction about what happened back then. It will only intensify your bitterness. It won't get your son back. The publicity might even cause him to reject you. You must learn forgiveness. What about his mother's feelings?"

"But I'm his mother!"

"I mean the mother who raised him," said Mrs. Lopez. "She wasn't part of any conspiracy, was she? She didn't know about this, did she?"

"I don't know," Deborah said. "I don't think she knew about it, but I'm not sure. Somebody should tell her."

"You have felt tremendous anguish from the beginning," said Mrs. Lopez. "Are you willing to inflict that kind of pain on her? It sounds like she's innocent of all wrongdoing. She's been a good mother to him. He's loyal to her. She's been a good friend to you. She's not expected to live long. Why cause her pain and anguish?"

"We were very close. She was almost like a mother to me. I don't know what to do."

"I think he's badly hurt over this, maybe as much as you are. Don't threaten the mother-son relationship between Mike and Betty Riggs. If you do, you'll lose him forever."

"It isn't fair," Deborah said.

"The world isn't fair, honest, or just," Mrs. Lopez said. "Right or wrong, what happened has happened, and there's nothing you can do to change it. You can still have a place in his life, but you must understand his feelings. If you don't, he'll reject you."

Deborah continued to cry. She thought of her broken relationship with her parents. She didn't want that with her son. Steve put his arm around her shoulder.

"What about your daughter? What are her feelings? You don't want to alienate her either?"

"No, we don't," said Steve.

"You had better tell her what happened. Be as kind as you can. Legally, she's not Mike's sister until a court decides that. She can marry him if she chooses. Don't try to force her one way or the other. Let her decide what she wants to do and accept her decision."

"Even if she chooses to marry him?" Deborah asked.

"Even if she chooses to marry him," the counselor said.

"But that wouldn't be right!" Deborah said.

"Maybe it wouldn't," Mrs. Lopez said, "but it would be legal."

"What about the church?" Deborah asked.

"Mike was baptized as Betty Riggioletti's son. She did it in good faith."

"We'd better talk with Bianca," said Steve. "Thank you for your help. We'll be back. We have a lot to work through."

"Call me any time. You have my home phone number, too."

X   X   X

Steve and Deborah found Bianca after her last class that afternoon.

"Bianca," Deborah said, "before you go to work, we need to talk."

"What did you find out?" Bianca could tell her mother had been crying.

"When I was in high school, I had a miscarriage."

"You told me about that a long time ago. Your parents didn't want you to marry Dad."

"There's more to it, something the doctor found out."

"What?"

"They didn't kill my baby. They used it to replace a defective baby inside another woman. She gave birth and raised it as her own. That lady was Betty Riggs. The baby was Mike."

"I'm engaged to my brother?"

"Legally, he isn't your brother," said Steve, "but, yes, he is."

"Legally he's the son of Betty Riggs and her late husband," Steve said. "You can marry him if you wish. We won't try to stop you. But biologically, he's your brother."

"What about Mike?" Bianca said. "I love him."

"We want him as part of the family," Deborah said. "You can still love him as a brother."

"I'm confused. I don't know what to do."

"The church counseling center is open tomorrow if you feel you need to talk with someone," Steve said. "Mrs. Lopez is there."

"Thanks, Dad."

"We've had a difficult day," Steve said. "We'd better go home."

"I work at Fast Fred's tonight," Bianca said. "Mike will be there. I don't know what to say to him."

"I don't know, either," Deborah said. "I still feel somebody needs to tell Betty."

X   X   X

That evening after work Mike and Bianca talked at Fast Fred's.

"I love you, Mike," Bianca said. "But I'm not sure about marrying you if you're my brother. I want us to be close. Please don't be hurt. Try to understand."

"I'll try," said Mike. He put his arm around her and kissed her on her forehead. "I love you. I don't know what's right. I don't want to lose you."

"I love you, Mike," Bianca said. "I don't want to lose you either."

"I've got to go," Mike said. "Mom's back in the hospital. Please don't tell her anything about this. I don't want her to know. It will kill her."

"I won't. I wouldn't hurt Granny for anything."

THIRTY SIX

May 21, 1985

Dr. Stanley Sisson, the seminar speaker, was already at the podium when Chuck Crawford entered the auditorium. Late, Chuck signed his name to the roll and sat down. All interns and residents were required to attend. The others present were junior and senior medical students, professors, and members of the Rey family.

These seminars took up real medical situations. The subject matter was never announced ahead of time and was often determined at the last moment. Chuck usually had little interest in the subjects discussed.

"This afternoon," Dr. Sisson said, "we have a case of identical twin sisters who married brothers about ten years ago. Childless, both sisters were referred to us some three years ago with ovulation difficulties. We treated them with fertility drugs with no improvement. Six months ago, we treated them with an experimental drug, and both became pregnant. Conception was by artificial insemination. The husband's sperm was used in each case. We did both inseminations on the same day."

Chuck Crawford came to attention.

"The first sister is carrying what appears to be a normal baby. Last week, she and her husband were involved in a serious automobile accident. He was killed. She is brain-dead and is being kept alive by a respirator because of the baby. She has shown signs of failing. It is doubtful she will last to term."

Dr. Sisson paused momentarily.

"The second sister has a baby with numerous chromosomal abnormalities. If it survives to term, it cannot live long after birth. This mother may

260

not be able to have more children. She and her husband would be glad to take first couple's baby, but it's not likely to survive a premature birth."

Dr. Sisson continued on with a detailed description of the medical condition of the women patients and their unborn infants. Then the floor was opened for questions and discussion.

Chuck was uneasy as he listened to various interns, residents, and medical students trying to impress their professors with technical questions. Finally, he raised his hand.

"Why don't you take the normal baby out of the brain-dead mother and use it to replace the abnormal baby inside the other mother? Maybe she can carry it to term."

Members of the family came to attention. This was the first positive thing they had heard.

"That's never been done before," Dr. Sisson said. "The babies are far too advanced to be interchanged."

"It has been done before," said Chuck, "and the operation was a success. Here the mothers are identical twins. There should be no incompatibility problem. The babies can be interchanged. The normal baby could go to term inside the living mother and be born normal and healthy."

"Where did you hear of this?" Another professor asked.

"I didn't bring the details," said Chuck, "but if you come to my lab after the seminar, I'll show you what I have, and if you're interested further, I might be able to put you in contact with the doctor who exchanged the babies."

"I am interested," said Dr. Sisson. "If what you say is true, this might save the life of the normal baby. Please stay a few minutes after the meeting."

X   X   X

After the seminar, Dr. Sisson, several interested doctors and residents, and members of the family followed Chuck to his lab. He showed them the test results and birth certificates of Mike Riggs and Bianca Cortez. Many were skeptical. At Dr. Sisson's request, Chuck called his father.

"Dad, this is a conference call. We have an unusual medical situation here. We need to do an exchange similar to the one you did in 1962 with Deborah Clarke and Betty Riggioletti. Dr. Stanley Sisson is here. He's the doctor in charge. Three other doctors from the Medical school obstetrics and gynecology department are here, too. Members of the family are also present."

"What are the details?"

Dr. Sisson explained the medical situation. Charles Crawford asked questions, and Dr. Sisson answered them.

"It's risky, at best," Dr. Sisson said. "I don't think I can do it."

"Dr. Crawford," Mrs. Rodriguez interrupted. "We don't understand all this medical talk. I'm the mother of the twin sisters. Please help us. It may be my only chance to have a grandchild. We'll pay you somehow."

"I'm Don Rey, the father of the defective baby. Please come out here. Please save my brother's baby. My wife and I want it."

"I don't know if I can," said Charles Crawford. "It's not a matter of money. I wouldn't charge a fee. I'm retired, and my health is not good. My physicians' license is still active, but my last surgery was three years ago. I would have to be invited by the medical school, and I would have to have help. I'm sure there are good physicians out there who could do it."

"Please, Dr. Sisson," Don Rey said. "If you can't do the operation, invite him to come out here and do it."

"We will have to meet with the rest of the department tomorrow and discuss this," Dr. Sisson said. "The Dean of the College of Medicine would have to approve it."

"I don't have to be the one that does the operation," Dr. Crawford said. "I'll be glad to assist in any way I can. I would rather have a younger person do it."

"We need to talk about this," said Dr. Sisson. "We will call you back tomorrow. Thank you for helping us in this matter."

"There is another matter," Chuck Crawford said after Dr. Sisson had hung up the phone. "What about Steve and Deborah Cortez? Can they stop Dad from helping in the operation?"

"They can't stop us from doing the operation," Dr. Sisson said, "but they might try to stop him from coming out here to help us. We need to talk to them. Try to get them here tomorrow morning, if you can. The earlier the better."

X   X   X

In her apartment, Angel answered the telephone on the first ring.

262

"Mrs. Benny, this is Carmita from the Nightingale Detective Agency in Pacific City. We have a big file of information on Deborah Clarke Cortez. Do you want us to mail it to you?"

"What about Betty Riggioletti? Any luck?"

"We think so, but we're not sure. A lady named Betty Riggs fits that description very well. We found her because she's Deborah Cortez's close friend. Betty Riggs is in the hospital now suffering from a heart condition. She's not expected to live very long. Deborah Cortez is her frequent visitor."

"I have some business to tend to today. I'll catch a flight tomorrow afternoon and come out there to see what you have."

"We'll stay open for you."

May 22, 1985

Mrs. Rodriguez and several of her family were at Chuck Crawford's conference room when Steve and Deborah arrived the next morning. Dr. Sisson joined them.

"Mr. and Mrs. Cortez? I'm Mrs. Rodriguez. We're the family Dr. Sisson talked about last night."

"Where's Mike?" Deborah asked.

"I don't know," said Chuck Crawford. "We tried to call him last night, but he wasn't home. Maybe he was with his mother."

In tears, Mrs. Rodriguez told Deborah and Steve about her twin daughters and their babies.

"Please help us," Mrs. Rodriguez sobbed. "Please don't do anything to Dr. Crawford. Please let him come here and operate on my daughters. Please let him save my grandbaby's life. It may be my only chance to have a grandchild."

"I don't know. I've been trying to forgive him." Tears came to Deborah's eyes. "I don't know if I can. He stole my baby!"

"Can we talk to the doctor about this?" Steve asked. "Who is he?"

"Dr. Sisson." Mrs. Rodriguez pointed to him. "There's no other way."

"I don't know what to do." Deborah was in tears. "I wasn't expecting this."

"I wasn't either," said Chuck. "This case came up at my seminar yesterday afternoon."

"Do you want to talk with Mrs. Lopez?" Steve asked Deborah.

"That would help." Deborah was still crying. "Dr. Crawford told me our baby didn't have a head. He stole my baby. He gave my baby to someone else. I don't know if I can ever forgive him. Mrs. Lopez says I must try."

"I'm going to call Mrs. Lopez and see if she can see us," Steve said.

"Tell her it's important," said Deborah.

"We need to resolve this before you visit Betty tomorrow morning," Steve said. "I don't think you should tell Betty anything about this."

"But she needs to know."

X   X   X

"Dad," Chuck Crawford said when he called his father about noon. "The department met this morning but did not reach a decision. They want you to come out here and meet with them. They also want you to bring your notebook. They will pay your expenses. I can get you a flight leaving in a few hours. Can you come?"

"Do they know I have cancer?"

"No, they don't."

"Don't tell them. I'll come if Syndi will come with me. I'd still prefer someone else do the actual operation. Don't say anything about this to your mother."

"I won't."

X   X   X

Charles and Syndi Crawford entered the airport terminal at six forty-five that evening, east coast time, and went to the ticket counter of Coast-to-Coast Airlines.

"We're the Crawfords. We should have reservations for your seven o'clock flight."

"Your tickets are here. Your flight is boarding at Gate H-7."

They checked their luggage and went to Gate H-7. They presented their tickets and boarded the aircraft. They started down the aisle of the plane to find their seats.

"Hello, Charles." Angel was sitting in an aisle seat near the front of the plane. "What a surprise. Where are you going?"

264

"Angel!" Charles was stunned. He paused momentarily. "We're on a vacation. What are you up to this time?"

"I'm going to find out where you got that fifty thousand."

Charles didn't answer. He and Syndi continued on to their seats.

"I wonder who he's going to see?" Angel said to herself. "Something tells me this is going to be a very interesting trip."

May 23, 1985

Deborah went to University Hospital the next morning. She took the elevator up to the cardiac care floor.

"I don't care what anyone else says, Betty needs to know." She said to herself.

Deborah got out of the elevator and went to the nurses' station.

"How am I going to tell her?"

She waited until a nurse came.

"How is Mrs. Riggs?" She asked. "Can she have visitors?"

"Don't stay too long. She's resting."

"Mike was my baby," Deborah said to herself as she went down the hall to Betty's private room. "They stole him from me. How can I tell her without hurting her. She did no wrong, but she needs to know."

X   X   X

Angel entered University Hospital through the emergency room exit. She took an elevator to the cardiac care unit. She moved briskly down the hall, and she saw Deborah entering Betty's room.

"Wonder who that is?" Angel asked herself. "I'm going to find out."

Deborah was almost in tears as she sat down.

"Hi," Betty said. "Is something wrong?"

Angel opened the door and entered the room.

"Deborah Clarke?"

Deborah turned around to see who had called her name.

"No, I'm Deborah Cortez."

265

"It's all the same. I was told you might be here. I have been trying to find you both for several years. It's strange that I find you here together."

"Who are you?" Deborah asked.

"I'm Angel Crawford Benny." She smiled wickedly.

"Dr. Charles Crawford's wife," said Betty.

"His ex-wife."

"What do you want?" Deborah was alarmed.

"How much did your parents sell your baby for?" Angel said to Deborah.

"Sell my baby?"

"Your parents sold your son to the Riggiolettis. My ex-husband forged the birth certificate. I want to know the details."

"I didn't sell any of my babies," Deborah said. "My parents didn't sell any of my babies either. You're crazy!"

"If you didn't sell him, he must have been stolen from you. Charles Crawford must have sold him to the Riggiolettis then. That's where he got the fifty thousand. This is your chance to get even. I want to know the details."

"I gave birth to my son," Betty said. She was disturbed. "He was not bought! He was mine! His birth certificate wasn't forged!"

"HE'S BETTY'S BABY!" Deborah burst into tears. "SHE DEDICATED HER LIFE TO HIM! GET OUT OF HERE!"

"YOU BITCH!" Angel shouted.

"Are you all right?" Betty asked Deborah.

"I'm fine." Still crying, Deborah rang for a nurse.

"Yes," Someone at the nurses' station answered.

"I'm Deborah Cortez in Betty Riggs's room. The doctor ordered her visitors be limited and be quiet. There is a woman here trying to start trouble. Mrs. Riggs doesn't need this, and neither do I. Please get her out of here."

"We're on our way."

"I'LL GET BOTH OF YOU FOR THIS!" Angel hurried out the door as the nurses came.

"Mike's my son." Betty was upset. "We didn't buy him. I gave birth to him. Dr. Crawford saved him for me. I won't do anything to help her disgrace Dr. Crawford."

"Don't pay any attention to her." Deborah was stunned by Betty's defense of Charles Crawford. She looked away as she sat down. "His ex-wife doesn't know what she's talking about."

"The doctor told me I have a weak heart," said Betty. "I won't live long."

"Make the best of the time you have left," said Deborah. She had tears in her eyes. "That's all you can do. None of us live forever."

"I'm glad Mike is marrying Bianca," Betty said. "He couldn't have made a better choice. I don't want them to put off the wedding because of my health."

"Don't worry about Mike," said Deborah. "We'll look after him."

A nurse appeared in the doorway. "We saw her leave."

"What happens if she comes back?" Deborah asked.

"We'll be watching for her."

May 24, 1985

In the wee hours of the morning, Angel returned to University Hospital. She paid the taxi driver and went inside. Dressed as a nurse, she moved unnoticed through the emergency room entrance into the main hallway. Holding her purse, she took an elevator to the cardiac care unit.

As Angel hurried by the nurses' station, a nurse looked up.

"That lady doesn't belong here," she whispered to her two companions. "She's not a nurse. Nurses don't carry purses while on duty. Let's see what she's up to."

Intent on her purpose, Angel did not see the three nurses following her as she entered Betty Riggs's room. She smiled as she put her purse down on the cart next to the bed. Betty Riggs was asleep.

Moving quickly, Angel took a disposable syringe out of its plastic wrapping. Hurriedly, she filled it from the vial she took from her purse. Then she injected it into a vein in Betty's arm.

The three nurses burst into the room. "Grab her!" One said as they saw Angel withdrawing the syringe from Betty's arm. In the brief struggle, Angel dropped the syringe. She grabbed her purse and ran out of the room. Two of the nurses were after her. The third called for the doctor on duty. Then she called security.

It was too late. Still asleep, Betty Riggs had a massive heart attack and was dead by the time the doctor arrived.

267

Three security officers saw Angel as she was trying to leave by the main entrance. The two cardiac care nurses were in hot pursuit.

Angel tried to hurry by the guards, but one of them grabbed her arm.

"LET GO OF ME!"

"No, you don't," he said as she tried to get away.

They took Angel into custody and held her until the third cardiac care nurse could come by.

"There's no mistake," they all said. "That's her!"

Then, against Angel's protest, the security officers called the police.

X   X   X

"Is that offer ready?" George Benny asked Mrs. Kerrick. They were in Benny's business office. He was going directly to Fast Fred's shareholders with a second mailing.

"Here it is. I have proofed it. Do you want any more changes?"

George read it again. "No, I'll take it to the printer now. It will be mailed out tonight."

"How many shares will it get?" Mrs. Kerrick asked. "The last offer didn't get us much."

"I don't know. I called Clarke's lawyer to see if I could get his support. He was out and hasn't returned my call. The Clarke Trust owns twenty-five percent of Fast Fred's. It would be a big boost if we could get those shares."

"What about the Ocean Spray Investment Company?" Mrs. Kerrick asked. "All we have is a post office box address."

"I don't know who to call," said George. "I might ask Morrison to do what he can. He managed Benny's there for years. He knows the territory. Maybe they'll answer this letter."

"Have you heard the news?" Mrs. Kerrick asked.

"What news?"

"Your step-mother has been arrested for murder."

"Murder?"

"Last night, they caught her injecting some kind of poison into a heart patient at University Hospital. The morning news is about to come on." Mrs. Kerrick got up from her desk and turned on the television.

268

George watched attentively as a news commentator reported the story.

"The George Benny murder case is about to be reopened," George said. "If I have my way, they'll strap Angel in the electric chair, and they'll let ME throw the switch."

"Why did she do this?" Mrs. Kerrick asked.

"Who knows," answered George. "We can't let her stupidity slow us down. I'm off to the printers. This needs to be mailed out tonight. I'll call Mr. Shyes after I get back from the printer's."

THIRTY SEVEN

May 24, 1985

"It's time for your medicine, Mrs. Clarke. You're overdue. You didn't take your pills at breakfast." They were in the kitchen of the Clarke home. The nurse had two pills and a glass of water in her hands.

"Let me have them," Victoria Clarke said. She pretended to put the pills in her mouth, and then she drank the water.

"I'll watch TV," she said as she set the glass down. She went into the living room and turned on the TV. Then she went into the bathroom. Mumbling to herself, she dropped the pills into the toilet and flushed it. "I don't need this stuff!"

She went back into the living room and turned off the TV. "Garbage!"

She entered the hallway and paused momentarily in front of the hall closet.

"Deborah's coming home! I know she is!"

"You need to rest," the nurse said from the kitchen. "You'd better lie down."

"NO! I'm going to get Deborah and bring her home!"

Victoria opened the closet to get a coat. Not finding one, she starred into the closet. As if by instinct, she opened the secret compartment.

She saw the thirty-eight special and the box of bullets she had hidden there several years earlier and picked up the gun.

"I'm going to get Deborah!" Victoria closed the closet door. "You are not going to stop me!"

The nurse came into the hallway and saw Victoria with the gun.

"VICKY! PUT DOWN THAT GUN!"

"I'M NOT VICKY! I'M VICTORIA! I'm going to kill Steven! Deborah's coming home!"

"Put down that gun!" The nurse took a few steps toward Mrs. Clarke.

"Steven's the cause of the trouble. I have Mexican grandchildren. He has poisoned them against me. They're growing up Catholic. They're going to school with Mexicans, Asians, and who knows what other trash. I hate him! Don't come near me! Deborah's coming home! I'm going to get her."

"Put down that gun!" The nurse took a few more steps toward her.

Victoria suddenly pointed the gun at the nurse. "I'll kill Steven!"

The nurse retreated to the kitchen.

Victoria squeezed the trigger. The hammer hit the empty first chamber. "Click"

"Your gun's empty," said the nurse. "Put it down." She started toward Mrs. Clarke. "Put down that gun! It's not loaded!"

"STAY AWAY FROM ME!"

Victoria waved the gun in the air. Her eyes glared with hatred. Out of control, she carelessly pointed the gun toward the side of her head and pulled the trigger.

The hammer hit the loaded second chamber, and the gun fired. Victoria Clarke fell to the floor. There was a large hole in front of her ear, and blood was oozing out.

"There's nothing I can do for her." The nurse was still shaking. She went to the phone and called Bill Hamilton's office.

"Mrs. Clarke found a gun and went into a rage. She shot herself in the head. She's dead."

"Was it suicide?" Bill Hamilton asked.

"No, it was accidental," said the nurse. "She was going to shoot me or Steven, I'm not sure which. She was delirious."

"Did you try to take the gun away from her? Did you grab for it?"

"No, I was about ten feet away. I never touched the gun. Call an ambulance and the police. I'll be here to let them in."

X   X   X

"You gave a good medical presentation," Dr. Sisson said to Dr. Charles Crawford.

He was meeting with the doctors in the medical school obstetrics and gynecology department and with Dr. Bernard Benz, the Dean of the College of Medicine.

"I still don't believe he did it," one of the doctors said. "Even if he did, what about the ethics question?"

"I don't like this," said another. "It sounds phony. I don't want any part of it."

"There's some good in the worst of us," said Dean Benz, "and some bad in the best of us. None of us are without stain. I have known Charles Crawford for many years. He's a good physician, and I believe him. The question is whether we are going to try to save the life of the Rey baby. We don't have to be concerned about the ethics of what happened some twenty years ago. If we do the exchange, who wants to be the chief surgeon?"

No one volunteered.

"We can make medical history here," the Dean said as he turned to Dr. Sisson. "What do you want to do?"

"I think we should do it," said Dr. Sisson. "We have nothing to lose. Dr. Crawford is the logical person to direct the exchange. He's done one before. I'll be Chief Surgeon if he'll help."

"What about Mr. and Mrs. Cortez?" A third physician asked. "Can we get them to agree not to prosecute or take civil action against us."

"I don't like it," said a fourth doctor. "Count me out,"

"The surgery's risky," said Dr. Crawford. "I don't want to do it by myself."

"You've done it before," said Dr. Sisson. "I'll head the team if you'll help."

"What about the ethics question?" A fifth doctor asked. "I don't believe he did all of this."

"There's no ethics question in the Rey case," said Dean Benz.

"What about on the east coast?"

"His presentation was oral," the dean said. "There's no formal transcript of what he said."

"But if he does it here," the doctor said," that's proof he could have done it then. Will we be drawn into a fight?"

"It's not an ethics question here," said Dr. Sisson. "We have the family's permission. We've got a baby's life to save."

"We talked with Mr. and Mrs. Cortez this morning," said Dean Benz. "We explained the situation, and the family talked to them. Mrs. Cortez is very upset, but they won't try to stop Dr. Crawford from participating in the operation. They were stunned by the murder."

"So am I," Charles Crawford said. "What about my ex-wife? Is she any threat?"

"The Assistant District Attorney in charge of the case thinks she's criminally insane," said Dean Benz. "The drug she used has been identified as the same one that was involved in the death of her second husband, George Benny. The vial found in her purse is the one stolen from Memorial Hospital in November of 1981. She will be charged with the murder of her second husband, too."

"When can we do the exchange?" Dr. Sisson asked.

"We can schedule it for Tuesday at seven in the evening," said Dean Benz.

"Betty Rigg's funeral is tomorrow morning. Syndi and I would like to attend it. They should be finished with the autopsy today."

"No one has a problem with you attending the funeral," Dean Benz said.

"We need to plan what we are going to do," said Charles Crawford. "I want Syndi to assist me. She's a registered nurse specialized in obstetrics and gynecology."

"We can do the planning tomorrow afternoon," Dean Benz said. "Those who want to participate, please stay. Those who don't can leave."

X   X   X

Mike got out of his car at his home in Ocean Spray. He had mail from the post office box in his hand. Once inside, he turned on the living room lights. He laid the mail to the unopened mail stacked on the kitchen table. Mike did not notice the envelope from Benny's addressed to the Ocean Spray Investment Company.

"I'll look at it all later."

Mike picked up the phone and called Fast Fred's central office.

"Carlos," Mike said, "this is Mike Riggs."

"I'm sorry about your mother," Carlos said. "Is there anything we can do?"

"Mother had everything taken care of beforehand," answered Mike. "There's nothing for me to do but be at her funeral. It's tomorrow."

"You're off on leave," Carlos said. "Fred made Chico night manager at the University Fred's until you're back."

"That's what I called about," Mike said. "I have two more weeks of leave after this one. I'm resigning effective when my leave time runs out. I won't be back. I'll send a written resignation letter in a day or so. I'm not mad at Fast Fred's. You won't have a hard time filling my position."

"I'm sorry to hear that," said Carlos.

"You people have been great, but Mamma's dead. My marriage is off. There's nothing here for me. I just want to sell out and start over somewhere else, some place where nobody knows who I am."

"Where are you going?"

"I don't know."

After the telephone call, Carlos found Steve at his desk.

"Bad news."

"What is it?" Steve asked.

"Mike Riggs called. He's resigning. He said he wants to go somewhere else and start all over."

"Where was he when he called?" Steve asked.

"He didn't say."

X   X   X

"Have you talked to Mike?" Steve asked Deborah that evening after dinner.

"Bianca's tried to talk with him," said Deborah, "but he won't talk with anybody, not even her."

"Betty's funeral is tomorrow. Have all the arrangements been made?"

"Betty took care of that several years ago," Deborah answered. "Mike's in no condition to make such decisions now."

"Will she be buried here?" Steve asked.

"She'll be buried beside her husband back east, but there won't be a graveside service."

"Will Mike go back there for the burial?"

"No," Deborah said. "Betty was emphatic about that. He is never to go there. The mob might try to kill him if he did. They might think he's coming back to claim his father's underworld empire."

"Did she know about Mike being our son?"

"She never knew," said Deborah. "I just couldn't tell her."

"I'm glad about that," said Steve. "Let's get the dishes done. Tomorrow will be a hard day."

THIRTY EIGHT

May 28, 1985

"The repair shop called." Deborah handed Steve her notepad. "The car is ready. The repairs were major. This is the amount of the bill."

Supper was finished, and Juan and Juanita were in their rooms doing homework. Bianca was working at Fast Fred's.

"I don't know what we're going to do," Steve said as he looked at the amount of the bill. "We'll have to pay it to get the car back. Somebody's not going to get paid this month. We don't have enough to pay everything."

"How much are we short?"

"About the amount of our house payment. If we could miss it, we could pay the others and get by."

"We've never missed a house payment before." Deborah was concerned.

"We've always managed to pay our bills each month," said Steve. "I'll have to go to the bank and see what I can work out. It won't be pleasant."

"Steve, someone's at the door."

"I'll get it."

Steve went to the door and opened it. There was an older man wearing a suit and tie standing on the front porch.

"Yes," said Steve.

"Steve and Deborah Cortez?"

"Yes."

"I'm Bill Hamilton, John Clarke's attorney from the east coast. Deborah's mother is dead. May I come inside?"

"Deborah, you had better come." With some hesitation, Steve invited Mr. Hamilton inside.

"Deborah, your mother accidentally killed herself last week."

"Who are you?" Deborah asked.

"I'm Bill Hamilton, your father's attorney from the east coast. I know you had differences with your parents, but they're both gone now. Your father had everything put into a trust. Your mother got the income as long as she lived. Once her affairs are settled and funeral expenses are paid, it all goes to you. May I sit down? I have some things to show you."

"Sure," said Steve. He was somewhat relieved.

Bill Hamilton sat down and opened his briefcase.

"I'm not sure I want it," Deborah said. "What strings are attached?"

"There are no strings." The attorney paused.

"We don't need their help," said Deborah.

"Yes, they have made mistakes," said Mr. Hamilton, "but they have helped you in ways you don't know about. That was the only way your father could show he still loved you."

"What do you mean?" Said Steve.

"When you got your house mortgage, it was quickly approved because John Clarke guaranteed the loan. You got the lowest interest rate the bank offered." The attorney handed Steve a copy of the guarantee.

"I was surprised at how fast it was approved," said Steve. He looked at the document. "I didn't think we'd get it."

"Once the mortgage was issued," Mr. Hamilton continued, "John Clarke bought it. The bank only serviced your loan. If you made a payment this month, it will be returned. The mortgage has been cancelled."

Mr. Hamilton handed Steve the cancelled mortgage papers.

"The mortgage release is being recorded now."

"We haven't made the payment yet." Steve looked at the attorney almost in disbelief.

"Your father helped you with your children's education. He was the Bishop's Discretionary Fund."

"I don't know," Deborah hesitated.

"If you don't accept your inheritance, it will be held in trust for your children."

"I'm sure she'll take it," Steve said. He turned to Deborah. "You deserve it for what you've been through. Juan and Juanita are still in St. Benedict's. We'll need the money to pay tuition and for their college. We don't want them to go through college the way we did."

"I don't want to keep that house!" Deborah was stunned. "Three or four generations of gangsters lived in it. No telling how many people were murdered there. Some may have been buried in the basement or even be hidden in the walls. I never want to live there. I don't want to move back to the east coast." She was in tears.

"We have a generous offer for the house from people who think it's perfect for a small museum," the attorney said.

"They can have it," said Deborah. "I don't want it!"

"The trust will sell it for you," Bill Hamilton said. "Among other things, the Trust holds stock in two fast-food chains out here. Your husband works at one of them"

"Huh!" Steve came to attention.

"You own twenty-five percent of Fast Fred's Hot Foods and twenty-five percent of Benny's Fast Foods. The Benny's people have asked to buy their stock back. They also want to buy the Fast Fred's stock. Your father didn't want us to sell anything without your approval. What do you want us to do?"

"Do they know who is getting the stock?" Steve asked.

"They know it's going to the Clarke daughter, but they do not know who she is or where she lives."

"The Fast Fred's stock is not for sale at any price," said Steve. "The Benny's stock isn't for sale either. Don't tell them anything! Benny's is trying to buy us out!"

"We have to hold the trust together until your mother's affairs are settled. That could take up to a year, but we will forward the income."

Deborah burst into tears. "I don't want to be rich again!" She went to her room crying.

Hearing their mother, Juan and Juanita came out of their rooms to see what was happening.

"I know it's a shock to her." The attorney took a manila envelope out of his briefcase and handed it to Steve as he got up to leave. "Here is a copy of the trust inventory and other legal papers. It includes copies of the death certificates. A check representing a partial distribution of this year's income is in the envelope, too."

"Thank you very much," Steve said. "She'll accept the inheritance."

"I'm sorry to come unannounced, but it was the only way I could be sure you'd see me. Here is my card. If you have questions, please call. We'll talk again soon. I want us to be on friendly terms."

"So do I," said Steve.

"When John Clarke set up the Trust, he made it plain, he was not concerned about you being Mexican. That's not a factor."

After Mr. Hamilton left, Steve went to their bedroom. Deborah was crying.

"Steve, I don't want the money! I didn't know the Bishop's Discretionary Fund was their money or we wouldn't have taken it. I didn't know they got our mortgage for us or we wouldn't have taken it. I want to pay all that money back!"

"We can't do that!" Steve said. "Fast Fred's doesn't pay that much. Let's talk this over."

"I don't want to live that way!" Deborah sobbed. "I don't want to be rich! None of our friends are rich! I don't want to live in a mansion! I HATE COUNTRY CLUBS! I don't want to be like my parents were! I don't want my children to grow up snobs! I can't take it any more of this!"

"We don't have to live that way," Steve pleaded.

"THIS IS ALL TOO MUCH!" Deborah screamed. "The Mike situation, Betty's being murdered, and now this! I can't handle it!"

"Do you want to talk to Mrs. Lopez?"

"I don't know! I can't take any more of this! I don't want to be like my parents!"

"I'm going to call Mrs. Lopez. It's an emergency. I'm taking you to the counseling center. Juan, you and Juanita will be ok by yourselves. Bianca will be home from work soon."

Charles Crawford was uneasy as Dr. Sisson and Chuck escorted him to the OB-GYN operating room. Syndi was there waiting in the hallway.

"The brain-dead patient is fading," said Dr. Sisson. "She isn't going to last more than a day or two, even on the respirator."

"Everything's ready," Syndi said as they entered the room.

The two sisters were on opposite sides of the room, one on the respirator, and the other, Susan Rey, under anesthesia. As planned, two surgeons had already begun the respective operations. In each case, the body wall and the womb had been opened. The baby was exposed inside its amniotic sac.

Dr. Crawford moved to the side of the brain-dead sister with Dr. Sisson.

"Her heartbeat is irregular," Dr. Sisson said. "Time is of the essence."

"Draw out most of the amniotic fluid," Dr. Crawford said to a nurse. "Save it in those sterile bottles on the counter. We may need it."

The nurse drew out the out most of the fluid with a large syringe.

"I'm going to cut the membrane," he said to a second nurse. "Hold the edges off of the baby with your fingers."

"I'm ready." She wore sterile plastic gloves.

Charles Crawford's hands trembles as he cut the amniotic membrane. As he paused to regain his composure, Dr. Sisson placed two clamps on the umbilical cord about six inches apart, but he didn't tighten them. Then they moved to Susan, the one with the abnormal baby.

"Draw out most of the fluid," Charles Crawford repeated. "Save it in those sterile bottles."

The first nurse drew out the fluid as she did with the other sister.

"Hold the edges apart," he said to a third nurse. "We don't want them to stick to each other." He handed the scalpel to Dr. Sisson. "You saw how it was done."

"I'm ready," the nurse said.

Dr. Sisson slit the membrane and clamped the umbilical cord.

"Watch out for the blood vessels!" Charles Crawford said.

The nurse's fingers held the edges apart.

Leaving the clamped umbilical stub inside the amniotic sac, Dr. Sisson cut the baby free and lifted it out.

"A defective baby boy. There's no way he can survive," he said as he handed the baby to a nurse. She put the baby into a jar of preservative for later examination.

The two doctors hurried to the first sister.

"Her heartbeat is more erratic," said a resident who had been watching her. "She's fading."

Charles Crawford lifted her baby out handed it to Syndi. He tightened the clamps, cutting off the circulation. Then Dr. Sisson cut the cord about halfway between the clamps.

"Get those plastic tubes," Charles Crawford said to the nurse, pointing to a sterile package on the cart. "This is the most critical part!"

The doctors and Syndi hurried with the baby to Susan Rey's side. Charles Crawford inserted one tube halfway into the baby's umbilical artery and another halfway into the vein.

"The fluid still inside the membranes should keep them from sticking to the fetus," he said as Dr. Sisson put the baby inside Susan's amniotic sac.

Dr. Sisson connected each tube in the baby's cord to its corresponding blood vessel in the umbilical stub. He stitched the ends of each vessel together tightly around its tube. Then he removed the clamps and paused momentarily to observe.

"Blood flow has been re-established," Charles Crawford said. "The fetus didn't start using his lungs. His heart's still beating normally. Let's hope he wasn't deprived of oxygen long enough to cause damage to the brain."

Dr. Sisson attached the cord ends together with stitches.

"Now add more amniotic fluid," Charles Crawford said.

"The second nurse injected more fluid.

"That's enough," Charles Crawford said. "Now let's overlap the cut edges of the amniotic membrane. They'll stick together."

He applied an adhesive, and then he overlapped and stitched the edges together as the first nurse held them in place. He pressed them together to seal them tight.

"That should hold. Add more fluid."

"Using a syringe, the second nurse finished filling the amniotic cavity with fluid.

Then Charles Crawford gave a sigh of relief. "So far, the membranes aren't leaking."

He stepped aside, and Dr. Sisson closed up the uterus and the body wall of the healthy sister.

"The surgery's done," he said as he turned to the donor sister.

"She's gone," the resident said. "Her heart stopped beating just after you removed her baby."

X   X   X

"Everything's gone well so far," Charles Crawford said to Mrs. Rodriguez. They were standing outside the operating room. "Susan has a good chance of carrying the baby to term. Chances are good it will be a normal C-section delivery and a normal baby boy."

"Thank you, doctor." She was in tears.

"It's not over yet. I'll spend the rest of the night in the doctor's lounge with Syndi. A nurse will be in Susan's room all night watching her. Dr. Sisson will check on her every two hours. The whole staff will be here at the hospital in case she needs us. She could still lose the baby."

"We don't know how to thank you, doctor," Mrs. Rodriguez said. "You know we don't have the money to pay for this."

"I'm not charging a fee," said Charles Crawford.

"No one else is either," said Dr. Sisson.

"Hi, Charles," Dean Barney Benz came up to him in the hallway. "We have all this on film. You have just made medical history."

"Thank you, Barney," Charles said, "but it's not over yet."

"Congratulations, Dad," Chuck Crawford said. "There are two ladies here to see you."

In tears, Deborah came up to Charles Crawford and put her arms around him.

"I'm Deborah Clarke Cortez. This is my daughter Bianca. We watched you through the window."

"I'm very sorry for the hurt you must have felt over the years. I have thought of you and Mike often."

"Thank you. What you did may not have been right, but if you hadn't done it, things would have been worse. My parents would have taken me to the butcher shop. Mike would have been killed, and I might have been, too. You are forgiven."

"Thank you."

"If you hadn't done what you did then, this baby wouldn't have been saved today."

"It's not over yet. We could still lose it. I hope things work out for you and Mike."

"Where's Mike?" Deborah asked Bianca. "I'm worried."

"I'm worried, too, Mamma, He told me he would be here. I don't know where he is."

THIRTY NINE

May 30, 1985

Charles Crawford and Syndi were at the airport the next morning waiting for their flight home. Dean Benz, Dr. Sisson, Chuck Crawford, Steve, Deborah, and Bianca were with them.

"Have you heard anything more about Angel?" Steve asked.

"I called my attorney back east this morning," said Charles. "He said the DA's office there had re-opened the investigation of George Benny's murder. This time, they feel they have enough evidence for a conviction. They're trying to get her back there for a trial."

"I talked with the district attorney here," said Chuck. "He said that, between the two murder charges, she'll probably be in prison for the rest of her life."

"I hope things go well for you and Mike," Charles Crawford said to Steve and Deborah. "Did you find him yesterday?"

"No," said Deborah. "We don't know where he is. He has finished his final exams for the semester. He'll graduate next week."

"He took Betty's death hard," said Steve. "They were devoted to each other."

"Did he say what his plans were after graduation?" Charles Crawford asked.

"Because of Betty," Deborah said, "he had planned to stay at Fast Fred's. He was a night manager at the University Fred's. He wanted to be with her to the end."

"What happens now that she's gone?" Charles Crawford asked

"He told Carlos he wanted to sell out and get a new start somewhere else," said Steve.

"There's something else," said Deborah. "I haven't told anyone, not even Steve. Mrs. Lopez sent me by the doctor's office yesterday afternoon. I'm expecting another baby."

"Congratulations," said Charles Crawford. "It's a pleasant surprise."

X   X   X

"We own twenty-eight percent of Fast Fred's stock," George Benny told Mrs. Kerrick. They were in Benny's Fast Foods central office. "Those damn Mexicans think they got a bargain."

"That's not enough," said Mrs. Kerrick. "We need over fifty percent."

"There are two large blocks of stock out there," said George, "one owned by the Clarke Trust and the other by the Ocean Spray Investment Company. If we get either one, we win."

"What happens if we don't?" Asked Mrs. Kerrick.

"If neither block votes, we still win. Get Fred Gonzales on the phone."

Mrs. Kerrick placed the call.

"Fred, this is George Benny. It's in the bag. I've got enough stock to win. Why don't you make it simple?"

"How's that?"

"Just get your board to accept our offer. Tell them it's over. The best thing they can do for your stockholders is to avoid a fight."

"I'll fight you to the end," Fred said.

"It didn't work," George said to Mrs. Kerrick after he had hung up the phone. "Get Bill Hamilton on the phone. Here is his number."

"Bill, this is George Benny. I sent you the offer we're making for Fast Fred's stock. We need your support. I'm counting on you. It's a great deal for your client."

"I read your offer," said Bill Hamilton. "I also have a letter from Fast Fred's. I sent it all to the Clarke daughter. I signed the proxy over to her. She can vote it whatever way she wants."

"I need her address," said George. "I want to talk to her."

"I told her you wanted to buy both the Benny's and Fast Fred's stock She doesn't want to talk to you. Send everything to me. I'll forward it to her. That's the way she wants it."

"We don't have the time, Bill. The stockholders' meeting is June 4th."

"I have done all I can," said Bill Hamilton.

"I don't know what the story is there," George said to Mrs. Kerrick after he had hung up the phone. "I thought I had Hamilton's support. The Clarke daughter's a loose canon. Get Morrison for me. We'll see what he can find out about the Ocean Spray Investment Company."

X   X   X

Steve and Deborah arrived home from the airport. Steve got the mail and followed Deborah into the house.

"Here's a large envelope from the lawyer," Steve said.

"Which lawyer?" Deborah asked.

"Hamilton."

"I'm not sure I want to see it."

Steve opened it and looked through the material. "He sent Benny's offer to buy your Fast Fred's stock and a blank proxy. We'll need the proxy at the annual meeting. You need to sign it. There's other material here from Fast Fred's."

"We've taken too much of that money already." Deborah burst into tears. "I don't want to be rich again. I don't want the stock. I won't sign any proxy."

She went to her room crying.

Steve followed her. "But we need that proxy to keep Benny's from taking over Fast Fred's!"

"I don't want the stock! I don't want the money!"

"Let's talk this over," said Steve. "If Benny's wins, I lose my job!

"I can't take it any more! It's too much! This, the Mike situation, Betty's death, the new baby, I can't handle it. I feel sick!"

"I'm going to call Mrs. Lopez now! Do you need to go to the hospital?"

"I don't think so, but I do need to see Mrs. Lopez."

X   X   X

Mike had been in the Pacific Coast University library all day reading about various states and localities. Sitting at a table in the reading room, he closed the book he was looking at and put it on top of a stack of books he had already reviewed.

"I'll go to Midwest University," he said to himself. "I'll sell everything here. I'll study to be a writer. I'll write under a pen name. Nobody will know who I am. I can be myself. I'll be far away from here. That's the only way I can forget Bianca."

Determined, he got up from the table and started out of the library.

"I'll put the house up for sale. I'll sell the furniture, give away Mamma's clothes, and clean out the place. I'll put all this behind me."

Mike hurried to his car.

"I won't tell anyone what I'm doing."

Mike got in his car and drove away.

He stopped by the post office at Ocean Spray on the way home and got the mail from the post office box. He looked through it and discarded the advertising and catalogs.

"I don't have time to read their quarterly financial report," he grumbled as he threw away the large brown manila envelope from Benny's without opening it.

He noticed an envelope from Mr. Tachonaka and started to open it but changed his mind.

"I'll look at it later. I don't feel like it now."

He put it with the other mail and drove home.

X   X   X

"I want to know who rents this box," Morrison said to the postal clerk at the counter at the Ocean Spray Post Office.

He showed the clerk a sheet of paper with the Ocean Spray Investment Company name and box number on it. He held a folded hundred-dollar bill conspicuously between his fingers silently indicating a bribe.

"I can't say," said the postal clerk. "You might be a postal inspector. I'd lose my job and my pension if I got caught telling you that. I can't do it."

"Can I wait here to see who gets the mail from that box?"

"You can only if I don't know about it," the clerk said. "The box was emptied about an hour ago. Lately, it's been two or three days before the mail's been picked up."

"This box number is the only lead I have," said Morrison.

"I'm sorry, I can't help you."

"I'm going to have someone watch that box," Morrison said.

"We don't want to know he's there or what he's doing," said the clerk.

"What happens if the person comes in?"

"Don't talk to him here. Get his car license tag number, whatever, but we can't let you contact him on post office property."

June 1, 1985

"We're not doing too well," said Fred. He was meeting with Carlos and Steve in his office. "We only have proxies for about fifteen percent of our stock."

"How is Benny's doing," asked Carlos.

"I don't know," said Fred. "George Benny called and said he had enough to win. He wanted me to get our board to accept his offer."

"What about the two large blocks?" Carlos asked.

"One is the Clarke Trust," said Fred. "Benny's may have that one."

"They don't have those shares yet," said Steve.

"How do you know?" asked Fred.

" My wife is the heir to the Clarke Trust. John and Victoria Clarke were her parents. Deborah was their only child. She disowned them when we got married. It's a long story. The attorney signed over the voting rights to her."

"She'll vote our way," said Carlos. His eyes brightened.

"It's not that simple," said Steve. "She doesn't want the money. She broke off contact with them years ago. She doesn't want the inheritance. She doesn't want the stock. I'm trying to get her to vote our way. She won't vote for Benny's, but she may not vote at all."

"Where is she?" Fred asked.

"She's at the church counseling center talking with her counselor. We don't want her to have a miscarriage."

"We don't either," said Fred.

"What about the Ocean Spray Investment Company?" Carlos asked.

"We don't know who they are," said Steve. "We only have a post office box address."

"Let's see what I can find out," Fred said as he reached for the telephone and dialed a number. "I have a good friend who is a stock broker. He owes me a favor. His company holds those shares."

"Is Mr. Tachonaka in?"

"Tony, this is Fred Gonzales.

"Hi, Fred, what's up?"

"Who is the Ocean Spray Investment Company?"

"The Benny's people called," Mr. Tachonaka said. "I wouldn't tell them anything."

"I just want people's names and how to contact them," said Fred. "Nobody will know where I got the information."

"Betty Riggs," Mr. Tachonaka said. "She's dead now. Her son is Mike Riggs. It's all his now. Because of his mother's death, he may not know about the Benny's fight."

"Is anyone else involved?" Asked Fred.

"Nobody. Betty held it in a life estate. Now that she's gone, everything is his."

"Including voting rights?"

"Including voting rights," said Mr. Tachonaka. "I sent him a proxy. He can vote any way he chooses."

"Thanks, Tony," said Fred. "He worked for us until after his mother's death. We may need your help in finding him. His proxy is important."

"Betty Riggs was the Ocean Spray Investment Company," Fred told Carlos and Fred. "It all belongs to Mike now. He can vote the shares any way he wishes. Tony sent him a proxy."

"Where's Mike?" Asked Carlos.

"We don't know," said Steve. "He wants to leave town and start all over somewhere else."

"We only have a few days before the stockholders' meeting," said Fred. "Let's find him before George Benny does."

X   X   X

At home, Mike had moved the few things he planned to keep into his bedroom. His mother's clothes were packed inside cardboard boxes.

"I'll take them to St. Benedict's Thrift Store on my second trip," he said to himself. "That will be a good place to take the furniture."

The phone rang, but he didn't answer it.

"This is more important."

He packed his father's tommy gun and some other things his mother had on a list into shipping boxes. He taped them shut and carried them to his car.

"Mamma wanted these things to go to the new Gangster Hall of Fame."

He got into his car and drove away.

X   X   X

"I went by his house," Bianca told Steve, "but he wasn't there. He may be staying somewhere else. A 'FOR SALE' sign is in the yard. I called the real estate agent, but she wouldn't tell me how to reach him."

"How about calling him?" Steve asked.

"The phone isn't disconnected," Bianca said, "but he doesn't answer it. I have left messages on his answering machine, but he doesn't answer them. How's Mom?"

"She's better. Her doctor had her admitted to the hospital to rest. They're afraid of a miscarriage. Her visitors are restricted to family only. She should be out Monday, unless there are problems."

FORTY

June 4, 1985

"Tony Tachonaka is still trying to find Mike," Fred said to Steve. They were in the St. Benedict's High School auditorium. "Nobody's seen him for several days. The meeting starts in thirty minutes. What about Deborah?"

"She's meeting with Mrs. Lopez at the church counseling center," Steve said. "Mrs. Lopez knows this vote is important. Maybe she can persuade Deborah to come."

"I'll stall the vote as long as I can," said Fred. "Let's hope one of them shows up. Otherwise, we lose."

X   X   X

Mike came home after six o'clock that evening. He found a note from the real estate lady on the kitchen counter. She had shown the house to a prospective buyer and had a contract on the house at the listed price."

"It's sold," he said to himself. "I'll call her tomorrow. Next week I can go to Midwest University and find an apartment."

He noticed the light on his telephone answering machine blinking. He played the messages, ignoring all but the last one."

"Mike, this is Tony Tachonaka, your mother's stock broker. Call me as soon as you get this message. It's very important." Mr. Tachonaka gave both his office and home phone numbers in the message.

Mike called Mr. Tachonaka at home.

"This is Mike Riggs, what's up?"

"Are you going to the Fast Fred's stockholders' meeting tonight? I sent you a proxy so you could vote your mother's shares."

"I've been busy. I haven't opened the mail for several days. Let me find it."

Mike went to the dining room table and sorted through the unopened mail until he found the envelope. Then he went back to the phone.

"Here it is. I'm opening it now. What's so important?"

"Benny's is trying to take over Fast Fred's. Do you want that to happen?"

"No! I didn't know anything about it."

"Your vote is very important. You own twenty-five percent of Fast Fred's stock."

"I have the proxy form. What time is the meeting?"

"It's at seven at the St. Benedict's High School auditorium."

"Can I still make it?"

"You'll be late, but you might make the difference."

"I'm on my way."

Mike went out the front door, got into his car, and started for St. Benedict's.

X   X   X

"There's nothing wrong with having money," Mrs. Lopez said to Deborah. They were at the counseling center. "It's a person's attitude that can be bad."

"I don't want to live like my parents did."

"You don't have to live that way. You must learn forgiveness."

"I don't want to live in a big house. I don't like country clubs. I don't want to give up my friends. My parents' friends weren't friends at all. They were so fickle."

"You don't have to move to a big house. You don't have to join a country club. You don't have to give up your friends. You don't have to change the way you live."

"But Steve is so upset about it. We can get by without the money. I don't want my children ruined. I don't want my family destroyed."

292

"Steve is upset because Benny's is trying to take over Fast Fred's. If that happens, Steve, Carlos, and the other Mexican-Americans in Fast Fred's management will lose their jobs."

"Fred Gonzales has been good to us.," said Deborah. "I don't want Benny's to take over Fast Fred's."

"You can stop it. Do you have the proxy form with you?"

"Steve put it in my purse. Here it is."

"Take it St. Benedict's High School auditorium, sign it, and give it to Steve. He'll do the rest."

Deborah paused for a moment.

"Has he been a good husband to you?"

"He's been a very good husband."

"Then trust him in this. You're already late."

Deborah hesitated, then got up. "I'm on my way."

"Don't waste time! You're late!"

X   X   X

Fred Gonzales opened the Fast Fred's stockholders' meeting at five minutes after seven. He began by going over the corporation annual report.

"We had a good year," he said. "Our revenue and net profits reached all-time highs. The Board has voted to increase the quarterly dividend ten cents a share."

"So far, we're ahead," George Benny whispered to Morrison. "We'll win if the Clarke daughter and Ocean Spray don't show up."

"I'll go to the door and try to keep latecomers out," said Morrison.

"Good idea," said George.

"Stockholders represented by George Benny have presented a slate of candidates to run against the present officers and members of the board." Fred said. He had stalled some thirty minutes. "You have a list of their names. I'll open the floor for discussion."

"I call for a vote," George Benny said from the floor. "You're wasting time."

Deborah arrived at the school. It was seven-thirty. She hurried up the steps and went to the auditorium.

"Lady, you can't come in." Morrison blocked her way. "There's a meeting going on."

"My husband's inside," she said. "I need to talk to him."

"This is a public meeting!" Steve had heard the commotion and saw Deborah. He got up from his seat and started toward the doorway. "She has a right to come inside."

Standing in the doorway, Morrison turned to Steve. "She's late!"

"She still has a right to come in!"

Deborah pushed her way around Morrison and gave her proxy to her husband.

"Are you OK?" Steve asked as they went to seats in the front.

"I think so."

"Sign here," Steve said as he filled out the proxy giving him the right to vote the shares.

"Who's she?" George Benny demanded.

"She's my wife, Deborah Clarke Cortez," said Steve. "She's voting the shares owned by the Clarke Trust."

Mike arrived, and Morrison blocked his way.

"I'm here to vote in the election!"

"You can't come in," said Morrison. "You're too late."

"Yes, I can!"

"No, you can't!" Morrison grabbed him to keep him from coming in.

"Let go of me! I'm Mike Riggs. I represent the Ocean Spray Investment Company. I own twenty-five percent of Fast Fred's stock."

"We'll give you a good price for it, thirty dollars a share." Morrison let go of Mike. "You'll make a nice profit on the deal. Just sign the proxy over to us."

"Let him in!" Fred ordered from the podium. "This is a public meeting."

Mike pushed his way past Morrison and handed the proxy to Steve.

"Sign here," Steve said after he had filled it out.

Mike signed and then sat down.

"We dispute the voting of the Clarke Trust shares and the Ocean Spray Investment Company shares," George Benny said. "They should be disqualified. Deborah Clarke and Mike Riggs aren't the actual owners, and they were late. Had the vote been on time, they wouldn't have been here to vote."

Mr. Solomon, Fast Fred's attorney, went to the podium and looked at the two proxies. "Everything seems to be in order. They are or properly represent the actual owners of the stock being voted."

"You'd better not dispute my right to vote!" Mike said as he stood up. "I'm Italian! I fight! You'll find out at your annual stockholders' meeting next month! I own twenty-seven percent of Benny's stock!"

Steve came to attention.

"Deborah owns twenty-five percent of Benny's stock. Twenty-five plus twenty-seven equals fifty-two percent. That's controlling interest. Let's take over Benny's. How about it, Mike? Deb?"

"Let's do it," said Mike. "I personally want to fire Morrison."

"I won't give you the chance," said Morrison. "I'll quit."

"We're going to challenge this in court," said George Benny. "Let's get out of here!"

Led by George Benny, his group walked out of the meeting."

"The present officers and directors of Fast Fred's have proxies for seventy-one percent of the stock," Fred said. "I declare them to be re-elected."

After the meeting, Fred, Carlos and Steve met for a few moments at the podium with Mike and Deborah.

"If we can get Mike's and Deborah's proxies to vote their Benny's stock," Fred said. "We can merge Fast Fred's with Benny's on our terms."

"You can have mine," said Mike.

"I'll do whatever Steve wants," said Deborah. She looked down at the floor. "I don't feel well."

"You have had enough excitement," Steve said. "I'm taking you to the hospital."

He took Deborah's hand, and they left together.

"Carlos," said Fred, "do you remember the expansion plans we drew up three years ago?"

"They're in the filing cabinet," said Carlos. "We couldn't get the financing."

"You and Steve get those plans out," Fred continued. "Assume we're taking over Benny's, and modify them accordingly. When we announce our takeover, we can offer to keep some of Benny's management. We won't keep George Benny, and we won't keep Morrison. We'll keep Mrs. Kerrick if she wants to stay. They have other good people who we may want. We'll have to expand to provide them with jobs."

"What about financing?" Asked Carlos.

"We'll raise money by issuing new stock," said Fred.

"Can we do it without hurting our stock price?" Carlos asked.

"I'll take care of that," said Mike.

"I'll retire once we take over Benny's," said Fred. "I'm going to recommend Steve for Chairman of the Board and CEO. It should go through. If you will stay, Mike, I'm going to recommend you for Steve's present position. I promised Martino and Sancho they could retire from the board after this meeting. Carlos, you and Mike can fill these positions now."

"I'll stay if you will help us through this transition," said Mike.

"I will," said Fred. "Meanwhile, I will meet with Mr. Solomon. We're going to have to watch George Benny to see that he doesn't pull a fast one."

FORTY ONE

To the Present

Bianca was at work at the Fast Fred's home office on the afternoon of August 31, 1985, when the phone rang.

"Bianca," the receptionist said, "it's for you."

"Susan Rey has gone into labor," said Deborah. "I'm on my way to the hospital. Can you come?"

"I'll be ready when you get here," answered Bianca.

Bianca and Deborah rode in silence as they went to University Hospital. Steve joined them at the emergency room entrance. He took Deborah's hand as they went to the maternity ward. The Rey family was already there. Susan Rey was already in the delivery room.

Dr. Sisson came out about thirty minutes later. "Mother and baby are fine. It was a normal C-section delivery."

Everyone applauded.

Don Rey turned to speak. "Susan and I are going to name him Charles Crawford Rey."

Deborah turned to Steve. He put his arms around her as she burst into tears.

"This should remove any doubt about Mike's birth," said Dr. Sisson. "He was really your child."

X   X   X

In November of 1986, Mike and Bianca arrived at an east-coast airport on a Coast-to-Coast airline. They got their luggage and made their way to a car-rental counter. A car was waiting for them.

As Mike drove into the city, he thought of the Benny's stockholders' meeting in July. It was a mere formality. The Fast Fred's board and officers were elected to replace the outgoing Benny's board and officers. Their first order of business was to approve a proposal merging the two companies. Benny's shares were to be exchanged for an equivalent number of Fast Fred's shares in a stock swap.

In September, Fast Fred's held a private stock sale to finance a further expansion. Mike and Deborah purchased all of the shares offered and donated them to the "Bishop's Discretionary Fund", an endowment fund set up in memory of Betty Riggs. Each year, the dividends from these shares are contributed to the St. Benedict's school. Mike knew his mother would have approved.

Arriving at their destination, Mike turned into the driveway of the new Gangster Hall of Fame. At the guardhouse, they signed the register "Mr. and Mrs. Michael Riggs" and received nametags. No, they weren't married, but it was important that their true identities not be known.

They drove up to the mansion and parked. Pausing for a moment, Mike looked around the yard. It matched the pictures in his mother's photo album.

They went up the steps and inside. About twenty people were waiting in the hallway. They were just in time for the next scheduled tour.

"The building and grounds have been restored to the days of the Riggiolettis," the tour guide said.

She pointed out the pictures of Maffi, his father, and his grandfather in the front hall.

"This was the Riggioletti home for three generations. They were major figures in the underworld."

She opened the hall closet and pointed to an open chamber. "This is one of the many hidden compartments in the house."

She paused momentarily to allow all of the tourists to see it.

"The industrialist John Clarke and his wife Victoria were the previous owners of this house," she continued. "The museum bought the house from the Clarke Trust. Mrs. Clarke hid a gun in that chamber and later used it to end her life."

Gangster memorabilia was on display in every room. There were pictures of gangland leaders on the walls and plaques beside displays describing various aspects of gangster life.

Betty Riggioletti's picture was in the kitchen.

"She was Maffi's wife," the tour guide said. "She moved to the west coast after her husband's death. She was murdered in a hospital there."

"Was it a gangland slaying?" A member of the crowd asked.

"We don't think so," said the tour guide, "but it's possible."

"Who killed her?"

"Angel Crawford Benny, a fashion writer. She's serving a life sentence without possibility of parole on the west coast. If she ever gets out, she faces first degree murder charges here in the death of her second husband, George Benny."

"Was she a gangland figure?"

"No, she wasn't. Her contacts with the mob were limited."

In Maffi's study, Mike recognized his father's tommy gun mounted inside a locked wall case.

"Maffi Riggioletti was an expert with the tommy gun," the guide said as she pointed to the weapon. "When Maffi wasted someone, he always had an ironclad alibi. The river, the tommy gun, and the alibi were his trademarks.

She turned and pointed to the bookcase behind the desk.

"There is a wall phone hidden inside this bookcase." She moved a panel, and the phone came into view. "It was a private line to a fictitious address. The police were never aware of its existence. Gangland business was conducted over this phone and not on the phone on the desk."

The tour guide paused momentarily making sure everyone could see the two phones.

"The bookcase also hides a stairway." She pushed a button, and a section of the bookcase moved revealing a flight of stairs. "These stairs lead to a tunnel that ends at a concealed entrance outside the back wall. It was designed to allow the Riggiolettis to come and go without being observed by people watching the front gate."

Going upstairs, they saw the room that was Mike's nursery.

"Betty and Maffi had only one child, a son," the tour guide said. "This was his nursery. His baby things were sold or given away by his mother before she moved to the west coast. We were able to purchase his baby bed. It's there in the corner."

"Did the boy grow up to be a gangster," one of the tour group asked.

"No, he's never been part of the gangster world. Betty changed their last name after Maffi's death and moved to the west coast. After her death, he donated some things to the museum in her behalf, but we do not know where he is at this time."

After the tour, Mike and Bianca drove to the cemetery and visited the graves of Michael Thomas and Betty Riggioletti. Then they went back to the airport to return to Pacific City.

X   X   X

On December 28th, Mike and Bianca were at the hospital with Steve when Deborah was taken into the delivery room.

"It's a girl!" Dr. Sisson said after the delivery. "Mother and daughter are doing fine."

"We're naming her Betty Riggs Cortez," said Steve.

Though not married, Mike and Bianca were named as godparents at the baby's baptismal service.

X   X   X

In March of 1986, Steve and Mike resigned their positions at Fast Fred's but kept their places on the board. They replaced two retiring members on the board of directors of Clarke Industries, but they did not become part of the day-to-day operations of that company. Deborah and Mike own more than half of the stock of Clarke Industries.

X   X   X

Dr. Charles Crawford died of cancer on March 22, 1987. Jason and Jeremy later graduated from Atlantic Coast University. Jason went on to medical school and is a practicing physician on the east coast. Jeremy is an engineer and lives in the midwest. Ellen and her husband live in New England where he practices law. Syndi sold the family home and moved into an apartment. Now retired, she sees all four of the Crawford children and their families often.

X   X   X

Dr. Chuck Crawford is a permanent member of the Department of Medical Genetics at the Pacific Coast University medical school. He married Joyce Bereund, a registered nurse, and they have two daughters.

X   X   X

Mike continues to refer to Betty Riggs as "Mamma", but he calls Deborah "Mom" and has begun to refer to Juan, Juanita and little Betty as his brother and sisters. He still treasures the Riggioletti family photo album, pictures of Betty Riggs, and other Riggioletti memorabilia. He has made no effort to change his last name or his birth certificate. Although not married or engaged, Mike and Bianca continue to see each other frequently.

Thank you for reading BETTY'S BABY. I hope you enjoyed the story. If you did, tell your friends, but please don't give away the ending.

Please consider reading my other books. Two are described on the following pages.

Sincerely,

Bob Cole

THE WARRIOR

BOOM boom boom boom! BOOM boom boom boom! BOOM boom boom boom! BOOM boom boom boom! BOOM boom boom boom!

The sound of an Indian drum introduces Bob Cole's action thriller THE WARRIOR.

Spike Dumpster and John Fooleman star as the scoundrels.

Dumpster has no redeeming qualities. "I'm a super scoundrel!"

John Fooleman is determined to build a network of nuclear power plants all across the country. "Nothing is going to stand in my way!"

Jim Kawatcha is the good guy. He is a pacifist American Indian. "I can not kill! I can not kill! I can not kill!" But he has to KILL, KILL, and KILL AGAIN!

Then there's Barb, a preacher's daughter, three generations of preachers. "If God gave me such fine equipment, surely he intended for me to use it."

The story is based in eastern Tennessee. Kawatcha tribal land is taken for the construction of a new type of nuclear power plant. Jim Kawatcha becomes an antinuclear protestor. Nuclear terrorism is involved. Barb plays a surprising role.

If you read no other book this year, you must read THE WARRIOR!

ISBN 0-7414-2314-6

Available from Infinity Publishing at www.BuyBooksOnTheWeb.com, or by phone, toll free, at 877-BUY-BOOK (877-289-2665). Also available from Amazon.com, Borders, Barnes & Noble, or through your local bookstore

CONTESSE

"CONTESSE" is an exciting story of a chase up the old Natchez Trace, a major pioneer trail running from Natchez, Mississippi, to Nashville, Tennessee.

"The year is 1799. I am Dennis De Villanee, a retired pirate turned **BUSINESSMAN!** I am known for my wicked laugh. I own **SATAN'S PLACE**, a gentleman's house of pleasure in Natchez, north of New Orleans on the Mississippi River.

"No girl escapes from my house of pleasure, heh, heh, heh, heh, heh, not even you!"

Contesse escaped. She meets three Pennsylvania brothers, and they flee up the Trace with De Villanee after them.

YOU MUST READ "CONTESSE"

ISBN 0-7414-2457-5

Available from Infinity Publishing at www.BuyBooksOnTheWeb .com, or by phone, toll free, at 877-BUY-BOOK (877-289-2665). Also available from Amazon.com, Borders, Barnes & Noble, or through your local bookstore.

Bob Cole has a PhD degree in a biological science from a mid-western university. He is also a Certified Public Accountant.

Bob has taught biology and chemistry in a small college and has worked in the business office of a large university. In addition, he has been in private industry and in government service. He his a student of history and enjoys classical music. He is currently doing research in an area of biology of personal interest. He has a novel in progress tentatively titled "BLACK".